The Mad O'Haras

By the same Author

The Turf-Cutter's Donkey

The Grey Goose of Kilnevin

Fiddler's Quest

The Bookshop on the Quay

The Dark Sailor of Youghal

Back of Beyond

Published by Poolbeg

The Mad O'Haras

PATRICIA LYNCH

POOLBEG

First published 1948 by JM Dent & Sons Ltd, London
This edition published 1997 by Poolbeg Press Ltd
123 Baldoyle Industrial Estate
Dublin 13, Ireland

The Publishers gratefully acknowledge the support of
The Arts Council.

A catalogue record for this book is available from the British Library.

ISBN 1 85371 721 5

Cover illustration by Eoin Stephens
Cover design by Poolbeg Group Services Ltd
Set by Poolbeg Group Services Ltd in Garamond 10.5/14
Printed by The Guernsey Press Ltd,
Vale, Guernsey, Channel Islands.

A note on the Author

Patricia Lynch was born in Cork in 1898. She was educated in Ireland, Britain and Belgium. As a young journalist she wrote an eye-witness account of the 1916 Rising. She wrote over fifty books, mostly for children, published the world over and translated into many languages.

She lived in Dublin with her husband, the writer RM Fox, and died in 1972.

Contents

1

Hanlon's

Grania O'Hara rubbed the sleep from her eyes, pushed back her red hair, and wriggled up against the pillow. Far away a dog barked – a lively, friendly, hard-working bark. Now he was coming nearer, his flock of sheep baa-ing before him.

Grania always woke early on Fair Day. From her narrow little shelf of a bed she could see through the round window, like a ship's porthole, which Uncle Christie had made for her twelfth birthday.

She could see dim shapes hurrying in the darkness, for there was no moon and a thin mist drifted on the morning wind. A bullock tossed its head and she caught the gleam of horns and flashing eyes in the light from a lantern.

A springless cart went groaning by, the driver standing upright. A boy's whistling sounded above the snorting of cattle and men's harsh, weary voices.

"Out all night," murmured Grania enviously. "I'll draw a picture of it in me book."

She was always painting and drawing on scraps of paper and bits of cardboard; special pictures were in her big, school drawing book.

Grania slipped from the bed and grabbed her clothes.

Her two cousins slept in the big bed under the square window, looking over the huddle of roofs and chimneys to the market-place by the river. Sally lay on her back, her sharp nose pointing to the ceiling, a mop of hay-coloured frizzy hair making a halo on the pillow. Norrie had one hand flung above her dark head and was smiling in her sleep.

No fear of waking them, yet Grania tiptoed from the room.

The landing and stairs were so dark she had to feel her way. The air was heavy with the smell of fresh paint and the banisters were sticky, for Christie Hanlon had been cleaning out his tins of paint and varnish. Grania thought of the smooth, empty stretches of wall and longed to fill them with trees, cows, or even sheep.

"If only Aunt Bridgie'd let me, I'd make this the loveliest house in Dromard. Then, one day, when I'm a famous artist, people would come from all over the world to look at me grand pictures."

She crept down to the warm kitchen, where the fire still glowed through the bars of the iron range, and pulled on her clothes. Her hand was stretched to the glass-fronted bookcase, where she kept her drawing book, when she started and stood listening, her fist against her mouth.

A queer sound – faint, yet she heard it through the lowing and baa-ing, the shouts and cries, the thud of hoofs and the rattle of wheels.

"Sounds like a baby," said Grania. "Yet it can't be!"

She went softly into the little square lobby between the kitchen and the shop, fumbled with the latch, and came out behind the counter.

The cretonne overalls and children's muslin frocks

hanging from rails were frightening in the dim light. They swung when she brushed against them, lifted the flap, and groped over to the big street door. As she turned the key, a bullock crashed against the shutters and the cry which had puzzled her became shriller and desperate.

"It is a baby!" thought Grania. "Those creatures will destroy it!"

She flung back the door. The darkness was lifting and the grey light made the lanterns dim. Most mornings she saw the road winding from the mountains empty and deserted. On this Fair morning it was crowded.

A flock of sheep filled the space before the shop, surging about a cart piled with crates of scolding hens. Grania didn't notice them. She looked down in bewilderment at a tiny black kitten, which tottered stiffly into the shop, mee-owing plaintively, made a dart, and butted her bare ankle with its head.

"The dote!" cried Grania, picking it up and snuggling it under her chin, glad of the furry warmth, for she was shivering.

She closed the door without locking it and walked back to the kitchen, the kitten complaining all the way. She found the jug of milk saved for breakfast and pouring out a saucerful, put kitten and saucer on the floor. The little creature licked and splashed so that its round black face was splattered with milk and Grania laughed as she watched.

"Black and white!" she said softly. "I do love black and white!"

As she spoke her eyes rested on the whitewashed walls. Uncle Christie had finished them on Saturday and the white was still unmarked.

"I wonder would Aunt Bridgie be mad if I did her a black cat," said Grania out loud.

She ran to the bookcase. One shelf belonged to her and in her cardboard box she found a stick of charcoal.

"Sit on the table, pussy, and be good!" she ordered, putting the kitten on the table. It yawned, stretched itself and, rubbing its head against Grania, began to purr.

"What's happened your tail?" she demanded.

The kitten's fur was long and thick, but its tail was only a stump and stuck out like a brush.

"I've never seen a cat with a tail like yours, never! It's only right you should have your portrait done. Keep still now!" said Grania.

The kitten stretched a paw, gave a few licks with its pink tongue, fell sideways, and was asleep.

Grania frowned. She wanted the kitten standing on its hind legs, the short tail showing.

With one hand she held it propped up, with the other drew an outline in charcoal on the wall. Before she had finished the room was bright with sunshine.

Grania was sitting on the table, the kitten on her lap, admiring her work, when unsteady feet stumbled down the stairs and Uncle Christie, yawning and grumbling, shuffled into the room.

"God bless an save us, Grania!" he cried. "Ye put the heart across me. What brings ye down this early?"

He stooped to pull his slippers on properly and saw the kitten.

"Where in the wide world did that come from?" he asked. "Will ye look at the size of it!"

"I found it at the shop door," Grania told him. "And there's its portrait. See the short tail!"

He started back and his niece gazed at him doubtfully. She wasn't afraid of Uncle Christie, but she wanted him on her side when Aunt Bridgie came down.

"I've never done a better picture!" she declared.

"God help ye when yer aunt sets eyes on it!" sighed the little man, shaking his head. "She'll skelp ye! Be off to the school before she sees it."

"You've forgotten again," Grania reminded him. "Haven't I left school? I'm turned fourteen!"

"So ye have! So ye are!" he agreed. "I'll give that wall a slap of whitewash. There'll surely be a drop left. There's no need to be annoyin yer aunt. She has great plans for ye!"

"You can't whitewash my picture!" cried Grania, standing in front of it. "When Aunt Bridgie see how lovely it is, she won't want to destroy it. Sure she won't!"

Christie Hanlon rubbed his hands through his curly grey hair so that it stood on end.

"God give ye a morsel of sense in that copper nob," he groaned. "Ye bring in a stray kitten, when ye know if there's one thing yer aunt hates worse than a dog tis a cat! Then ye black her clane wall. She'll be ragin when she sees it. Here she comes!"

He caught up the kitten and stowed it in his pocket.

"Not a word!" he muttered. "Leave me to deal with this. Pop on the kettle and stir the coal!"

The fire was still glowing in the stove and the kettle was singing. Grania knew Uncle Christie was wise. A good cup of tea might make all the difference.

Mrs Hanlon ran downstairs. She was only half-dressed and had flung on her coat. Her thick brown hair hung over her shoulder in a long plait and her eyes were drooping with sleep. But she was always in a rush.

"What brings the pair of you down this early?" she asked cheerfully. "Ah, Grania! You're the good child! That's right, the big cups. Pon me word I'm parched with the drought. Twill be a grand Fair Day!"

She dropped into the arm-chair by the window and gazed round the clean kitchen. Her eyes opened wide, she leaned across the table, her lips pursed.

Grania looked despairingly at her uncle.

"Sure the child meant no harm!" he said quickly. "Lave it there till the next time the walls need a brush. Twill be something to look at!"

Mrs Hanlon slapped the table. The cups jumped in their saucers. Uncle Christie sat at one end of the bench against the wall, Grania squeezed close beside him. It was their favourite seat, especially when they were in trouble.

"Listen to me, Grania O'Hara!" exclaimed Aunt Bridgie. "There's an end to this nonsense. I promised your poor mother I'd make a lady of you, and a lady you'll be. Make up your mind to that! The minute Mrs Fogarty enters the shop we'll settle you. Tis time you were thinking of the future instead of scribbling on the walls, making a holy show of me good house, and me treating you like me own child!"

Grania put her head on the table and burst into tears.

"I don't want to learn to be a dressmaker with Mrs Fogarty!" she sobbed. "I hate Mrs Fogarty and I hate dressmaking!"

"Whisht! Whisht now!" murmured Uncle Christie consolingly.

"Hate dressmaking, indeed!" cried Mrs Hanlon. "Might I ax, me lady, what you do like?"

Grania lifted her head. She tried to blink away her tears. Her brown eyes danced.

"I want to be an artist. I want to make pictures!"

Her aunt folded her arms.

"God give me patience. Here am I striving to do me best and all you want is to be like old Barney Rearden, chalking Brian Boru and Wolfe Tone on the pavement of the bridge!"

She stopped and stared about her.

"What's making that queer noise? Where is it?"

The kitten had been struggling to escape from Christie Hanlon's deep pocket. Now it was mee-owing its loudest. With a chuckle, but trying to look solemn, he pulled out the rumpled little thing and set it on the table.

"There's the cause of the mischief, though, mebbe, Bridgie, twill bring us good luck!"

The kitten staggered across the table, sat down in front of Mrs Hanlon, and began to purr.

"Put that cat out of my house, Christie Hanlon!" she exclaimed. "You know well I'll not have animals in the place. Who brought it in?"

Christie shook his head.

"It walked in itself. Turn it away and ye turn your luck away, as well as doing a bad, cruel thing!"

Mrs Hanlon believed in luck and she was kind.

"Well enough!" she said. "You can choose, Grania, the lad on the table or the kitten on the wall!"

2

Two Artists

Grania tried not to look at the kitten on the wall. She knew she would never draw a better one. The kitten on the table fixed its round, unwinking eyes on her face and purred. It sounded sure and safe.

"You know I can't choose but the one way," grumbled Grania. "Aunt Bridgie! It isn't fair!"

Sally and Norrie rushed downstairs breathless.

Norrie wore her pink frock and the new grey hat with the wide brim which blew off in every breath of wind.

"A cup of tea in me hand!" she gasped. "Mr Murphy will murder me. I've been late twice this week!"

Sally was smart in her navy suit and a red tammy pulled sideways over her fair hair. She was easy to draw. But though Grania thought Norrie lovely she could never be satisfied with any picture she made of her.

"I'm not yet clever enough," she told herself. "But one day –"

"Is me rasher ready?" demanded Sally. "Grania! You might have put on the pan – it wouldn't hurt you!"

Grania jumped up.

"Start on the bread, Sally. The rasher and egg will only take a minute."

"Will you look at what young Grania's been scribbling on me clean wall!" exclaimed Mrs Hanlon.

Sally, gulping her tea, barely glanced at the wall. But she poked her finger under the kitten's chin and studied it critically.

"That's a good cat! Is it a stray? We'll not be bothered with it long. The owner will be searching."

"The ridiculous creature!" said Mrs Hanlon. "There's cats with long tails an cats with no tails. But whoever heard tell of a cat with a tail like a brush an it no longer than your finger!"

Grania put her head over the kitten.

"It's mine! People who let a kitten that size stray on Fair Day have no right to it!"

"It's good luck, anyway!" Sally assured her, jigging about on her chair, for she never sat still. "Put a name on it and not a soul can take it from you. That's the law!"

"You'll clean up the wall before we eat our dinners in this room!" Mrs Hanlon told her husband.

"Sure! Sure!" agreed Uncle Christie, searching on the mantelpiece for his pipe.

"What harm if Grania does draw a cat on the wall?" asked Norrie, coaxing her mother with her big blue eyes. "Can't you leave it till she's tired of it?"

"When did Grania get tired of her scribblings?" demanded Mrs Hanlon. "Will I ever forget the show she made of me yard? I had all the make-games in Dromard up to get a squint at it!"

"I made a lovely flower garden for you!" protested Grania.

"Flowers painted on the wall of a yard!" retorted her aunt. "Did anyone ever hear the like!"

"Heaps of people said it was grand," drawled Sally, spooning the sugar left in her teacup.

"Making Grania more foolish than she is!" snapped Mrs Hanlon. "Time you were on your way."

Sally chopped the rind off her rasher and pushed the plate over to the kitten.

"Will you look at the clock!" she cried suddenly. "Fly, Norrie! Your hat's back to front. But what harm?"

Grania, the kitten on her shoulder, followed her cousins through the shop, for when Sally and Norrie were in a rush they never shut doors. As they went out, their high heels clacking on the cobbles, two men in thick frieze overcoats went by, driving one cow. A boy, riding a horse, a dog trotting close behind, came down from the mountain. Then the road was empty.

"Grania!" called Mrs Hanlon.

She was making a fresh pot of tea. Uncle Christie, sitting at the end of the form, was toasting slices of bread.

"Slap on the butter, allanna!" he said. "Then we'll be off to the job."

"You'll be off to the job on your lone, Christie Hanlon!" declared Aunt Bridgie. "Grania can help me in the shop. When she's prenticed to Mrs Fogarty she'll have something better to do than trotting at your heels with a can of paint!"

"Where's the luck you should be bringing me if I can't go with Uncle Christie and I'm to be a dressmaker?" Grania asked the kitten.

"Let the child come, this once, Bridgie!" pleaded the little man.

"For the last time," agreed Mrs Hanlon. "You needn't look so sorrowful, Grania! Wait till you uncle paints up

AND GRANIA O'HARA DRESSMAKER over the shop. There'll be a proud day for us all!"

Grania tried to smile.

"What will ye call the wee fella?" asked Christie, holding out his cup for a fourth filling.

The kitten was on the floor gazing at the fire.

"What can you call a cat but Puss, or maybe Tom?" demanded Aunt Bridgie. "And anyway, what right has a cat to a name like a Christian?"

Grania considered, her head propped in her hands.

"I'll call him Timmy Fuzz!" she decided, looking up.

"Timmy Fuzz? Timmy Fuzz?" repeated Uncle Christie, slowly. "Haven't I heard that name before?"

"Don't you remember the gollywog you gave me when I was six?" Grania asked. "He had striped trousers and a red coat. I loved him! A dog ran away with poor Timmy Fuzz one Fair Day and I never saw him again!"

Uncle Christie nodded.

"I remember. Ye cried yer eyes out over him – ye poor scrap – until I got ye to draw him for me!"

Aunt Bridgie pushed back her chair.

"You always encouraged her, Christie Hanlon. That's what has her the way she is. Now, if you're going, for pity's sake go! Grania O'Hara! Will you comb that head of hair and wash yourself? Off now! You can leave the kitten. I'll not eat him. Timmy Fuzz, moryah!"

"You'll wait for me, Uncle Christie?" asked Grania from the door. "I'll not be too long."

"Sure, we've all the time there is," said Christie Hanlon. "Thanks be I've no need to dress up, an me paints and brushes is ready. But we'll need to call on Danny Molloy for me ladder. I lent the loan of it to the scoundrel the whole of a week ago. He gave me his word he'd leave it back here the next day."

"You've no right to be lending your tools," Mrs Hanlon told him. "Isn't it time Danny Molloy had a ladder of his own and he a gutter cleaner?"

"Ye're right, Bridgie, ye're dead right!" agreed Christie, strolling out to the yard.

The kitten was following him but Mrs Hanlon picked it up.

"Stay where you're bid," she said. "Look at your picture disfiguring me wall. Look at it! And what am I to do with the child? I'm not that fond of Mrs Fogarty meself, the ill-tempered old scandalizer!"

The kitten scrambled down, rubbing its head against her ankles, then rushed round and round her, rolled over, and fell asleep on its back, paws folded, its tail limp.

Mrs Hanlon pressed her lips together to prevent a smile as she watched it thoughtfully.

Christie disappeared through the gate of the yard and went round to the front. There he could lean against the grassy bank opposite, where country people said good-bye to their Dromard friends on Fair Day.

He was proud of the tall narrow house which shook in every storm. Draughts came in under doors and windows; the chimney smoked, stairs and floors creaked when no one stirred. But to the farmers and dealers coming into the town it looked gay and friendly.

When Christie had any paint left over from a house painting or decorating job, he used it on his house and shop. The big front door was bright green, the window frames and sills red, and over the big shop window he had scrawled in fat, gold letters, BRIGID HANLON HABERDASHER.

He was so pleased with his work he was always stepping out to admire it. He pretended to find fault with the way Bridgie built spools of cotton into pyramids, draped skeins of knitting wool between piles of tape, cards of darning cotton, packets of needles, and boxes of pins. Ribbons coiled like snakes, ties and collars dangled on little brass rails, and pattern books were ranged against the glass. But he was almost as conceited about Bridgie's work as his own.

He stood there, his coat and trousers splashed with colour, his pockets filled with nails, screws, and bits of wire, planning fresh ventures with paint, cement, and wood.

Only for Fair Day every Thursday he would have been the happiest man alive. But when the drovers with their herds and the farm carts, drawn by big trampling horses, came splashing mud over the paint and glass, Christie had no peace until he spent all Friday washing and polishing the dirt away.

"There isn't such another shop in Dromard, nor in all Ireland!" he muttered. "An tis all our own here, where the cobbles end an the mountainy road begins. But isn't it terrible not to have an inch of pavement betwixt us an the hoofs of animals. I'm very vexed wid all the work they heap on me, so I am."

His bright blue eyes twinkled, his big tweed cap slipped over one ear as he darted back to gather up cans and brushes.

He was still sorting them in the shed when Grania, her hair smooth, stiff and clean in starched blue frock and polished shoes, looked in on him.

"Uncle Christie!" she said breathlessly. "I'm going to

paint a picture of the marketplace with all the stalls and animals and people. And I'll paint one of the bullocks coming down the main road in the early morning. Have you seen them – pushing and tossing their horns and their eyes shining, and men with big caps like yours, and sticks and lanterns? You'll be proud of me then! You will, won't you, Uncle Christie?"

"Deed an I will!" he agreed, puffing his pipe as they went down to the Main Street. "Will ye take a grip on them brushes, Grania, an not be losing them on me!"

There were steps at the bottom, with iron railings at the side, and they stopped to look at the crowds on the pavements, in the roadway, swarming in the shop doorways, and streaming up to the marketplace, over the bridge from the tree-lined Mall.

"Tis the world's pity ye're not a boy, Grania," sighed her uncle. "Ye cud be me prentice an we'd paint the whole of Dromard between us. Famous, we'd make it!"

"Twouldn't make any difference!" declared Grania. "I'd have to be a gentleman instead of a lady, that's all!"

"Now I come to think," said Uncle Christie, "tis no manner of use calling at Danny Molloy's. He'll not be there!"

"But the ladder will!" Grania told him.

He took off his big cap to scratch his head.

"Keep quiet while I'm thinking. I'm right, Grania, he'll not be there! An Nano Molloy won't be there – as it's Fair Day, she'll be stravaging off somewhere – and the childer will be in school. We'll only be wasting our time to call."

"Isn't that Danny Molloy?" asked Grania, screwing up her eyes. "Look! On the hump of the bridge, leaning over, staring at the water!"

Christie nodded.

"Tis himself! If he leans an inch further he'll be in the river. Now wouldn't you think he'd lave back the ladder an I doing him a good turn!"

"Will we go after him?" asked Grania.

"We will not. I wouldn't give him the style of it! An I don't need the ladder on this job. We'll finish at Mr Donnelan's an, on the way back, we'll call on Mister Borrower Molloy. We'll cut round the back now to save time."

"Not go through the marketplace!" exclaimed Grania. "How can I paint a picture of the marketplace, Uncle Christie, if I never see it?"

"Right enough!" agreed Christie. "Right enough. I'd hate to miss an inch of it meself. Stick out yer elbows an mind yer feet!"

They went down the last step and were caught up by the crowd. A calf butted Grania and, backing away, she was pressed against a cart of cabbages. Squeezing between two countrywomen with large baskets, she reached the pavement and, keeping close to the shop windows, edged along.

Her uncle could not be seen. Grania didn't trouble to look for him. She knew where he'd be found. At the door of Kearney's Stores she wedged herself against a packing-case on the high step and gazed over hats and shawls, heads of horses and bullocks, to the men standing up in carts, to the grey spire of the chapel. Blue smoke drifted from the chimneys, screaming children rose into the air on boat swings, pigeons flashed and hovered.

"If I could put it all into the picture!" thought Grania. "But if Aunt Bridgie does make me a dressmaker, what chance will I have at all?"

Uncle Christie was outside Murphy's sweetshop, clutching his pots of paint in his arms and struggling to keep his place amongst the tugs and thumps of envious children. The window was piled with toffee – coconut toffee, toffee in square tins, Everton toffee in silver packets, fig toffee in a great block, and neat rounds of almond toffee, which Grania thought best of all. Fair Day was toffee day at Murphy's.

The shop was as crowded as the space outside the window. Farmers were buying bags of toffee to munch while they bargained, or to take home. Women were laying in a stock till the next Fair and children were clamouring at the counter, tapping like leprechauns with their ha'pennies and pennies.

From the doorway Grania could see Norrie, a clean white overall over her pink frock, breaking toffee with a tiny hammer, weighing, tipping the sticky lumps into a paper bag, tossing the money into a machine which showed the price in neat black figures. Norrie hated Fair Days an the sticky toffee. She enjoyed selling boxes of chocolates, wrapping them in pale green paper hanging in a roll at the back of the counter, and tying white tape, with MURPHY CONFECTIONERS DROMARD printed on it, about the parcel.

"Is it yerself, Grania?" cried Christie. "Go along in. I'll treat ye to a round of that almond stuff."

Grania knew he'd eat most of it, but she moved with him and he forced a passage up to the scales.

"A round of the nut toffee, Miss, and break it small, if ye plaze, Miss Norrie Hanlon!" he said, laughing.

"Daddy, you shouldn't eat toffee in the morning! It's not good for you, or Grania either. You won't eat any dinner!" Norrie told him.

"Indade then an I'll ate me dinner!" chuckled Christie. "Corned beef, carrots, and dumplings; why wouldn't I ate me dinner? Parcel up the toffee, like a good gerrul, Miss Sticky Fingers!"

She frowned at her father, then she laughed.

"You should be buying Grania chocolates now she's grown up, Daddy!"

She began tapping with her hammer at a mountain of plain toffee and Christie almost changed his mind.

"Only I wouldn't disgrace me own daughter before strangers I'd ax Norrie to change this for a half a pound of mixed toffee," he whispered to Grania. "Think of it – fig an coconut an Everton an the almond as well!"

"Who heard of such a thing?" demanded Grania, wishing he had dared.

"How proud we are," he mocked her, and they were out again in the sunshine with the smells and noises of the Fair around them.

3

A Golden Apple-Tree

Christie Hanlon pushed slowly along to the corner and, peering through the glass door of Miss Mooney's, watched Sally sitting at a desk writing in a big account book.

The window was elegant with a wax lady's head on a stand draped with purple silk. On a fold of the silk lay a silver-backed brush and comb. Sally arranged the window every Monday, curled and trimmed the customers' hair, and did the accounts. Miss Mooney had promised to make her a partner when she was twenty-one.

"I've three clever little gerruls, so I have!" declared Christie proudly. "Will ye keep a tight hold on them brushes, Grania!"

They went behind a creaking turf-cart with green branches waving all round the closely packed brown sods, through the narrow alley beside the chapel. Miss Fogarty's was at the end and, though Grania wanted to run past it, her feet dragged and Christie had to wait for her.

Mrs Fogarty herself was seated in the big square window behind a sewing-machine. Beyond her, four girls in black overalls were sewing at a long wooden table.

"On Monday," thought Grania, mournfully, "there'll be five!"

The dressmaker folded her arms and leaned back as Grania and Christie passed the window.

She looked with scorn at Christie's crumpled clothes, gay with splashes of paint, and his bulging pockets. Grania was so neat and tidy she almost smiled, but she didn't like the colour of the girl's frock or her cloud of ruddy hair.

"I don't like her!" murmured Grania, as Uncle Christie raised his cap.

The little man screwed up his face.

"The house is a bit dreary like. That's what vexes me. Tis the narrow alley an the high wall opposite mebbe. But sure every one can't live at the top of the town!"

"Tisn't the house that matters. It's Mrs Fogarty!" persisted Grania.

"Don't I know she's a desprit one for pimping and prying. That's the town's knowledge!" said Christie. "But she's a decent, respectable woman an yer aunt says she'll make a gran little dressmaker out of ye. Ye'll be comin to an from wid Sally an Norrie. Ye'll love it, so ye will, Grania!"

"I won't, Uncle Christie! I won't! How would you like to be a dressmaker?"

That made them laugh and they were still laughing when they reached Mr Donnelan's house on the far side of the railway track.

It was new and Christie Hanlon had painted every bit of the woodwork. He had only to finish the trellis by the side gate and his work was done.

"Uncle Christie," said Grania, as they crossed the road.

Her soft tone made him glance round suspiciously.

"I don't know what ye're after!" he exclaimed. "But tis no use coaxin. Yer aunt says ye're to be a dressmaker an a dressmaker ye'll be. Didn't I get round her to lave ye the kitten! Isn't that enough for one day?"

Grania shook her head impatiently.

"I'm not talking of that, Uncle Christie. It's something quite different."

"Out wid it!"

"You know Mr Donnelan's front door?"

"Why wouldn't I? Isn't it there forninst us?"

"Look at it, all flat and plain! Wouldn't he be pleased if I painted a golden tree on it? You have the little tin of gold paint ready mixed. An apple-tree with little golden apples! I read about one painted on a door, over in foreign parts. Can I, Uncle Christie?"

"It sounds grand," he answered doubtfully. "I'll not be denying it sounds grand. But would Mr Donnelan like it? He's the bank manager, you know! I wouldn't think a bank manager would have much of a wish for a tree on his front door – an apple-tree, ye say?"

"He would, Uncle Christie! I know he would! He'd come along on a cold grey day and there'd be his golden apple-tree welcoming him! It would make him happy every time he went into the house."

Christie Hanlon pushed open the gate.

"If I'm not losing me memory, yer Aunt Bridgie wasn't too happy every time she looked at the flower garden ye painted for her."

Grania slipped her hand through his arm.

"This is different!"

Christie Hanlon was feeling pleased. His pocket was

bulging with almond toffee, a good job was nearly finished, and he hated to refuse Grania anything.

"Have it yer own way," he said, unlocking the front door. "Let's hope Mr Donnelan doesn't ate us! Put a lump of the toffee into yer mouth to give ye strength."

She began at once. He looked at her hair tumbling over her flushed face, her thin strong hands lifting the lid of the tin. Then she glanced up, her brown eyes misty with joy.

"Uncle Christie, I'll never forget this for you as long as I live!"

Christie hummed as he worked on the trellis at the side. Out here, where the wind blew up the river from the sea, the air was fresh, not like the sleepy, shut-in town, where people drank tea all day to keep themselves from falling asleep.

Wasn't he the lucky man! thought Christie. A job like this was worth six months of small, niggling repairs and he had done the work well, good paint, good brushes. He'd like Bridgie to come up and see it – Sunday, after Mass, maybe.

Grania meant to paint the little tree in the middle of the door. But she began too low down with the trunk. Then two branches spread wider than she intended, so she painted up the door until all the space was filled.

"It's foolish not to use all the paint!" she thought.

A messenger boy from Doran's, the grocer's, cycled past the house. He saw Grania painting and stopped. Two women with heavy market bags leaned against the fence and propped their bags on the pathway.

"That's a queer way for a man to be having his door painted, an he a bank manager," said the younger, a fat woman with a red face and a thick black shawl wrapped round her, though the day was hot.

"Sure, doesn't every one know Mr Donnelan has a great consate of himself? Is there another man in all Dromard would make a holy show of his house that way?"

"Mebbe he doesn't know what the young gerrul's doing," suggested a man with a creel of cabbages on his back.

He walked on, shaking his head.

The women and the messenger boy went off. But every moment someone stopped to stare and wonder. Grania could hear them talking but she was too occupied to listen to what they said.

She filled in the last leaf. Now she must paint the apples. There would have been many more only a good deal of the gold paint was on the ground before the door, on Grania's bright blue dress, her hands, even her hair, and her nose had a golden tip.

Christie Hanlon, finishing his own work, stepped softly along the path and watched her. Would she be happy with Mrs Fogarty, wearing a black pinny an making dresses for other girls?

"Sure she used to love dressing up her dollies," he thought. "An the child must learn something!"

How grand it would be if Mr Donnelan was as pleased with his door as he should be! Other people might want trees painted on their doors and Grania needn't be prenticed to that old one. But who ever heard of a girl earning her living by painting apple-trees? And Bridgie mightn't be too pleased!

Grania stood up and saw him.

"Look, Uncle Christie!"

She was so proud she could hardly speak. He patted her shoulder and silently they admired the golden tree. Neither noticed the people staring over the gate.

Quick footsteps on the gravel startled them.

"Here's himself!" Christie told Grania.

"How're ye, Mr Donnelan?" he called. "The job's done, but the floors will be needin a good scrub."

Grania had seen Mr Donnelan behind the high solid counter of the bank, when she went in one day with her aunt. He was tall and grey – grey clothes, grey eyes, grey hair.

"He's terrible serious and cold-looking," she thought, "like an iceberg. It's all those sums he had to do."

"I'm pleased with your work, Mr Hanlon," he said. "Is this your little girl?"

"Me niece, Grania!" explained Christie.

Mr Donnelan held out his hand. Grania shook her head.

"I'm all over gold paint," she said. "See what I've done for you?"

"I see!" said Mr Donnelan. "A good many other people have seen it too. Shall we go inside?"

Christie opened the door. They went in and stood in the hall. The bank manager closed the door slowly.

"Was that all your own work?" he asked Grania.

She nodded.

"If I lived on a road where no one passed," said Mr Donnelan, "every time I came in the gate and saw your golden tree I'd be delighted. But I wouldn't want to live in a house with a crowd always staring at the front door."

"Mebbe you'd like it on the inside?" asked Grania.

"There's not a scrap more gold paint!" said Christie quickly. "Not a scrap!"

"Have you some thin, very thin brown paint?" the bank manager wanted to know.

Christie laughed.

"Why wouldn't I?"

"Could you paint over this tree, so that those who knew it was there could see it but no one else?"

"I could!" declared Christie.

Mr Donnelan smiled at Grania, who smiled back doubtfully.

"You do understand?" he asked. "It was good of you to paint me the golden tree. I heard about the garden of flowers you painted and I want you to have the best box of paints in Dromard. It's in O'Driscoll's window. You'll see to it, Mr Hanlon?"

He gave Christie a pound note, raised his hat, opened the door, and went out. He had to squeeze through the people at the gate.

"Uncle!" said Grania. "He did like the tree!"

"He was impressed!" declared Christie. "I could see it in his eye and the way he looked at ye. And here's the pound note to prove it. A pound note – mind ye! A man that hands money out that way desarves to be manager of the biggest bank in all Ireland!"

"And yet my tree must be painted over and no one will ever see it!" sighed Grania.

"Tis a lovely tree and ye did it!" declared her uncle. "He'll know it's there. Take a walk round the garden while I give it a coat."

"No!" said Grania. "I'll do it. It's my tree."

She should have felt unhappy but she was thinking of the box of paints in O'Driscoll's window.

4

The Paint-box

As they passed Mrs Fogarty's on their way back to the marketplace, Grania gazed at the far side of the alley. She would have to go to the dressmaker's soon enough. Until then she would think only of painting and drawing. But Mrs Fogarty saw her and the splashes of paint on her dress.

"What have those two been up to now?" she wondered.

The Fair was less crowded. Cattle were marching out of town and only a few calves lay in the straw of their pens. A man standing up on a cart was auctioning saucepans and Christie stopped to listen. Grania tugged his sleeve.

"Suppose someone else buys the paint-box!" she whispered urgently.

He loved auctions but he trotted on, never even stopping at Reardon's bakery, though the smell of hot doughnuts swept out to tantalise him.

They turned down to the Mall with grand shops along one side and a grass walk with seats between the trees and the river wall.

O'Driscoll's was the biggest shop in Dromard – bigger

even than the draper's – with two huge windows and a wide door in the middle set back from the pavement. The wooden box of paints, with its hinged lid thrown back, was guarded by account books standing on end, with drawing-books ranged in steps down to the glass. There were boxes of crayons and small metal boxes of paints. Grania saw nothing but the wooden box with its tubes and brushes.

They tiptoed in. Christie set down his paint-pots and looked about him.

"Will I speak for it?" he asked.

Grania nodded. She couldn't say a word.

The lending library was in the centre of the shop, and so many people were changing books there was no one to sell the paint-box. Christie thought how grandly the women were dressed. The day might come when Grania would be making their frocks. Twas what Bridgie wished. Pity the child had so little liking for it!

Grania didn't mind waiting. She wondered if the golden tree were as beautiful as it had seemed. Uncle Christie thought it was grand. But he was always kind. He'd hate to say her tree had too many branches or that the apples weren't quite round.

She turned her back on the shop and looked out on the Mall. The seats under the trees were empty, the humped bridge deserted. The wind was tossing the leaves so that their grey undersides showed.

"That's a queer grey," she thought. "How would I get that shade?"

She reached over and plucked the wooden paint-box from its nest.

"Put that down! How dare you touch the window!"

cried Mrs O'Driscoll, rushing from the book counter and seizing Grania's arm.

Christie's face turned red. He blew out his lips.

"Whisht, Mrs O'Driscoll, ma'am! There's no need to scarify the child. We came in to buy the box of paints an we've been standing on our feet waiting till it's a miracle our footwear isn't in holes. What price is on the box?"

"One guinea!" Mrs O'Driscoll told him scornfully.

She still held Grania by the arm. Grania clutched the paint-box.

Christie brought out the pound note. He hunted in his pockets for a shilling and found sixpence and twelve halfpennies.

"Ye can parcel the box an I'll want a receipt!" he said sternly. "An I'm sorry to say it, Mrs O'Driscoll, but ye've a quare way of treating customers. Only Grania's in a hurry for her paints I'd send up to Dublin for em!"

Mrs O'Driscoll had been sure he would never sell that box. It had been lying in the window since Christmas!

"I'm sorry, Mr Hanlon!" she exclaimed. "I'm very sorry. You've a right to be vexed with me. But –"

She shook her head, went off with the money and the box, looking back in a puzzled way.

Christie laughed and wiped his hands on his trousers.

"That one can't believe we've a pound between us, Grania!" he said.

The customers at the book counter were staring at Christie and Grania, and whispering to one another.

"Now why didn't we go back home an clane ourselves a bit before we ventured inside this place?" grumbled Christie. "Look at them, passing remarks an jeering us. Sure they've no manners at all!"

"Here's me box of paints!" said Grania.

Mrs O'Driscoll gave Christie the receipt and handed Grania the box, neatly wrapped in brown paper.

"I've put in a drawing-book too," she said.

Now she was smiling and trying to look friendly.

Grania was so delighted she could scarcely see where she was walking. It still seemed impossible that all those brushes and tubes of paint could be hers! She stumbled from the shop and bumped into Christie as he turned one way and she turned the other.

"Mind now, Grania, or ye'll tip the paint pots, God help ye! Ye're in a state! Don't ye know the way home?"

He laughed as he looked at her face.

"Sure, child, ye look as if ye'd found the crock of gold! Ye'll have great times wid all them paints!"

Grania nodded. Her eyes were filled with wonder. She kept on squeezing the box to make sure she still had it. Dromard had never looked more lovely. She thought kindly even of Mrs Fogarty and was ashamed that she could have imagined Mrs O'Driscoll sharp and unfriendly.

"Would ye mind if we went round be Danny Molloy's?" asked Christie. "I see he's gone from the bridge, so there's a chance he'll be home an it's on me mind I'll be needing me ladder badly."

Grania didn't care where they went.

Christie had to nudge her with his elbow to take the turning away from the marketplace to the row of thatched cottages which belonged to the days when Dromard was the village above the river. They found the gutter cleaner sitting on his window-sill, a big tabby cat on one side of him, a black-and-white dog at the other.

Danny was a small wizened man, very talkative and so

lazy he found it almost harder to go to bed than to get up. He pushed the dog from the sill to make room for Christie. But he remained standing and tried to look angry. Grania stood beside him hugging her parcel.

"How's yerself, Christie?" asked Danny. "An how's the young one?"

"Gran!" replied Christie. "Have ye finished wid me ladder?"

Danny Molloy took the pipe from his mouth.

"Ladder! What ladder?" he asked in amazement.

Christie glared indignantly at him.

"The long ladder I lent ye last Wednesday an that ye promised to send Jimsy back wid!" he snapped.

Danny shook his head.

"Be raisonable, Christie Hanlon! How could a small lad like Jimsy carry a long ladder through the town? Anyway, I lent it to old Dempsey. I knew ye wouldn't grudge it. An he gave me his solemn word he'd lave it in on ye the minit he'd finished a job he was after doin, down be Barnakeel."

"Barnakeel!" gasped Christie. "Why, Danny Molloy, man! How am I to get me ladder back from Barnakeel! An me wid a job waitin to be done as early as I can start in the mornin."

Danny held up his pipe.

"Ye're wrong, Christie, quite wrong. Ye misunderstood me – down be Barnakeel was me words. Tis this side of Barnakeel, not right there. Don't be wrongin me now!"

Before Christie could reply, a barefooted boy poked his head out of the door.

"Me mammy says not to be vexing Mr Hanlon, for his old ladder is round at the side an I'm to give him a hand back with it."

He followed his head and stood grinning in the doorway.

"Pon me word!" said Christie.

"Isn't that grand now!" interrupted Danny. "Sure it slipped me mind. I have that much to think about. Dempsey came to borrow the loan of yer ladder. But I wouldn't let him lay a hand on it. No, says I –"

"Twas me mammy," put in Jimsy. "She wouldn't let ye lend it, an can we start now, Mr Hanlon, for tis a long way up to your place an I've to do me messages?"

Grania watched her uncle and Jimsy bring out the ladder. She saw how Jimsy took one end on his shoulder while her uncle put the other end under his arm. Then the two of them carefully stepped into the roadway.

"I couldn't do that," she thought. "I'm bigger than Jimsy, but I'd drop if I had to carry half that ladder."

"Safe home, now!" called Danny Molloy. "An remember, if ever ye need a man's help, send for me."

Christie hummed fiercely and Grania walked silently beside him.

As they drew near Reardon's bakery he pulled out a threepenny piece and gave it to her.

"Three buns, Grania," he said. "The lad at the tail could do wid a bite as well as ourselves!"

Grania left them and ran into the shop.

"Three doughnuts," she asked Mr Reardon. "Sugary ones if you can!"

Mr Reardon picked out three and dropped them slowly one by one into a paper bag. Then he leaned across the counter.

"Is yer uncle taking Danny Molloy's Jimsy on?" he asked. "He'd be wiser to try him for a month. The lad's dacent and quarely fond of work. But look at his da! Just look at him!"

Grania held out her hand for the bag.

"I want to catch up with them: that's why I'm in a hurry," she explained.

"An I hear Mrs Fogarty's taking another prentice," continued Mr Reardon. "I suppose she's fixed it up with yer aunt to larn ye the dressmaking. Tis a warm trade, so it is, Grania. But I'm sorry for ye, me poor child, to be starting wid that old one!"

Grania said nothing. Now, with that parcel under her arm, it didn't seem possible she would ever be a dressmaker.

"Stand up to her, that's me advice," and Mr Reardon, leaning right across the counter, looked straight into Grania's eyes. "But sure, she's an old slave-driver an ye're not one to speak for yerself. Ah, well – there's a jam tart for a bit of comfort. If ye were my little girl I'd sooner send ye picking cockles on Barnakeel strand than prentice ye to Mrs Fogarty!"

Grania ate the jam tart as she hurried after her uncle and Jimsy. They had stopped for a rest and, when she reached them, they all sat down on a high step to eat the doughnuts.

"You won't be acting this way when you're wid Mrs Fogarty," said Jimsy enviously. "You'll be too proud. Sure you're the lucky one, Grania!"

5

Seven Ducks on a Bridge

The doughnuts were soft with a thick, crisp crust. As they ate, the powdered sugar showered over their clothes and on the rough pavement. The sun shone and the smells of the Fair rose above them like a dense mist.

Grania licked her fingers. Christie Hanlon blinked contentedly. Jimsy blew up the paper bag and burst it with a slap.

"Ye young divil, ye!" said Christie amiably. "Have ye no regard for people's feelins?"

"The paper was too sticky," complained Jimsy. "If I'd a clean decent bag I'd show ye! Look, Grania! There's Barney Dillon. Me father was telling me how he's drawn the one picture since he settled on the bridge. Would ye believe that now?"

"Grania would not believe it!" declared Christie. "She has a little sense left!"

Barney Dillon came shuffling along, a thin, lanky, worried man, with a bald head, carrying a little canvas bag of coloured chalks. He sniffed all the time he talked. Grania didn't like Barney. But she was sorry for him.

"How's yerself, Barney?" called Christie, for the pavement artist was passing without a word or a look.

He started, swung round and stopped.

"Poorly, poorly," he answered, "I didn't see yez. I was thinkin would it be the pills or the powder, the doctor told me to take first in the mornin or last at night?"

"Doesn't every one, barring yerself, know tis always the pills at night an the powder in the morning!" exclaimed Jimsy scornfully.

Barney shuffled opposite the boy.

"A young lad like yerself shouldn't know the manin of a pill or a powder. Ye're a bit too cute fer me likin, Jimsy Molloy!"

"Don't mind Jimsy. Don't mind him," exclaimed Christie, anxious for peace. "How's trade, Barney?"

"Bad, Mr Hanlon! Bad! The people of Dromard has no regard at all for art. No regard at all. There's no livin in it. No livin at all!"

"I've often wondered, Barney," said Christie, "why ye chose the bridge. Tis a windly, cocked-up class of a place. An people either hurry by or hang over the wall lookin at the river. Too fast or too slow – that's how they are on the bridge. Now – down beside the chapel, or at the end of the Mall – that's the place, Barney. That's the place!"

Barney sniffed.

"Ye're wrong, Mr Hanlon. Ye're wrong! Ye think ye're right but ye're wrong! I cudn't live in Dromard widout the bridge – ye can say what ye like. Tis me studio an me art gallery. An artist should never be down among the people, but set above them. Ask Grania there – she knows!"

Grania flushed with pleasure. Mebbe Barney Dillon wasn't so bad after all! If Jimsy wasn't there she'd show the old pavement artist her paint-box.

Barney shuffled along a little further so that he came close to her.

"I was wonderin, Grania, if ye cud do a bit of a drawin for me above on the bridge. I heard how ye put a golden tree on Mr Donnelan's front door. Do one on the bridge, Grania, an I'll keep it there all the days of me life!"

"Sure Bridgie wouldn't be too pleased if Grania did that," objected Christie. "An how did you hear about the tree on Mr Donnelan's door? Twas only done five minutes ago! Anyway there's not a drop of gold paint left."

"If Grania does the drawin an you sit there lettin on ye did it yerself, tis cheatin, Barney Dillon!" cried Jimsy.

Barney sniffed at him.

"Mind yer business, lad! This is a matter between artists. Draw a tree for me, Grania! I'd be a proud man to be sittin there wid a golden tree. But sure any kind of tree would do. A gold one would be wasted on the numbskulls of Dromard!"

Grania smiled. She wouldn't draw a tree for Barney: she'd draw something he'd like better. But Uncle Christie was talking.

"I'm sorry, Barney. Grania can't do what ye're axin. Her aunt would be vexed. She'd be more than vexed. She'd be ragin!"

Grania stood up.

"She needn't know, Uncle Christie."

He shook his head.

"God between ye an harrum, Grania O'Hara! Ye mightn't tell. Barney mightn't tell. Dear knows I wouldn't. But could young Jimsy here kape his mouth shut? Ten minutes after ye'd drawn the picture, the whole town of

Dromard would know. Sally would know, Norrie would know, an ye think yer aunt wouldn't, ye poor innocent!"

"Sure there's not a soul passin over the bridge, Mr Hanlon!" urged Barney. "An she'd never be seen from the marketplace."

Grania was thinking. If she did this – if she set the whole town talking – maybe Mrs Fogarty wouldn't want her for an apprentice. But Aunt Bridget would be angry and disappointed. If only she needn't know!

"Let me do it," she coaxed Christie. "Please!"

"Quick then!" he said. "Yer aunt will ate us when she hears."

They went on to the bridge. Barney shuffled ahead, spread out his chalks, put down his cap for the pennies, and waited. Christie and Jimsy stood with the ladder so that Grania was hidden.

"I'll use your chalks," she told Barney. "I haven't any of me own."

She was thrilled as she knelt there, smiling and fingering the chalks.

She drew a row of ducks, first a big white duck, then green, red, blue, yellow, black, each smaller than the one before. Last of all came a tiny, primrose-coloured duckling. They were all different; the white fat and contented, the green dancing, the blue cocking its head up, the red scolding, the yellow timid and side-ways, and the black ready to fight the world, the duckling bobbing gaily along – seven ducks marching over the bridge at Dromard!

Grania sat back on her heels. Through the parapet she could look down on the shut-in town that woke up only on Fair Days. It had been a wonderful day, but she felt it might be the last of youth and freedom.

"I can't be prenticed to Mrs Fogarty!" she cried out. "Uncle Christie, I can't!"

There were tears in her eyes and she gazed up at him so reproachfully that he was ashamed.

"What can I do?" he asked. "There's your Aunt Bridgie set on havin DRESSMAKER up over the shop. And since the day the new coloured sign was put up outside Regan's Medical Hall the longing has her tormented."

"Is she that set on it?" sighed Grania.

"She is indeed! She was always terrible ambitious, or we'd still be in the one-room cabin where we started. Sure I was content enough wid me bits of jobs – paintin here, roof work there, runnin up a wall or fence. Ses Bridgie – we're gettin nowhere an we'll be old before we know where we are. We'll go into business, ses she. An bedad we did, though sorra wan of me knows how we done it. She was certain Sally would be a dressmaker. Well, ye know Sally! She wouldn't take a needle to her stockings till her toes were pokin out. Then she had great hopes of Norrie. But me gay Norrie wouldn't hear of the dressmakin!

"When she seen ye so great wid the dollies, and ye for ever dressing em up, the heart riz in her. Twelve dolls ye had at the one time an she never refused ye a bit of silk from the shop. Never!"

Grania nodded sorrowfully. It was all true.

"Uncle Christie! I was only pretending with the dolls. I let on they were people in stories – Red Indians and pirates and kings and queens. If I could make the kind of clothes I made for them, maybe I wouldn't mind being a dressmaker. But just to fix up ordinary clothes – I can't!"

She scrambled to her feet. The line of ducks seemed to

be marching away into the future. The big white one winked at her.

"Let's be off out of this!" whispered Christie. "There's one of Mrs Fogarty's young gerruls crossin the bridge. I'm just hopin she never laid an eye on ye!"

He tugged at the ladder. Jimsy, who had been gazing in wonder at the ducks, turned to help, tripped and sprawled in the roadway. He was up in a moment and, with Grania keeping close, the ladder swung stiffly as Christie and the boy hurried away from the bridge.

"All I'm praying is," said the little man, "that it won't be all over Dromard before we get home, how young Grania O'Hara was down on her hunkers on the bridge, chalkin ducks for Barney Dillon. Tis bad enough to do it, but to be seen doin it is the most desprit thing of all!"

6

Dinner at Hanlon's

As they came up the hill Grania and Christie could smell the dinners of the neighbours. The O'Mahonys, next door, were having bacon and cabbage. They never had any other dinner. The odour of red herrings drifted down from the Reillys' open window. The whole world could tell it was Thursday because of the smell of fried sausages, onions, and white pudding, which came over Mrs Dempsey's half-door.

"I wonder, if ye had the choosin, which dinner's the best," said Christie, sniffing and smacking his lips. "Take a sniff, Grania! Now isn't it a tantalising position for a man?"

Grania laughed. She was ready to laugh at Uncle Christie, or the smells of dinner, or herself.

"The best dinner is the one we're going to have," she told him. "Is there any one in Dromard can make dumplings like Aunt Bridgie?"

Jimsy groaned with pleasure and hunger.

"Ye're right!" agreed Christie Hanlon. "There is not. Light as a drift of smoke an very satisfying. Jimsy! Let ye go round the back. We'll rest the ladder here. Tell her we're comin!"

He turned to Grania.

"We're in a shockin state. We'll creep in through the shop!"

Christie thought Bridgie was in the kitchen. She wasn't. She was in the shop, serving Mary Martin, Mrs Fogarty's eldest apprentice.

Mary was thin and tall like her mistress. She wore a black overall with two big pockets. Her fair hair was pulled back tightly and tied with a bow of black ribbon.

"The image of an orphan, God help her!" thought Christie, compassionately. "I'll not be too pleased to have me little Grania lookin that way!"

Grania was feeling just the same. She clasped her wooden paint-box and the drawing book before her like a shield and stared at Mary Martin. Mary stared back, her eyes goggling, her mouth falling open.

Bridgie Hanlon pretended not to see them.

"The narrow ribbon, is it, Mary?" she asked. "You'll not forget to tell Mrs Fogarty I'll be waiting on her after dinner."

Christie lifted the flap of the counter.

"In wid ye!" he muttered, to Grania, and glared at Mary so ferociously she was terrified.

"Yes, ma'am! No, ma'am!" she stammered, grabbing the ribbon, without waiting for it to be wrapped, and running from the shop.

Bridgie swung round to Christie and Grania.

"Ye pair of omadhauns!" she cried. "What ailed you to come through the shop! You had to show yourselves to that little gossip, Mary Martin, looking as if you'd fallen in a tub of paint! You're a perfect show, Grania O'Hara! I was an eejit to let you go running wild with that Christie Hanlon! And he with a coat and trousers looking as if they were made from a rainbow! There's Mary Martin off to tell Mrs Fogarty the news!"

"What harrum, Bridgie, woman, if Mary Martin did see us and we after doin a good job of work! Who's Mary Martin, anyway?"

Christie gave Grania a push and they bundled through into the kitchen.

"Clane yourself grand!" he ordered. "Wait till I tell her about Mr Donnelan an the apple-tree! We'll burst out wid the story when Norrie and Sally are in. But not a word about Barney Dillon an the ducks – mind now!"

Grania changed her frock. She thought the splashes of gold paint a great improvement. But her hair was sticky, so were her hands. Soap and rubbing only made her skin sore.

"I'll have to get some turps from Uncle Christie," she decided. She came into the kitchen as Norrie and Sally ran through from the shop.

"Daddy! Is it true? We heard you bought Grania the big paint-box in O'Driscoll's window!" exclaimed Norrie, pulling her chair to the table. "It's all over the town!"

"A whole guinea!" jeered Sally. "How could it be true? Where'd Daddy Christie get twenty-one shillings?"

Christie grinned. He was thankful they hadn't yet heard about Grania drawing on the bridge.

"Sit down, Jimsy," said Bridgie. "Your mammy knows where you are. No need to hurry. Eat a good dinner."

She was cutting up the dumpling. Grania looked down at her plate, at the red slices of meat, the crumbling wedge of dumpling, the glistening carrots, and the big floury potato. She had never felt so hungry. But she stood up, went over to the windowsill and untied her parcel.

Norrie's fork was halfway to her mouth. It stayed there. Sally's mouth was full and she nearly choked. Christie pushed his plate away.

Jimsy, munching carrots as quickly as he could, gazed in wonder.

"I bought it!" said Christie. "But twasn't me own money. Where would I find all that amount? Twas Mr Donnelan paid Grania twenty shillings for a golden apple-tree she painted on his dure. She's to have the best box of paints in Dromard, ses he, givin me a note!"

Bridgie put her elbows on the table.

"What's all this figarie?" she demanded. "Christie Hanlon! Where did you get all that money to waste on a box of paints?"

"I'm tellin ye, Bridgie! I'm tellin ye! Mr Donnelan gave it to me!"

"For Grania painting an apple-tree on his door! Don't ask me to believe that. Will you all stop staring at Grania as if she was growing horns and eat the good dinner that's on the table!"

They ate silently.

"I'd like to see that same tree!" said Bridgie suddenly.

"Well then, ye can't!" Christie told her, his mouth full of dumpling. "Tis painted out!"

"What's that?"

"He didn't want a crowd of the eejits of Dromard at his dure admiring the tree day and night, so we put a coat of thin paint over the tree. But if ye went up close and looked sideways, ye cud see it – apples an all!"

"If Mr Donnelan had given me the money I'd buy that blue hat in O'Farrell's and gloves to match," sighed Norrie.

"You were born lucky, Grania!" declared Sally.

Grania chased a piece of carrot round her plate. She held it up on her fork and gazed at it solemnly, with a quick glance at her aunt.

"If I can earn a whole twenty shillings for painting one tree, I don't see why I have to be a dressmaker," she said.

"An what about what you did up on the –" began Jimsy.

A glare from Christie Hanlon warned him to be silent and luckily Bridgie hadn't heard.

The kitten was sitting on the table between Grania's plate and Christie's. They had both been feeding it. Now it reached out a little black paw and knocked a piece of carrot to the floor. Instead of leaping down it looked over the edge of the table, then up at Grania.

She put her head down so that her brown eyes were on a level with his green ones.

"Timmy Fuzz! You've brought me luck already. Now you'll save me from Mrs Fogarty – you will, won't you?"

Bridgie Hanlon was angry.

"Put that cat off the table, Grania! And when Mrs Fogarty talks to you, you'll behave yourself and not disgrace me! I wonder a man like Mr Donnelan, with daughters of his own, hasn't more sense!"

Grania settled the kitten on her lap. He put his front paws on the table and peered about, purring with content.

"There's a ring at the bell. Run, Grania!" her aunt told her.

"I wonder you have any customers at all, stuck up here," grumbled Sally. "You might as well be keeping a shop for goats. Why can't we live on the Mall?"

"Or on the market square!" suggested Norrie.

Mrs Hanlon was too pleased with her shop to be

vexed, even if she hadn't been so proud of her daughters. Besides she was too perplexed about Grania to answer. The girl put Timmy Fuzz on her shoulder and went off.

"I'd hate to think of the child being unhappy," said Christie. "Bridgie! Can't we see if there's anythin in this painting business?"

Grania heard him as she went into the shop. A little girl, whose head scarcely rose above the counter, wanted a paper of pins. Grania went with her to the door and stood looking out.

A goat trotted daintily up from the town. Behind it came six sheep, one after the other, and last of all a boy in trousers so large they came up to his chin, and a battered hat which sat on his shoulders.

"I should put that in me book!" thought Grania. "Now wasn't there something else I meant to draw?"

She flung back her head to remember, then started so that the kitten dug its claws into her frock.

Over the high bank opposite she saw a horse, a shaggy mountain pony, against the sky. It reared on its hind legs, swung round so that she could see the boy riding it, sank back, and came sliding down the bank, bringing a shower of sods and stones with it to the roadway.

The boy leaned forward and Grania thought he would be pitched to the ground. She put up her hand, clutched the kitten, and stepped out on the cobbles.

The pony stood trembling. The boy swung his leg over and jumped down.

"I'm looking for Grania O'Hara!" he said.

Grania gazed at his tanned face, his grey eyes and thick fair hair, the loose clothes he wore and the bright orange scarf tied about his neck. His legs were bare, but he wore fine brown boots with tasselled laces twisted about the ankles.

"He's surely a tinker," she thought. "Though who ever saw a fair tinker?"

"I am Grania O'Hara," she told him.

"I'm Desmond Burke," he said.

They stared at one another. The door into the shop swung open and Aunt Bridgie's voice called:

"What's keeping you, Grania?"

The flap of the counter banged. She came across the shop and stood behind Grania, looking over her head at the strange boy and the shaggy pony.

"What are you wanting, young lad?" she asked.

"I'm Desmond Burke," he answered. "And I've come for Grania O'Hara!"

7

The Rider from the High Bog

Mrs Hanlon stood against the door, her arms folded. "Who sent you?" she demanded. "Why was there no letter?"

She pushed Grania inside.

"Go back to the kitchen!" she snapped.

Grania didn't move. She stared at the boy, then at her aunt.

Mrs Hanlon sighed.

"You'd as well come in. Take the horse round to the yard. The gate's open."

Grania followed her aunt.

"Who is he, Aunt Bridgie?" she asked. "What does he mean – he's come for me?"

Mrs Hanlon did not speak until they were in the kitchen. Norrie was pouring the tea. Sally and her father were doing a crossword puzzle. Jimsy had returned home.

"Christie!" said Aunt Bridgie. "Desmond Burke's here. You remember young Desmond?"

Christie blinked.

"I do indade!" he answered. "Has he run from them savages? The poor lad! Where is he? Let him come in an welcome!"

"He hasn't run away!" Mrs Hanlon told him. "He's come for Grania. Here he is to speak for himself. Come along in, Desmond Burke!"

The tall, sunburnt boy strolled in, his lips pursed as if he were whistling. He stared at the girls and frowned, looked at Christie and smiled.

"How are you, Mr Hanlon?" he asked.

"Gran! Gran!" cried Christie, jumping up to shake hands. "Ye're that stretched since I last saw ye, I'd not have known ye, Des. Why – ye're almost a man!"

Norrie put her elbows on the table. She was puzzled.

Christie went on fussing with the stranger, trying to make him welcome but looking very uneasy.

"Sit down now and take a cup of tay. Norrie! Sally! This is Des Burke, a kind of a cousin of Grania's."

Sally looked at the boy scornfully with her pale blue eyes.

"I didn't know Grania had any cousins – barring us," she declared, tossing her frizzy hair. "Where'd he spring from?"

The boy sat beside Christie.

"I rode over the High Bog from Castle O'Hara," he said.

"Oo!" screamed Sally. "It's the first time I ever heard of Castle O'Hara! Would you mind telling me where it is, your highness?"

Grania leaned against the wall beside her drawing of the kitten. Timmy Fuzz bit her ear gently, and she lifted him from her shoulder without moving her eyes from Desmond Burke's brown face.

Norrie gave her sister a dig and shook her head reproachfully. She pushed a cup of tea across the table to the boy and cut a plate of beef for him. Mrs Hanlon sat in the big wooden armchair, her finger tapping the arm, her face worried.

"Who sent you, Desmond?" she asked.

He sat silent a moment, then looked straight at her.

"Who'd have the right to send me, only her mother!" he declared.

Grania, startled, swung round to him.

"Me mother!" she cried in amazement. "I have no mother!"

As long as she could remember she had lived with Aunt Bridgie and Uncle Christie. Why had she never heard of her mother before?

Desmond Burke pushed away his plate and stood up.

"So that's what they told you!" he exclaimed. "Tisn't right! You have a mother – Eily O'Hara, and she's living yonder at Castle O'Hara!"

"Castle O'Hara!" cried Mrs Hanlon. "Is that the name you have on it? I'm not surprised. Listen to me, Grania!" she turned to the girl. "You have a mother, God help her! She's me own sister, Eily. And when your father died she brought you here to me, a small, wee child, and made me promise to bring you up as my own and not let on that she was living. She had a dread of you growing among them savages, for that's all they are! The Mad O'Haras is what they're known as. I can't believe she sent for you, Grania! Tis a wicked trick, so it is!"

Grania listened in silence, her face pale. She could not understand. She looked at her uncle. His head was bent. He put his pipe back on the mantelpiece. Then he took it down again.

"But why didn't you tell me I had a mother?"

demanded Grania. "Why didn't she stay here with you, and me? Couldn't she, if she'd wanted to? But why did you never tell me?"

Mrs Hanlon put her arm about Grania.

"Don't think hard of me, allanna! Twas your mother's wish. She could have stayed. She was me favourite sister and Christie there had a kindness for her. But the place where the O'Haras live – they call it a castle, others call it a cave – belonged to your father and she was determined you shouldn't be done out of your rights. She wanted you to be brought up properly, not mixed in with those O'Hara savages. When you were old enough she meant to tell you."

Grania shut her eyes. She wanted to think and she couldn't, with all of them looking at her that way. She felt stunned. Could it be true? But how could her mother leave her like this? Then her face brightened.

"I've a mother of my own!" she thought. "And I've a real home!"

She opened her eyes and smiled at Desmond Burke.

"I'm glad my mother sent for me," she said, speaking slowly but proudly. "It's grand not to be an orphan any more!"

"Grania!" exclaimed Mrs Hanlon reproachfully. "Haven't I always treated you like my own child?"

"You have indeed!" agreed Grania. "Only I can't help being thankful I needn't be prenticed to Mrs Fogarty after all."

"Is that how you feel?" murmured Mrs Hanlon sorrowfully.

Christie Hanlon was horrified.

"Ye'll not lave us,Grania!"

She looked from him to her aunt.

"I can't bear to leave you!" she said. "But I do want to know me own mother. I wish I'd known her all these years. Didn't she want to know me?"

Bridgie Hanlon sighed.

"Poor Eily did it all for the best. She wanted you to be a lady and I never had the heart to cross her. I'm terribly fond of her. But I can't understand her sending for you now. Desmond Burke! If tis a trick of the O'Hara's, I'll never forgive you!"

The boy looked down at his plate.

Christie coughed loudly.

"Sure tis no harm to have her go there for a visit. Didn't I always say twas wrong not to let Grania know her mother? Never fear – Eily won't keep her there. Grania'll be comin back to us an, mebbe, Eily with her!"

"I wonder!" said Mrs Hanlon.

"What's to hinder us going to see her?" asked Sally.

She was thrilled at the thought of a castle, even a ruined one. But Mrs Hanlon shook her head.

"Tis the welcome you'd get at the end of your journey, that's the drawback, Sally!"

"She'd be very welcome," Desmond muttered. But nobody believed him.

He looked at Grania.

"We should be on our way. If the pony has to carry two, we mightn't reach the castle before dark, and there's no moon tonight."

Grania clutched her aunt's hand.

"Should I go?" she asked doubtfully. Suddenly she was afraid.

"If your mother wants you, child, I suppose you must,"

replied Bridgie. "But the last time I saw her, she didn't let on. I can't understand it at all!"

"Is it far?" asked Sally.

"Far enough!" was Desmond's reply.

"Pack the child's things, Norrie! There's the girl!" said Mrs Hanlon. "She can have the cardboard box the stockings came in. Tis strong and empty. Wear your thick coat."

Grania had never seen her aunt idle before. Always when she sat down she had knitting or mending in her hands. Now her fingers trembled and she was biting her lips.

"She's fretting for me," thought the girl.

"I won't go!" she said suddenly. "Me mother didn't want me all these years. Why should she want me now? I'll stay here with you, Aunt Bridgie! You're the one I love!"

Yet as she spoke Grania knew that her going was settled. No one answered her. Sally had slipped out of the kitchen and was making friends with the pony tied in the yard. Only Grania and Norrie knew how she loved horses. She wished she had been a boy, so that she could ride in races. Instead she worked in the ladies' hairdresser's on the Mall.

"Pack up yer paint-box, Grania!" whispered Uncle Christie. "Twill comfort ye!"

"I'll not go without Timmy Fuzz!" decided Grania.

"There's a box under the counter," said her aunt. "You can have that too and the onion basket will do for the little cat."

Norrie came down with the big cardboard box neatly tied.

"Here's some thick string," she told Desmond, giving

him a handful. "You'd best fasten on the box. I daren't go near a horse!"

"Bogtrotter doesn't bite!" exclaimed the boy. "He's the quietest creature on four legs."

"That's a quare name for a horse," said Christie, rubbing his hair.

The cardboard box from under the counter had a hinged cover and looked like leather. Grania had been coaxing her aunt for weeks to give it to her. Now she had it without asking. All her treasures went into it – the new paint-box and drawing book, her pencils, crayons, bits of charcoal.

Desmond went out with Norrie carrying the boxes. Grania was alone with her aunt and Uncle Christie. Already she felt strange.

"I'll come back!" she told them. "You know I'll come back!"

"Poor child," sighed her uncle.

"It's only natural I'm glad to be seeing me mother!" explained Grania. "But you're the ones I know. Maybe she just wants to have a look at me."

"Maybe," agreed her aunt.

She put a piece of flannel in the onion basket. The kitten, sleepy and indifferent, curled round in it.

"God help the pair of ye!" said Christie.

They went out through the shop. A barefoot boy, his hands in his pockets, his tangled hair over his eyes, walked beside a black cow away from the town. Then the road was empty as far down as the market-place.

"Twill be desprit widout ye, Grania!" said Christie.

"I'll miss you terribly," declared Norrie, squeezing in

between them. "Coming in to dinner and tea – and no Grania! I'll never be used to it, never!"

"I'm in two minds not to let you go," murmured Mrs Hanlon. "That lad's been raised by the O'Haras. You'd never know what games they'd be up to. Tricksters – all of them."

"I'm an O'Hara too," thought Grania.

Desmond came round the side of the house from the yard, leading the pony. Sally was on its back, her hair tossed, her eyes delighted.

"I'm off with young Desmond," she cried. "He's going to practise calling me Grania! We won't let on he's bringing the wrong girl."

"Come along down out of that!" commanded her mother. "Haven't we enough trouble?"

"I've always wanted a horse," said Sally. "I'd sooner have a horse than a diamond necklace!"

But she slid to the ground, for Mrs Hanlon looked worried and, though Sally wanted to ride a horse, she wasn't prepared to set off to the O'Haras. Desmond swung himself up in front of the two boxes. Grania stepped on the big stone, which was there for that purpose, and scrambled behind him. Norrie handed up the basket with the sleeping kitten.

"God bless ye, Grania!" said Christie, patting her hand.

"Be a good girl and let me know how things are," and Mrs Hanlon stood close to Bogtrotter so that Grania could lean down and hug her.

Now that she was leaving Sally and Norrie, Grania remembered how kind they had been, petting her when she was little, standing up for her, the best sisters in Dromard. Only they weren't her sisters at all!

"Hold tight!" warned Desmond. "Take it easy, Bogtrotter!"

The horse cantered a little way up the road, swung round and leaped. Grania was looking backwards, gazing down at the sad, friendly faces lifted to hers. Then four sure hoofs came down on the grass, the bog lay before them, and Hanlon's was left behind.

8

Through the Gap

Grania shivered though she had on a thick brown coat and her velvet tammy was pulled over her ears.

A cold wind whipped back her hair. She was so close to Desmond she could not see where they were going. She dared not look back. On the left the bog stretched to where the sky closed down. Above the boy's head rose a line of jagged, dark blue mountains.

Bogtrotter sprang from tussock to tussock of dry grass, leaped over deep cuttings, and trotted along crumbling banks. He splashed through a stream and the water his hoofs tossed into the air glowed like amber. Golden brown pools, fringed with late forget-me-not, spread about grey rocks. High above, chattering birds swarmed dizzily. Grania tilted her head to watch when Desmond's voice startled her.

"Take a grip of me. We're going over the deepest hole on the High Bog!"

She was suddenly terrified – of her companion, the loneliness, and her journey's end.

"Why did Aunt Bridgie let me come?" she wondered. "If only I could get back home! Still, I'm not an orphan any more. I'm like other girls!"

Grania smiled. She was going to her mother. There was nothing to be afraid of. And now she'd never be a dressmaker!

A stretch of heather, blue-purple, red-purple – a gorgeous cloud dropped on a brilliant green meadow made her gasp. She hadn't known there were such colours.

"There was I all those years and never knowing what was in front of the shop," she thought, marvelling at the busy crowded life of Dromard.

"You'd sink in that green stuff so deep not a soul would know you'd passed this way," Desmond told her over his shoulder.

"It isn't grass?" she asked, trembling at the danger though it was behind them and Bogtrotter's hoofs were clattering on stone.

He laughed.

"Grass indeed! That's waterweed and there's no bottom to the water it grows on. But this was a road in ancient times. Isn't it well for us to have it?"

"Mm mm!" agreed Grania, her teeth chattering with the pony's unsettling trot, and clenching her hand tightly in Desmond's belt.

Once the boy turned half-round and took a long steady look at her thoughtful face, with the brown startled eyes framed in a tangle of ruddy hair.

He had been grinning mischievously. Now he frowned.

"She's only a little girl!" he muttered. "Maybe I've been too clever!"

Where three silver birches guarded a flat slab of glittering rock he stopped Bogtrotter and dropped to the ground.

"Listen to me!" he said. "I was joking your aunt. Eily – that's your mother – young Mrs O'Hara, never sent me for you. She'd sooner jump into the Haunted Pool! She hasn't a notion what I'm after doing. We'll turn, and I'll have you back with the Hanlons before they know you're really gone!"

Grania sat silent, staring at him. He could see tears in her big solemn eyes.

"Me mother didn't want me?" she asked in a small voice.

Desmond felt uncomfortable. He was ashamed and sorry.

"Sure she wants you. But she didn't send for you," he explained. "Isn't she for ever boasting how you're being educated to be a lady! It was this way. When she goes down to the market every Thursday, Judy – she's your aunt – does the cooking. Well, she can't cook! And the uncles, that's Phil and Jer and Terry, couldn't stand it any longer, and she didn't like it any better herself. So they planned to bring you up to the castle and you can do the cooking when your mother's away."

"I can't cook!" and Grania looked at him doubtfully. "But I can paint pictures!"

Desmond frowned.

"Much use that will be. If you can't cook you're no better than Judy. I wanted to please Phil. But I might have known there's no use in trying. We'll be getting back."

Grania's eyes flashed with anger.

"Telling lies!" she declared. "You should be ashamed. Making a mock of me!"

The boy laughed. His white teeth made his face seem even darker.

"I told no lies, Grania O'Hara. I said – who but your mother would have the right to send for you? That's all! We'll turn back!"

Grania thought what returning would mean. She wouldn't see her mother, and that wasn't all! By this time Aunt Bridgie would have heard about the ducks on the bridge. She'd be real vexed and there was always Mrs Fogarty. She made up her mind.

"We will not go back!" she said. "You brought me this far. You'll take me the rest. Anyway, I'll see my mother. If I knew how to ride I'd leave you standing!"

Desmond was delighted.

"Wasn't I right to come for you? In two days you'll be standing up to Judy! Your mother needs someone with her around. Even if you can't cook, it's worth while!"

He scrambled up on Bogtrotter, and the pony started off at a steady pace which bounced Grania up and down, but Desmond didn't seem to mind.

Grania asked question after question. What did her mother look like? What kind of a place was Castle O'Hara? Would there be room for her?"

"We don't use half the rooms," Desmond told her. "The castle's been there since the Danes, or Cromwell, or – ah, for years and years! And the walls are three feet thick. If Phil lets you stay, he's the one that counts, and if he gets any more horses, I'll teach you to ride out with me."

"Castle O'Hara doesn't belong to Phil!" said Grania. "It's me mother's and mine. Didn't Aunt Bridgie tell me?"

Desmond reined in the pony and, twisting about, stared at Grania in amazement.

"Don't let Phil or Judy hear you talk that way!" he warned her.

"Isn't it the truth?" asked Grania.

"I suppose it is! But remember – they're not called the Mad O'Haras for nothing!"

"I'm an O'Hara too!" came the answer.

Desmond laughed. But Grania could tell he was anxious.

They rode uphill over the overgrown road, with the line of mountains rising before them.

"Is it far?" asked Grania. "I'm so tired!"

"You can be thankful it's not raining. It's desperate up here in the rain."

The road twisted, and between two high rocks they came to a narrow gap which went right through the mountains.

Overhead the sky was still blue, but they rode in shadow. The wind among the rocks had a mournful sound and Grania felt lonely. The kitten, sleeping in the basket, was her only friend. The boy was a stranger who had played a trick on her, and Hanlon's was far away.

They rode down the wooded valley where a stream, rushing between steep banks, fell suddenly, flinging spray so high the trees were dripping, the long moss and ferns grew in every crevice.

The light, which had been golden on the bog, was green, as though they were sinking beneath the sea. The water crashing over rocks and stones, the wind wailing high in the trees, bewildered Grania. Her eyes were closing with weariness, her body ached, yet still they rode.

She thought of Hanlon's warm snug kitchen, with Timmy Fuzz's portrait on the wall. Her hand was cramped with holding his basket and she longed to see his little black face. He was awake now and mewed faintly when a sudden jump disturbed him.

What would Uncle Christie be thinking? What would Aunt Bridgie be saying about her? And Norrie and Sally?

A yellow light shone through the trees above them.

"That's Peg Lanaghan's!" said Desmond. "She's a queer one, makes her own candles and has a road all to herself. We're as near Castle O'Hara as makes no difference."

Grania forgot her weariness.

"I never dreamed I'd live in a castle!" she murmured.

The stream turned. But they kept straight on towards another light – a red one.

"Is that the castle?" asked Grania.

"It is not. Tis the old pensioner's cabin – Thady Connor. The uncles are always tormenting him."

Grania was cold and frightened.

"Why should they torment him?"

"You ask too many questions!" protested Desmond. "You'll know soon enough!"

He kicked his heels against the boxes, whistled a tune, broke off, started another, became silent.

The pony stepped cautiously. Night had come. But there was a glimmer of stars and every sound was clear and sudden.

Trees grew taller as they passed, rocks were black and silver. Grania had never seen so much sky before. It made her feel small and unhappy.

"I wish I could go home!" she thought. "I want Uncle Christie!"

She looked straight down into a pool glittering with stars.

"The Haunted Pool!" Desmond told her. "There's

strange tales about it. Listen now! There are dogs at the castle. Don't move till I get at them. They're a bit wild and you'd be scared."

"The kitten!" cried Grania.

"Do as I tell you!" said Desmond impatiently. "Then they'll not touch you or the kitten. The Castle, Bogtrotter!"

The pony's hoofs rattled on a stone causeway, water glinted on each side. A dark pile rose before them and, in the centre, Grania saw the red glow of a fire.

Bogtrotter stopped so suddenly she bumped against the boy. Four dogs, little grey shadows, rushed forward, growling and leaping.

Grania held the basket with the kitten in it close against her. She could hear its frantic mee-ows through the uproar.

"Don't be frightened, Timmy Fuzz," she whispered, so terrified herself she could hardly speak.

"Down, Oscar!" shouted Desmond. "Quiet, Finn! Bran – back, back! Maeve, I'll murder you!"

He sprang to the ground. The dogs crouched at his feet, their heads raised to the stranger. Grania could see their shining eyes and grinning teeth.

Desmond led the pony up against the doorway. He pulled Grania to the ground.

"Here she is!" he said. "Grania O'Hara!"

He gave a tug at Bogtrotter's reins and strode away, the dogs jumping round him, leaving Grania alone at the entrance to Castle O'Hara.

9

Castle O'Hara

Grania stared about her, no longer frightened but curious and excited.

A great fire of turf and logs sent heat and light across the room. The square oil lantern, hanging from the centre of the ceiling, left the corners dark and mysterious.

An old woman, leaning forward on a short thick stick, sat on a low wooden chair, her feet on the hearth. She was close to the blaze, yet she wore a thick, black shawl over her shoulders belted in at the waist. On her feet were men's thick boots and she had a blue-and-white checked apron. Her dim, peering eyes were friendly though she could barely see Grania standing in the doorway.

"If she isn't wearing a real red petticoat!" thought the girl.

Every moment she could see more. A square table was set under the lantern which sent its shifting light over the playing-cards scattered there. At one side, a young woman with red hair and blazing blue eyes lounged in a wooden armchair.

"She must be Aunt Judy!" decided Grania.

Opposite, on a high-backed settle pulled out from the wall, three young men sat side by side. At first they looked so much alike that Grania blinked. Then she saw the likeness was in the colour of their hair and their brown faces, for one was fat and his eyes were foolish, the one in the middle had eyebrows which darted up and down, though his eyes remained steady. The third, the handsomest of the three, had a thin bitter face and mocking eyes.

"He's Phil!" thought Grania. "Phil, Jer and Terry!"

They stared at her till she looked away, not knowing what to do. Desmond had no right to march off and leave her there!"

"Who is the strange young gerrul?" asked the old woman. "Come over to the fire, child. Who brought ye here?"

Before Grania could answer, a voice spoke from the dark corner beyond the settle.

"No stranger, ma'am! But my own daughter, Grania O'Hara!"

Someone very like Aunt Bridgie, only younger and slighter, came with a little rush to Grania and hugged her so that she nearly dropped the basket with Timmy Fuzz inside.

"Are you *really* my mother?" asked Grania. Her voice trembling. She felt a strange excitement.

"I am indeed, Grania! But you shouldn't be here? Who brought you? What's happened in Dromard that Bridgie let you come? I had no word! Tell me – what is wrong?"

She stood back from Grania, her face alarmed and puzzled.

"Desmond Burke came for me," answered the girl. "Aunt Bridgie thought you had sent for me. But I know you didn't."

Desmond came in and closed the door. Grania's mother turned to him.

"What possessed you, Des? What were you dreaming of? What made you do such a thing?"

A strange noise came from the settle. Two of the brothers were laughing. The fat one beat his hands together and giggled. The other hid his face in his hands and shook with laughter.

Phil leaned forward.

"Des did what I told him, Eily. I wanted to see your grand young lady of a daughter. Now I've seen her, the lad can take her back!"

For all her tiredness Grania was so indignant she put her hand on the door.

"I'll go back to Dromard," she said. "I can understand why my mother didn't want me here."

"The poor child!" exclaimed the old woman. "Deed and ye'll not stir a step. Come over to the fire and let me look at ye – me own Kevin's little gerrul!"

Judy jumped up in a rage, scattered the cards, and struck the table with her fist.

"We want no Hanlon spies in Castle O'Hara!" she cried. "Let her go back where she came from!"

"Grania has a right to be with her mother," said old Mrs O'Hara. "Don't make me ashamed of ye, Judy!"

"Out she goes!" cried Judy.

Eily put her arm round the girl protectingly.

"If Grania goes, I go with her and we'll never come back!" she declared. "I should never have left her so long."

"Now I know she really is my mother!" thought Grania.

Judy hesitated.

"The Lord pity us!" groaned Terry, jerking up his eyebrows. "If I have to eat another bit of Judy's soda bread I'll not have a tooth left in me mouth!"

Judy glared at him. Suddenly Grania pointed to the cards scattered on the table.

"You should be thinking of the luck that's in the cards for you, instead of making trouble," she said.

"What do you know about cards? Surely Bridgie wouldn't have cards in the house?" protested Eily. "Doesn't she hate them as much as I do?"

"She'd never have card playing," explained Grania. "But Sally taught me how to tell fortunes – just for fun!"

"You can tell fortunes with the cards?" asked Judy in wonder.

"I can, and in the teacups!" boasted Grania.

"Then sit down and do the best you can for me!" ordered her aunt.

"The child needs rest an a bite an sup!" objected old Mrs O'Hara. "Sure she's scarce able to stand on her two feet. She's come a long hard journey to a strange place and ye'll let her be, Judy! Take off yer coat, pet, an come over to the fire till I get a look at ye."

Grania was thankful to sit down. She was so weary she could scarce keep her eyes open. Timmy Fuzz was scratching and mee-owing, so she lifted the lid of the basket and let him out. But he stayed there, looking about with round startled eyes.

"Tis gran to have ye sittin there foreninst me, as your own father often sat," declared the old woman.

"My father!" murmured Grania.

"Ye're the spit of him," her grandmother told her. "It does me eyes good to see ye. Sure I have a grah for ye already."

The friendly voice sounded muffled and confused. Grania's eyes closed and she did not open them until a cup of tea was put in her hand and a hot bacon sandwich laid on her knee.

One sip of that strong sweet tea and she was wide awake.

"That's good tinker tea, child. Twill rise the heart in ye!" chuckled the old woman.

The three men and Judy were eating at the table. Desmond sat silently on a box at the back of Mrs O'Hara. Eily poured tea, cut bread and bacon, then drew forward a chair beside Grania.

"How could you, Des, even if Phil wanted it?" she asked reproachfully. "Twas a cruel trick!"

"Twasn't just him telling me," muttered the boy. "I wanted you to be be happy."

"The lad was right!" declared the old woman. "Ye have a lonely life, Eily. The child will make up for it."

"Desmond told me the truth when we were halfway," said Grania. "But I wouldn't go back. I wanted to come!"

"She takes after me!" cried Mrs O'Hara. "She has the same spirit. Didn't I run away from a decent farm to take up wid a rovin tinker?"

"You're making a fool of the girl with your old chat!" exclaimed Judy. "Isn't it time you dropped that nonsense about tinkers!"

"I'll not stop me talk for any one!" retorted the old woman. "Ye've a bad, hard tongue in yer head, Judy O'Hara, an yer temper's the same. I'm yer mother, an I'm telling ye!"

She muttered indignantly until Grania's mother put a saucer of hot apple pudding in her hand.

"Bedad! Ye're the queen's cook, Eily!" she said.

Mrs O'Hara laid her hand on Grania's.

"Are ye clever too?" she asked. "Wasn't there talk of prenticing ye to the dressmaker?"

"There was!" replied Grania. "But I don't want to be a dressmaker. I'm going to be an artist."

The old woman put her head on one side as she scraped the saucer with a bent spoon.

"Whisha, child! What's that at all?"

Without raising her head Grania glanced round at them all.

Her mother was sipping a cup of tea. Desmond ate apple pudding from a basin he clutched against his chest. The brothers and sister ate and drank steadily at the table. But they were all watching her. Even the four dogs, lying at the door crunching bones, had their eyes on her.

"They mightn't think it so foolish as Aunt Bridgie did," she thought anxiously.

"I can paint pictures!" she said. "I painted a golden apple-tree on Mr Donnelan's door – the door of his new house, he's the bank manager. He gave me a pound for it so that Uncle Christie could buy me the box of paints and brushes that's been in O'Driscoll's window since last Christmas. It was too dear for any one else to buy. It cost a guinea! There it is!"

She pointed at the square parcel Desmond had placed with the others on the window seat. Their eyes followed her pointing finger.

It was so like what had happened earlier in the day in the Hanlons' kitchen that Grania wondered if she were dreaming.

"I'll show you," she said.

She brought the big cardboard box over to the table. Judy pushed away the saucers and cups with a clatter, to give her room, and Desmond untied the string.

Grania let the lid fall back, pulled out the paint-box and opened it. The brushes arranged in order of size and held with bands, the tubes of paint, their colours printed on them, were so lovely she hardly dared touch them.

"That's a queer toy!" said Judy harshly.

"An it cost a whole guinea?" asked the old woman. "Bedad! That must have been a gorgeous gold tree ye painted on the man's door!"

"And I did a black kitten on the wall in Aunt Bridgie's kitchen!" boasted Grania.

"I'd love to look up an see this little lad's picture on the wall!" exclaimed Mrs O'Hara, rumpling the kitten's fur.

Grania was afraid he would be frightened or hurt. But Timmy Fuzz yawned, stretched himself, and clawed his way to the old woman's lap. There he settled and purred so loudly the dogs looked at him with suspicious eyes.

"If the wall was a bit whiter!" murmured Grania. "It's terrible dirty!"

Desmond picked up a sack from the corner, stood on a box, and rubbed a stretch of the wall clean. It wasn't white, but compared with the rest of the room it seemed white.

There were half-burnt sticks lying on the hearth. Grania chose three – two thick and one thin. Then, standing on the box, she began to sketch.

"Sure, that's not a pussy cat!" grumbled Terry.

"Can ye not keep yer mouth shut, and hide yer ignorance?" jeered Phil.

"I must draw this better than I've ever drawn before!" thought Grania.

She forgot the watchful eyes. Desmond stood beside her holding the blunt sticks ready. When she had used up the thick ones, she touched in lighter strokes with the thin. At last she stepped down.

The old woman was laughing silently. Grania, startled, looked at her uncles. They were staring at her in a puzzled way. Judy, her arms folded, was shaking her head angrily as if she were having an argument with herself. Desmond was smiling and only her mother seemed unchanged – sad and patient.

"Don't you like it?" asked Grania, backing against the wall. "Would you sooner I drew a cat?"

Old Mrs O'Hara sat up straight.

"Think of me when yez are all about yer business, lookin at meself up there, the stick in me hand and the pot oven on the hearth! We'll have great times, so we will, Grania and me! Desmond Burke! Ye did a grand thing when ye brought that child away from them shopkeepers in Dromard an tis meself that ses it!"

"No!" cried Eily. "I wanted her to be a lady. I worked for it. I paid for it. I won't have her here!"

"I knew it!" exclaimed Judy. "That's where the good money went. You set them two Hanlons up in a shop, so they'd help you make your daughter a lady. You took good O'Hara money out of this place where it was needed. You're no better than a thief and that's the truth!"

"Twas my own money!" protested Eily. "I'd a right to do as I pleased!"

"Twas O'Hara money!" declared Judy.

"Ah, she has ye there, Eily!" crooned Terry, rubbing his hands. "Judy has ye there, Eily!"

Grania picked up the sack Desmond had used to clean the walls.

"Shall I rub it out?" she asked.

Old Mrs O'Hara was so alarmed she dropped her stick and groped for it in the turf ash. Desmond picked it up.

"Ye'll not rub out me picture!" she cried. "Ye'll not lay a hand on it. Take the sack away from her, Des, there's the lad!"

Grania thankfully dropped the sack.

"Aunt Judy!" she said quickly. "Don't be vexed. One day I'll earn more money than ever my mother spent on me. And now I'll tell your fortune!"

She spread out the cards. Judy and her brothers sat with her at the table.

"In sevens first," explained Grania.

She was conscious of Phil staring at her drawing of the old woman. The dogs had left their bones and were lying at his feet. Old Mrs O'Hara was talking to Timmy Fuzz, whose green eyes were fixed on her face. Eily, pale and sever, sat by herself, holding her sewing to catch the light, but away from them all.

"She should be with Aunt Bridgie," Grania told herself. "She doesn't belong here!"

10

The First Day

"That's all I know!" declared Grania, yawning and wondering where she would sleep that night.

"One more sup of tay?" suggested old Mrs O'Hara, lifting the blackened teapot.

Grania was ashamed to say she didn't want tea which had been stewing for hours. Her mother had vanished, so had Desmond and, while she was still pretending to sip the strong, thick tea, the three uncles and the four dogs slipped out.

As they opened and closed the door, a cloud of grey mist swirled in. Grania shivered and moved closer to the fire.

"If you could tell dreams, I'd be thankful," said Judy. "I have the dreams-books, but they're packed with old rubbish!"

Grania blinked silently.

"Your bed's ready, Grania!" called her mother softly, from the shadows at the foot of the stairs. "You'd best bring the kitten with you."

Grania put the half-finished cup of tea on the table and picked up Timmy Fuzz. The old woman's arms were folded and her head sunk on her chest. Did she sleep here, wondered the girl as she looked about for her parcels.

"Everything you have is in your room," Eily told her, leading the way up a narrow stone staircase, a flickering candle held above her head.

At the top a narrow passage ran the length of the house. Eily pushed a door at the end and stepped into a small square room as bare and cold as a cell.

She set the candle in a pool of its own grease on the window-sill.

"We'll talk tomorrow. God bless you, child!" she murmured and was gone, leaving Grania wide awake now and clutching the kitten for comfort as she gazed about her.

The walls were stone, the roof slabs of stone resting on thick rafters, and the small square window was set half through the thick outside wall.

"It's like a prison!" thought Grania.

A wooden chair, with her nightgown over the back, stood beside the low bed. Her paint-box and the cardboard cases were on the floor. Her best frock and coat hung on hooks behind the door.

Timmy Fuzz leapt to the floor and stalked round the room sniffing curiously. Grania tried to look from the curtainless window. But it wasn't made to open and mist pressed against the glass.

"I do wish I hadn't come!" she murmured.

The candle flickered, and, terrified of being over-taken by the dark, Grania pulled off her clothes and scrambled into bed.

She remembered she hadn't said her prayers. But she was growing sleepy and she dreaded the cold floor.

Hiding her face in her hands she whispered all the prayers she knew.

The candle cast shadows on the walls and floor. They seemed to have a life of their own. Her face, as she moved, made a black shape so strange it was amusing. Timmy Fuzz trotted across the floor and a huge beast stretched up over the ceiling.

Grania pulled the bedclothes to her chin and lay thinking.

"This very morning I didn't know I had a mother. Will she make me go back? I think she likes me. I know I like her! I can't go back now, and I won't be a dressmaker!"

"Jump up, Timmy Fuzz, and keep me warm!" she coaxed.

Grania was asleep before the candle guttered out. The kitten snuggled at the back of her neck and walked into her dreams – a little black, friendly spirit.

She again painted the golden apple-tree, not on Mr Donnelan's door, but on the wall of the big room downstairs. As she painted, it grew, rising through the roof and across the fireplace, out by the window. She slept soundly.

Fierce barking and a terrified mee-owing startled Grania awake. The door was open wide. Timmy Fuzz, his fur on end, his tail as broad as it was long, was perched on the window sill and the four dogs were leaping at him.

Jumping from the bed Grania caught up her shoe and tried to beat them away. Oscar, the biggest, showed his teeth in a snarl. She ran behind a chair and saw the kitten spit at one dog and scratch another on the nose. They dropped to the floor as Eily, with Desmond behind her, rushed into the room.

"Take the dogs away!" cried Grania. "They might have killed Timmy Fuzz!"

"I'm sorry, Grania!" said the boy. "I didn't know what was happening."

And out he went with the four dogs trotting amiably at his heels.

She cuddled the kitten in her hands and stroked its fur until it began to purr jerkily.

"Go back to bed," her mother told her. "I'll bring your breakfast. Don't fret! The little fellow isn't harmed."

Grania was thankful to stay in the warm bed. She was afraid of this rough, wild place.

Her mother came in carrying a battered iron tray with a brown teapot, a chipped enamel mug, and a plate of hot, buttered toast. She propped Grania up with pillows, wrapped a shawl about her, and settled the tray on the bed.

"I've never had breakfast in bed before," said Grania. "I love toast, hot and buttery."

Her mother looked at her gravely, then smiled.

"You had a hard day. A little petting won't hurt you," she said.

The toast was cut in fingers. The butter was strong and deep yellow, and Grania liked its flavour. But the tea had a strange taste. Last night she had been too tired to notice.

"Isn't the milk a bit queer?" she asked.

"Goat's milk," explained her mother. "I've grown used to it."

The kitten finished the crusts and drank a saucer of milk so doubtfully they both laughed.

"Listen now," said Eily. "I couldn't talk to you before the O'Haras. But now I must. You can't stay here, Grania.

Though dear knows I'll be lonely without you. Once a month I'd go to Mass over at Dromard just to have a look at you. But I didn't dare speak for I feared you'd ask to come here and I wanted you to grow up a lady. I didn't care how hard I worked. I didn't care for anything but that. You do understand, Grania, why you must go back, don't you?"

"I wish you had told me," whispered Grania, for her voice was trembling and she was afraid of crying. "Even with Aunt Bridgie and the girls and Uncle Christie I was lonely! I can't go back. I can't!"

"They were good to you?" asked Eily quickly.

"Terribly good," Grania assured her. "But it wasn't like having a mother. Then there's Mrs Fogarty!"

"Is she so bad?" Bridgie thought it a great chance for you. If I did let you stay, Grania, what would become of you?"

Grania twisted her fingers together.

"Could I be an artist?"

She couldn't look at her mother. Aunt Bridgie thought her drawing childish nonsense. Even Uncle Christie thought it foolish because she was a girl and couldn't go painting houses with him. As she spoke, Grania felt hopeless.

"An artist!" echoed Eily.

Kevin had written verses. She had a bundle of them hidden in an old chest. She gazed at Grania, longing to help her.

"How do you become an artist?" she asked.

Grania shook her head.

"I don't know! But there are so many pictures in shops and books there must be plenty of artists in the world.

Sister Mary Joseph thought I was good. She taught me all she knew. But she wanted me to be a teacher."

Eily sat up eagerly.

"Would you like to be a teacher? We might manage it."

Grania sighed.

"If it wasn't for Mrs Fogarty, I'd almost sooner be a dressmaker!" she declared.

"If only we had someone to advise us," said Eily, looking at Grania's downcast face. "I want you to be happy. That's all I ever really wanted."

Grania laughed.

"But I'm happy now. I have you. I have a room to myself and I'm living in a castle. It's wonderful. Do let me stay!"

Eily picked up the tray.

"I don't know what to do. If only that foolish boy had told me what they were planning. Yet I can't feel sorry now you are here. I'm a terribly silly woman, but I'm more contented than I've been for years."

"Let me stay!" coaxed Grania.

"I must think. Maybe in a day or two you'll be running back to Dromard and going down on your knees to Bridgie to take you in."

Left alone Grania dressed slowly. With the kitten in her arms she went cautiously down the steep stairs.

Even on a summer day they were dark unless a door above was left open. Indeed in that house there was never much light.

The big kitchen was empty and she went through the open doorway.

A wide stream flowed before the castle with a causeway of rough stone across it, leading to a road which dropped steeply. A hundred yards along, the stream turned suddenly, dashing over rocks and sending up a continuous cloud of spray. The noise of its fall made a wild humming which bewildered the girl.

To the left the gold and purple, the green and brown of the bog, rose gradually to the blue mountains. Before her, as far as she could see, white-tipped waves surged tumultuously towards the horizon.

"Ye'd never grow tired of looking at it, never!" said a voice so close Grania started, for she thought herself alone.

Her grandmother was sitting on a stone bench against the wall.

"I been watching ye," she declared. "Twas the self-same way poor Kevin would come out an stare around as if he'd never before set eyes on the bog or the salt say! When twas green an grey, wid great hills an valleys he'd say twas the way it should be. An when the waves leapt up, cold and bitter, an the sky shut down, he'd think it grand. But when the sea was blue an wild wid the white horses racin the way it is now, he told me all the beauty of the world lay there before us. A strange lad, Kevin!"

"Could he paint pictures?" asked Grania.

"I dunno, rightly. But he could write poetry. He was clever an he was good. The best of them! Whisha, we didn't know how happy we were while we had him!"

"What was he like?"

"A bit like Phil, more like yourself, child. An very friendly. He had great plans for the castle, great plans. An Phil thought the world of him. Phil was always terrible jealous an he had no kindness at all for poor Eily, no kindness at all!"

"Isn't he very unreasonable!" exclaimed Grania, indignantly.

Mrs O'Hara wrapped her shawl more closely round her.

"Onraisonable's the word, the very word! Twas Kevin lavin the castle to you an Eily that tormented him. Phil couldn't understand it at all. Yet twas the right thing to do."

Grania was puzzled.

"Why can't he be friends with me mother? Wouldn't she be friends with him?"

"She would, child, she would! Sometimes I think if she'd only stand up to him, he'd have more regard for her. But she's as gentle as that little fella in yer arms, an she never scratches.!"

The kitten jumped to the ground and scampered to the edge of the stream. Grania ran after him. He stood on his hind legs, then rolled over and lay on his back.

"Take a hold of him, pet, while I butter his paws!" called the old woman, stumbling into the kitchen.

"Look now what I have for ye," she muttered, coming out with two lumps of butter. While Timmy Fuzz licked one she rubbed the other on his paws, then put him on the ground. Propping himself against Mrs O'Hara's foot the kitten cleaned his paws, bit his nails, yawned, and curled up sound asleep.

"You're a dote!" Grania told him. But he did not hear.

"That lad will never stray!" her grandmother declared. "Butter a cat's paws when he is rale young an ye needn't be troubled when he goes gallivantin. Ah, sure a cat's great company, as good as a dog."

"I hate those dogs!" exclaimed the girl.

"They're grand dogs, aich an ivery one of them!" protested Mrs O'Hara. "Another day an the kitten will be sleepin wid them."

Grania leaned against the sun-warmed wall, thinking dreamily of all that had happened since she set out with Uncle Christie yesterday morning. She felt that weeks had passed.

"Will ye listen to the grand threshin machine they have over at Farrellys'," said the old woman. "There do be times when I'm longin for the ways I used to know: choppin up nettles for the hins an they scutterin about the dure, mixin the food for the pigs wid them shufflin along to get all that's goin, an milkin cows instead of wild, old goats. Still an all I'm comfortable the way I am!"

The strong sweet air made Grania restless.

"I should be helping my mother," she said.

Her grandmother patted her hand.

"Ye'll find her at the pool below the high rock. An don't be lonesome about them ones over at Dromard. Tisn't at the world's end it is!"

"But it will never be the same," thought the girl.

As she ran towards the high rock the wonder of living where there were no other houses, and where sea and bog changed colour every moment, made her happy again. Her grandmother was right: Dromard wasn't at the world's end.

Eily was kneeling beside the pool. She had a creel piled with clothes and she soaped a sheet on a wide flat stone.

"I've come to help you!" announced Grania, dropping down beside her.

Her mother turned with a smile and shook her head.

"There's no need, child! I'm only soaping the clothes and putting them to soak. After dinner I'll squeeze them and spread them to dry. When Mrs O'Hara does the ironing tomorrow, she'll let you do the folding. But you could do something for me now."

"Anything!" declared Grania.

"You could pick blackberries. Thady O'Connor brought over a jug of cream he got from Peg Lanaghan and I'd like to make a pudding for the dinner."

"Pick blackberries!" cried Grania. "I'd love to!"

She jumped up. Her mother caught her frock.

"Listen, Grania! Don't set your heart on the painting. I'm not sure yet. But tis what you want?"

Grania nodded.

"I'd sooner paint pictures than do anything else in the world."

"Get a creel in the house!" Eily called after her.

Grania ran on. Her grandmother, now smoking a short black pipe, blinked at her.

"What's the hurry, child? Sure, ye're young yet!"

"I'm off to pick blackberries. I want a creel."

"There's a wee one be the hearth. The best blackberries is up at the back of the castle. Folly the path beyond the sheds."

Timmy Fuzz was stretched on the old woman's lap. He stood up as Grania came running out. Mrs O'Hara pressed him back with her warm heavy hand.

"Don't be rushin, lad, till ye've the feel of the place. An Grania will be comin back."

Grania followed the path around the side of the castle between the sheds and the turf pile, twisting about the rocks so that at every turn the mountains were before her.

The roots of the brambles were damp, their branches lay on the hot stone and the berries were swollen as large as grapes. Grania settled herself on a slope covered with short, dry grass and leaned back luxuriously, stretching her hand to the gleaming clusters.

She lined the creel with big dock leaves, but it was long before the bottom of it was covered for she could not stop eating the ripe, sweet berries.

"Why did we never come blackberrying on the bog?" she pondered. "No one in Dromard bothered about blackberries."

Distant barking roused her. But she could trust her grandmother to protect Timmy Fuzz. Now she picked steadily until the creel was piled with the wild fruit.

"We'll need a big pudding," she thought. "I'm terribly hungry and how many of us are there? Six – no, eight!"

Crooking her arm about the creel, Grania wandered back. Her uncles sprawled on the stone seat by the door, the dogs with them.

"It's a grand day!" she said.

Not one answered. The men's blank, sullen eyes stared beyond her. The dogs sniffed her ankles. Holding her head as high as she could, Grania walked into the kitchen.

Old Mrs O'Hara was cutting onions; her mother was rolling a lump of dough on the table, and Desmond, working a huge bellows with both hands, blew up the fire under the steaming cauldron. Judy, her elbows on the table, was looking through a pile of dream books.

The big kettle sang on the hearth and a pot oven sat in the hot ashes, with red turf piled on the lid.

"Are the berries ready?" Eily asked. "No leaves or twigs?"

Grania tipped them into a bowl and made sure they were fit for the pudding.

Her mother rolled the dough into an uneven square, slipped it on to a buttered paper, lifted the sides in her hands, while Grania poured in the berries. Now she closed up the opening and wrapped the whole in a clean cloth, tied the ends, and slipped it into the cauldron.

By this time the potatoes and onions had joined the rabbits in the pot oven, and a tempting smell filled the room.

Timmy Fuzz trotted up and down before the fire. He rolled over, squeaked, leapt on the table, jumped down, sprang to Grania's shoulder and purred in her ear.

"I'm hungry too!" said Grania.

"Did you roll yourself in the bramble berries?" asked Judy. "You'd best clean yourself in the stream. You're a fright and that's the truth!"

"Here's a clean towel and a piece of soap, Grania," said Eily. "Don't be long."

Grania went on towards the waterfall. It wasn't as easy as she imagined to wash in the rushing water, and by the time she had finished her sleeves and the front of her dress were soaked.

The plates were ready on the table. They were all cracked. But as Desmond held them out one by one for her mother to fill, Grania longed to be sitting down eating.

Her place was between Desmond and Judy. Eily and the old woman had their dinner by the fire. The kitten crouched between them, eating his saucerful of mashed-up stew. The dogs crunched big beef bones over by the door. Oscar, the biggest of the four, slouched over and tried to share the kitten's dinner. Timmy Fuzz hissed and the old woman gave the dog a tap on the nose which sent it off grumbling.

"They'll be friends before night," said Desmond.

"It's lovely stew!" murmured Grania.

Her mother smiled at her.

"Sure it takes tinkers to make rabbit stew!" chuckled Mrs O'Hara.

No one else spoke.

If the stew was good, Grania thought the blackberry pudding, with cream poured over it, even better. She was beginning not to mind the goat's milk, but she still found the tea bitter.

The uncles sat side by side on the settle, rolling and smoking cigarettes. Judy gazed into her empty mug.

"I had a strange queer dream last night," she said. "Read the cup, Grania!"

Grania took the mug, twisted it round three times, and turned it upside down. When she looked again the tea-leaves had made a pattern all over the inside – the pattern of an apple-tree.

She gazed at it and saw again the golden tree on Mr Donnelan's door.

"There's happiness and success," she said slowly.

Judy snatched the mug and stared solemnly at the scattered tea-leaves.

"Happiness and success? Happiness and success!" she repeated. "I might have believed it once!"

With a scowl she flung the mug over the half-door. They heard the splash as it fell in the stream.

"It's a lie! Where's my happiness to come from? And success!"

Judy glared at Grania.

"You little trickster! Soft and sweet and sly, like your mother! But you'll not trick me.!"

She jumped from her seat and rushed out.

The three brothers had been listening intently. Phil stood up and stretched his arms above his head.

"Success and happiness at Castle O'Hara!" he jeered. "The girl must be a fool!"

Grania went up to her room. The window seemed smaller. The walls were once more like those of a prison. Picking up her drawing-book and the new paint-box she stood leaning against the bed-rail.

"What's wrong with the O'Haras?" she asked herself. "They hate the place and yet they stay. It's queer, but I couldn't bear to leave the castle. Only I'm not like them – I don't hate it!"

11

The Wasteland

When Grania lived at Dromard she was longing to draw and paint every moment of the day. Now she had her wish.

Coming through the empty kitchen one morning she found Mrs O'Hara on the stone bench outside, knitting a stocking, while Timmy Fuzz slapped at the ball of wool as it moved. Grania sat beside them.

"Don't mind me, pet!" said her grandmother. "If I'm in the way, I'll shift meself. Bedad! We're comin up, wid a painter in the family."

Grania opened her paint-box and fingered the tubes of paint. She laid her palette on the bench and at once the kitten sat on it.

"Ye rascal!" chuckled the old woman, lifting him off. "Ye'll destroy the child!"

Grania laughed and looked across to the sea. The wind had died and the waves were no longer tipped with white, but rolled heavily, endlessly, dark green, grey.

Her drawing-book rested on her knee and she turned the pages. It wasn't the one Mrs O'Driscoll had given her but the one Sister Mary Joseph had bought her as a parting gift. The first page was crowded with tiny sketches. Here was Uncle Christie, his pockets bulging, a pot of paint in either hand; Mrs Fogarty; Aunt Bridgie, big, smiling, a rolling-pin under her arm; Sally and Norrie, but Norrie was scribbled over.

"I never could do Norrie!" thought Grania.

Her mother stood beside her looking at the drawings.

"You did those!" she marvelled. "Oh, Grania! Paint a picture of the sea, or the waterfall, or the mountains – something beautiful!"

"Aren't people beautiful?" asked Grania, her head on one side.

"Give the child time!" protested the old woman. "Sure she's still a stranger. The sea takes getting used to an she'll not be herself yet awhile."

Desmond came along with the bucket of water and stopped to look at the sketches.

"Did you draw them yourself, without anybody to help you?" he asked.

Grania nodded and turned the page.

There was the bridge with Barney Reardon on his hands and knees, chalking. Danny Molloy, leaning against the borrowed ladder, stood watching. There were only a few lines in the drawing but Grania knew it was good.

The rest of the book was empty. Grania closed it.

"I can't draw today!" she said.

"An why would ye" demanded her grandmother. "I'd love a dish of musherooms for me tay. Would ye go gather them with Des?"

Desmond darted in the house and came back with the creel Grania had used for the blackberries.

Eily took the paint-box and put it under her arm with the drawing-book.

"Be careful, Des," she said. "We want no more trouble."

"Any one can have musherooms for the gatherin, wherever they grow!" declared Mrs O'Hara. "That's the law!"

"Much she cares for the law!" murmured Desmond, laughing at her over his shoulder.

He ran, swinging the creel, across the causeway. Grania followed, trying to run as he did. But she was used to the pavements of the town and her foothold was slippery and uncertain.

Desmond waited for her above the waterfall, by the ruins of a stone bridge. Two supports thrust up from the water in the middle of the river and, at each side, stone blocks made a steady platform. The boy lifted a long moss-grown plank which lay in the grass and pushed it across. He ran over and stood on the other end.

"Come over while I hold it!" he called.

Grania stared at him in dismay.

"I couldn't!" she cried above the noise of the waterfall.

"Are you frightened?" asked Desmond.

She nodded.

He rubbed his head, not knowing what to do. Grania looked at the plank. It was long. It was narrow and slippery. As Desmond ran across she had seen it bend and sway. But he was holding it firm.

"I'd hate him to think me a coward!" she told herself.

Desperately she put one foot forward.

"I'll fall in! I know I will!" she thought.

She took another step. And there she was, walking a path so frail it seemed each moment would send her toppling into the foaming water, for the bridge had been built at the edge of the fall.

Desmond came to meet her, stretching out his hand so that he seemed to be pulling her.

At last his fingers gripped hers. He stepped backward and they huddled side by side on the tiny island of stone in the middle of the stream.

"You did that fine!" declared Desmond. "Keep still now while I push it to the far side."

She held the creel and watched while he balanced himself and the plank, swinging it round until the end rested on the other bank.

"Why doesn't someone build a proper bridge?" asked Grania, dreading the second venture.

"There was a proper bridge," shouted Desmond, to make himself heard above the rush and tumult, "before the O'Haras destroyed it."

He pushed and tested the plank until it was wedged tightly.

"Now cross!" he said. "I'll come after you."

Grania didn't mind this crossing. The wide stretch of the bank made her feel safe.

The grass was long and rich on this side. There were few rocks and a thick wood sheltered the slope. A fence of posts and wire ran from the wood in a line with the stream, guarding a herd of cows.

"They're the Farrellys'. Wish we had cows!" muttered Desmond.

"Why don't the cows feed this side of the fence?" asked Grania.

"This is O'Hara land," replied Desmond.

"Then why don't we have cows?" persisted Grania.

Desmond frowned.

"The Farrellys used to rent this land from Kevin. When

he died Phil stopped that. There was a path across here to the bridge and the Farrellys used the road down to Kilvaragh. Your uncles destroyed the bridge, so now the Farrellys have to use a rough track three times as long instead of the road, and cross by the ferry."

"What made them destroy a bridge?"

"The Mad O'Haras!" said Desmond. "No reason at all. There was a law case over it. The Farrellys lost; the O'Haras won. And Eily says it was the worst thing ever happened to them!"

They went as far as the trees. Then, dropping to the ground, squeezed under the wire. The cows were at the lower end of the field and didn't stop feeding to look at them. Grania couldn't see any mushrooms. But Desmond found one, then four growing together. After that the ground seemed covered. There were fine big one, little pink-and-white fairy cups, ordinary ones, big enough for flavour, not large enough to be coarse, and one like a dinner plate.

Grania, wearied of stooping and standing up continually, stood idle, looking down upon a white-washed farmhouse with a stone wall enclosing a flower garden in front and an orchard at the back.

Even at the distance it had a pleasant, comfortable appearance. There were white curtains to the windows, the gate was painted, and the path up to the door was bordered with sparkling pieces of rock.

The door stood open and an enormous tabby cat lay stretched there. In the orchard, hens scratched beneath the trees and, on a turf pile at the side, was perched a black cock. The sound of its crowing came thin and clear.

Suddenly a brown-and-white collie stepped over the cat and walked along the path, its head thrown up.

Grania laughed.

"You'd think it was sniffing a strange smell," she said.

Desmond didn't hear her. The creel was filled but he was trying to pile on a few more.

The collie barked, sniffed again then, rushing to the gate, leaped over and, running backwards and forwards, barked his loudest.

Desmond swung around.

"Run!" he cried. "They'll be after us!"

A giant of a man with a pitchfork over his shoulder, strode in sight from behind the turf pile.

"That's Big Bill Farrelly!" explained Desmond, as they ran towards the wire.

The dog raced in front of the man. Luckily he kept stopping to bark and Big Bill delayed himself by shouting. Two young men rushed through the orchard, calling out as they came.

Desmond reached the fence first, put the creel on the other side and wriggled underneath. Grania could not keep up with him. She stumbled and slipped, while the shouts and barks, instead of making her quicker, seemed to hold her back.

"Hurry!" called Desmond.

Grania was gasping when she reached the fence. As she tried to roll under, her frock caught in the barbed wire. Frantically she tugged until the stuff tore. Then on they ran. The long grass caught at Grania's feet, but she wasn't so breathless now and reached the bridge only a little way behind Desmond.

He had left the plank in place. Grania crossed without

thinking and held the creel of mushrooms while he pulled the long awkward board from one side to the other.

The three Farrellys stood side by side. The dog would have leapt into the stream but the youngest hauled him back.

"Ye young thieves!" shouted Big Bill. "I'm warnin ye! From this day out I'll keep watch an if ye trespass on my land I'll not leave a whole bone in yer bodies! Remember now! I have planks that will cross the river as aisy as yours!"

They stood still there while Grania and Desmond crossed the second gap and pulled the plank after them.

"They're horrid!" declared Grania. "Do they sell mushrooms?"

"They used to," Desmond told her.

"I wish we hadn't taken them," said Grania.

Desmond grinned.

"They're good mushrooms!" he said. "And I never lost one!"

Mrs O'Hara was still on the stone bench when they reached the castle.

"That's a gran creel of musherooms ye have there, Des, lad! Put em here, till I skin em. Grania, ax Eily for two plates. Des, ye can help wid the skinnin, an tell me what happened. I can see the Farrellys chased ye. But what harrum?"

Eily was cutting a loaf on the table. She looked round with a smile. But it vanished when she saw Grania's downcast face and torn frock.

"Did you hurt yourself?" she asked, her hand to her mouth.

"The Farrellys chased us!" Grania told her indignantly.

"They didn't catch you?"

"I'm ashamed!" said Grania. "It isn't fair to be hated for something I can't help!"

Eily went on with her bread-cutting.

"You're an O'Hara! I'm sorry, Grania, but you'll have to grow used to people disliking you because of the others. Even Des has to put up with it. Now change that frock and I'll see if I can mend it."

Grania leaned across the table.

"Why don't you make them behave?" she urged. "If it's our place you can make them!"

Eily stopped cutting.

"I can't live without peace," she said. "And I'm afraid of their tempers."

"I'm not!" declared Grania.

Eily laid down the knife and stared at her. Unexpectedly she laughed.

"I don't believe you are!" she exclaimed. "And I've never seen them friendlier with any one. Of course, you're an O'Hara too and they seem to be proud of you. But don't cross Phil, not until you're older and understand more."

Grania changed into her blue school frock with a white collar. It was too short, but Eily liked to see her in it.

"Bridgie told me how smart you looked going to school and I never saw you," she said.

When the bread was cut Grania laid the table. Already she was growing used to chipped plates, battered knives and forks, and mugs instead of cups. Her mother sliced rashers from a piece of bacon hanging on a hook in the rafters. She cut them as quickly and thinly as a machine, and Grania stood admiring her.

"Plates, Grania," called Desmond.

She ran out with two of the big plates. Already a pile of mushrooms without stalks or peel was stacked on the bench.

"Lave one plate for the stalks an skins, allana!" said the old woman. "We'll have gran soup tomorra!"

Eily was turning the rashers in the pan when Judy came in swinging a market bag. She was flushed and bad-tempered, and began scolding the moment she entered.

"That road's a disgrace! Bogtrotter nearly broke a leg a dozen times. And I had to hand out every penny I carried for cheese and fruit at the new shop. Someone will have to bring money into this house or we'll starve!"

"No starving tonight!" declared Grania. "We brought home a creel full of mushrooms!"

Judy flashed a sharp look at her.

"I have me nose, thank God! Did the Farrellys see you?"

"They did!" replied Grania. "Why can't we be friends with them?"

Judy leaned forward, her fist clenched on her knees, her eyes blazing.

"Friends!" she exclaimed. "Friends with the Farrellys? Do you know they had the law on us, turned informers, tried to take our rights away?"

Grania was about to answer. Her mother stopped her.

"Grania's only a child. How could she understand the rights or wrongs of a neighbours' quarrel, Judy?" she asked.

Desmond and the old woman came in with the remainder of the mushrooms. Then followed the brothers and the dogs. They carried six rabbits which they flung into a corner. The kitten, high up on a shelf, peered down curiously but without fear as the dogs stretched themselves before the fire.

"You'll have to sell the horse!" announced Judy.

The men stared at her. Phil laughed.

"Sell the last remaining horse?" he asked.

"We've no money!" exclaimed Judy. "We can't live without money!"

Phil looked at her thoughtfully.

"After tea I'll go down to Kilvaragh. Where's the new pack of cards?"

"Who in Kilvaragh will play cards with an O'Hara and Phil O'Hara at that?" asked Judy.

Phil drank a cupful of scalding tea without taking the cup from his lips.

"When we were out on the High Bog I saw a strange ship come into the harbour. A fair-sized one. There's not much fun in Kilvaragh."

He ate a plateful of the fried mushrooms and cleaned up the gravy with a piece of Eily's crumbly soda bread. She was frowning.

"Just like Aunt Bridgie!" thought Grania. "This is why they both hate cards!"

Phil went off while they were still drinking tea. Terry and Jer stood up to go with him but he waved them back.

"I'm riding!" he said.

Desmond brought the pony to the door. He had brushed its coat and trimmed its mane and tail.

Phil put his hand on the pony's neck and jumped up. Away he rode, over the causeway, then down out of sight.

12

Eily's Story

Before the month was over Grania no longer thought of her room as a cell. Eily turned out a big chest of old clothes and pieces of stuff, and Grania had made curtains which draped the window and cut off a corner. In the corner she hammered nails to hang her best dress and coat. An old crimson rug served as a bedspread and even Judy admired the result. But she had to find fault.

"You're making your own room grand enough," she said. "You'd never think of putting a bit of colour in your mother's room. Still, it serves her right, the way she cocked you up!"

Grania tried not to smile triumphantly.

"I'm painting an apple-tree on the wall so she'll see it every morning when she opens her eyes. I haven't enough gold paint to make it like Mr Donnelan's, but there'll be two gold apples and red and yellow ones."

Judy tossed her head.

"You have an answer to everything. You're too clever by half!"

Grania wondered would she have enough paint to do pictures on all the walls. She could hardly believe that she would only be praised if she succeeded.

Grania helped her mother make beds and sweep floors. She brought water from the stream and went with Desmond to carry in turf. Aunt Bridgie had taught her to clean windows so that it was hard to see the glass. But the O'Haras cleaned only the inside. Rain and wind had charge of the outside.

"I clean the windows here!" Desmond told her, when she wanted to wipe steam and smoke from the kitchen window.

"Aunt Bridgie wouldn't call them clean!" she declared, longing to show how they could be polished.

Desmond grinned, crumpled a piece of newspaper, and had the window gleaming while she watched.

"Windows should open," Grania grumbled.

"Sure, child, if tis air ye want, isn't the door enough?" asked her grandmother.

But every hour carried her further from the clean, ordered life of Dromard and she had never been so happy.

She sat by the half-door, trying to paint the rocks which rose beyond the stream. The shadows gave her the most trouble.

"I can't do them!" she thought. "They're all wrong. Shadows should be grey or black, but those look purple. Why isn't there someone to teach me? I don't know enough! If only I could paint shadows!"

"I wonder will Phil win the money to settle Danny Morgan's bill, let alone the Rattigans'. They should be paid – the dacent people!" murmured old Mrs O'Hara, pressing the bellows up and down.

Jer and Terry had been discussing Phi's chances of success at card-playing with the sailors down in Kilvaragh.

"There's that robber, Andy Mahon, clamouring to be paid for my boots," said Judy. "And I need a new frock."

"Sure that old wan down in Kilvaragh can't cut a frock fit for a tinker woman!" exclaimed Mrs O'Hara. "She should be at the fish peddlin! She made a disgrace of ye wid the last frock she stitched!"

"I could make you a grand dress!" declared Grania, glad to turn away from the troublesome shadows.

Judy looked at her scornfully. Then she wondered, her chin resting on her clasped hands. Slowly she raised her head.

"Are you joking?" she asked.

"I don't want to be a dressmaker, but I did make this frock myself!" Grania explained. "Aunt Bridgie helped me with the stitching but I did the cutting. Of course I had a pattern."

"I've a lovely length of cashmere," said Judy. "A gorgeous green it is. But if you spoilt it I'd slaughter you!"

Eily sat bolt upright, a heap of undarned socks and stockings spilling from her lap.

"If you wanted to make dresses, Grania, why wouldn't you be taught to do it properly?"she asked reproachfully.

"Stitch, stitch, stitch!" sang Terry mockingly.

"I like making things," Grania answered. "But I couldn't bear to be shut up day after day with Mrs Fogarty. And I'll make a grand frock for Aunt Judy!" she added.

Old Mrs Fogarty laughed and clapped her hands.

"Pon my word, Eily, she's like her da! He had always an ever to be makin somethin. But he had to do it in his own way. I'd love to see her contrivin a green frock for Judy. Tis time there was a bit of style an cultivation at Castle O'Hara!"

"We'll buy a paper pattern on Sunday at the Widda Dooley's!" decided Judy, her elbows on the table, her hands clutching her tawny hair. "Isn't it a terrible pity we haven't a decent trap to drive down in! My green frock 'll be ruined sitting in that dirty old cart!"

"If we had a decent trap, itself would be shattered to bits on that divil of a road!" grinned Jer.

"We had a good road when the Farrellys used it. They never minded mending and making!" put in Eily, speaking quietly but darning so quickly, the long tail of wool twirled and knotted until she had to break it.

Judy turned in her seat.

"Quit talking about the Farrellys!" she cried. "Haven't I told you time and time again not to be bringing them up – thieves and informers!"

"You leave my mother alone or I won't make your frock!" threatened Grania.

Judy half rose from her chair, then sank back.

"You'd better make a good frock, or twill be the worse for you, you impudent young strap!"

Her blue eyes met Grania's brown ones and they both laughed.

"She's a match for ye, Judy girl!" chuckled the old woman. "Now, Eily, don't look so vexed. Sure, the O'Haras always was quarrelsome, an Grania's an O'Hara, God help her! There's no getting away from it."

"I'm sorry," said Grania. But it was to her mother, not Judy, she spoke.

Terry and Jer were playing cards, and when they played cards they cared nothing for what was happening around them. They sat with their legs stretched, their muddy boots sticking out from under the table. Judy, her mind filled with the vision of the green cashmere frock, glowered at them with contempt.

Grania sat gazing at her aunt. To her own amazement she was feeling pity for Judy.

"It can't be much fun to have no friends and nothing to do," thought the girl. "My mother and granny take care of the house. Des does the work outside. The uncles snare rabbits and deal in horses. She has no life at all!"

"Why are you staring at me?" demanded Judy suddenly. "Are you wanting to paint my portrait!"

"Twould be a gran picture if she did, and you in the new green frock!" declared the old woman, delighted at the idea.

"Yet she'll never look lovelier than she does in that faded blue!" thought Grania.

Judy leaned forward, her hair glowing like a halo about her frowning face.

"We're wrong!" she said, laughing. But her blue eyes were bitter. "Grania's feeling sorry for me! Why wouldn't she? Isn't it terrible to be cooped up with a pair of card-playing tinkers! There they sit, idling their lives away! And look at the place! If Kevin had lived, he'd have made the castle the pride of Kilvaragh. But I'll be ashamed to come in here in the new green dress!"

Judy's mournful voice made no impression on her brothers. They sprawled on the settle, the dogs at their feet shifting continually and gazing longingly at the door. The slapping of cards on the table went on without a pause until Judy was exasperated.

"Jer," she exclaimed. "Do you not hear a word I'm saying? Terry! Take those muddy boots out of my sight!"

She snatched at the broom leaning against the wall

and gave Terry, who was nearest, a crack across the leg.

With a howl he drew in his feet and gazed wildly at his sister.

"What ails ye, Judy?" he asked. "Was it accident, or was it maleecious?"

"Drop them tantrums, Judy!" said Mrs O'Hara sternly. "I'm ashamed of ye, scarin the poor child out of her wits, an Eily's disgusted wid ye!"

Grania wasn't the least scared. But when she saw her mother standing at the half-door, gazing despairingly across the causeway, she was sorry. She went over to her.

"Don't mind," she whispered, slipping her hand into Eily's. "If I make her a lovely frock, she may become quite good-tempered."

Eily pulled open the lower door and they walked out across the causeway.

Grania glanced back at the dark building. It looked a real castle in the evening light – grey and square, with turrets at each end. Mrs O'Hara had told her it was only a blockhouse built as a watchtower for soldiers when the Rebels were in the hills. But to Grania it was indeed a castle.

Down in Dromard there would be lights in the houses. The streets in the lower town would be dark. Up here sunlight still splashed the mountains, the river sped in a golden flood, and the bog pools were mirrors reflecting rushes and clouds.

"You want to be an artist," said Eily. "Now you're talking of making a dress for Judy. Besides, all the artists I ever heard tell of were clever men, old, I expect, and you're only a little girl. All these years I thought of you going to school, learning nice manners, and growing into a lady. I thought I'd be proud of you. Now you're settling in here – one of the Mad O'Haras!"

"Well, I am an O'Hara!" protested Grania. "And I like it better than being little orphan Hanlon!"

"Did they call you that?" asked Eily indignantly.

Grania laughed.

"Only for fun. But you can't think what it means to have a mother of your own. Aunt Bridgie used to be always talking about her lovely sister, who married a tinker. My father wasn't a tinker, was he?"

They walked on away from the waterfall, away from the stream, along the path where Desmond had brought Grania that first night.

Eily shook her head.

"Kevin was no tinker! He loved the land. His father was a tinker and old Mrs O'Hara was a farmer's daughter who ran away from home to marry him. They lived in a van and often slept at the side of the road. You'll hear all about it soon enough."

Grania's eyes were wide open with interest.

"But how did they come to own a castle?"

Eily seated herself on a flat rock and Grania perched beside her, her legs drawn up, her hands clasped round them, and her chin resting on her knees.

"Twas Kevin bought the castle!" said Eily proudly. "All the O'Haras are clever with horses, but he was the cleverest of them all! He didn't play cards and he kept his money, so when his father died and his mother grew tired of wandering, he could make a home for her. Twas down in Dromard at a fair I met him. He was showing a big fierce horse that every one was afraid to look at. He handled it so that it was like a carriage horse. Kevin was wonderful that day. Phil was there too. But I didn't notice him. Kevin was always good-tempered, with a ready laugh. Phil was the sour one. But he stood by Kevin."

"Don't stop! Please go on!" urged Grania.

"I was a wild young one, Grania, and very head-strong," said Eily thoughtfully. "I wouldn't listen to Bridgie, though she was terribly upset. I married him and came up here to live. We were so happy, it's like a dream now."

She sighed and looked away across the stretch of bog to the mountains. Grania kept very still.

"Why didn't Aunt Bridgie like my father?" she asked.

"She never knew him. She didn't see him as I did, riding that horse at the Fair, and she never came here."

Grania was puzzled.

"But when you took me to Aunt Bridgie. Why didn't you stay too?"

Eily stood up, straight and slight, but every bit as determined as Judy could be.

"I wouldn't let Judy and her brothers take away your rights. Castle O'Hara is yours and I'll not let them rob you!"

13

Sunday in Kilvaragh

"Hurry or you'll be late, and there's no waiting on Sunday morning!"

Half-asleep, Grania blinked at the flickering candle flame and saw her mother smiling back at her as she went out through the low doorway.

The sheepskin on the floor beside the bed was snug to her bare feet, but she shivered as she washed in the tin basin rattling on a box set endways against the wall.

"What was I doing this time last Sunday at Dromard?" pondered Grania.

The week stretched away and away behind her. Riding over the High Bog, Grania had ridden from one world into another.

She combed her thick curly hair, very like Judy's, over her face. Hurriedly she flung it back and ran to her drawing-book.

"How can I draw here?" she cried, forgetting the day and the need for haste.

Blowing out the candle she groped her way down the staircase, her fingers brushing against the rough wall.

The big kitchen seemed crowded as she reached the last step. Phil sat on the table swinging one leg. He switched with an ash-plant at the dogs who prowled restlessly under the table, out and back again. Terry, his eyebrows jerking up and down, was fixing a black tie in front of the cracked looking-glass which hung between window and door. Jer, nearer than she had seen him before, was polishing his boots.

Mrs O'Hara wore a long black fur coat, kid gloves, and a bonnet with a feather, perched at the back of her head. Surmounted by such splendour her face looked harsh and weather-beaten.

Grania was pleased that her mother looked quite as elegant as Aunt Bridgie.

But Judy sat on one chair with her foot cocked upon another, trying to force the buttons through the holes with a hairpin.

"I've never seen any one else wear button boots," thought Grania.

As she watched, the hairpin bent and Judy flung it from her.

"Who's been meddling with me button-hook?" she demanded. "I can't leave a thing out of me hands but it's lost. And that was the last button-hook in Kilvaragh. I'll be driven to wearing lace-up boots!"

Then she saw Grania standing on the stairs.

"Eily! Will you look at that half-asleep daughter of yours! Does she ever wake up? Get ready, girl! Are you such a heathen you don't know we go to Mass on Sundays?"

Grania knew this was no time to be thinking of drawing. She ran back to her room, changed to her best frock, and was in the kitchen before Judy's boots were fastened.

Eily was on her knees before Judy, buttoning the boots with her fingers. Grania hated to see her mother kneeling there while Judy, arms folded, gazed above her head over the half-door.

"She's like a warrior queen!" thought the girl, half admiring, half angry.

As Eily rose from her knees, Desmond came to the door leading Bogtrotter harnessed to a rough cart.

Phil put the old woman's armchair into the cart and fastened it to the side with a thick rope. She was still munching soda bread as he helped her up. Desmond sat in front with the brothers crowding him off the seat.

"I'll walk!" said Grania. "That little pony can't pull all of us!"

"She's right!" declared Desmond.

He thrust the reins into Phil's hands and jumped to the ground.

The dogs barked and snapped at Bogtrotter. Timmy Fuzz stood on the stone bench mee-owing in great distress. Grania lifted him to the moss-grown gutter.

"I'll be home again," she told him. "Don't fret!"

"If he stays there he'll be safe," she said to Desmond.

"If it's the dogs you're worrying about, you needn't. They'd protect him now!" he assured her.

But Grania was glad to see the kitten out of their reach. Already the cart was rumbling away, the plume in Mrs O'Hara's bonnet waving in the wind. Desmond was crossing the causeway.

"We'll have to walk back as well," he grumbled as she joined him. "And it's all uphill."

"Is this the way to Dromard?" asked Grania in surprise, as they hurried along an overgrown road which plunged down into a valley of rocks.

He shook his head.

"Look! There's Spain straight ahead, and over the way lies France!"

Grania could see nothing but tumbling waves where he pointed. Overhead, cloud galleons were surging towards the horizon where a great city of domes and pinnacles rose against the sky.

"They're only clouds!" she thought. "But such colours!"

They changed as she watched, all colour faded, domes and pinnacles sank into the grey mass.

"I don't mean you can see France or Spain," Desmond was saying. "I'm showing you where they are."

"Is it Kilvaragh we're going to?" asked Grania.

"It is! Did you think we were going to cross the High Bog to Dromard?"

Grania had eaten nothing. She had taken a sup of cold black tea and now she was hungry. As she tried to keep up with Desmond she thought longingly of the Hanlons' pleasant kitchen. Whatever the haste the tea was always well-made, bread and butter decently piled on a plate. The wind flung a stinging drizzle in her face and she shrank inside her thick coat.

"We'll take a short cut!" exclaimed Desmond. "Think of their faces when they see us waiting for them at the top of Kilvaragh!"

Desmond made the rough journey easy. He swung her down from rocks, lifted her over gaps, held back briars, and showed her how to leap from rock to rock. Suddenly he pulled her forward.

"The Farrellys!" he said.

Where the Varagh river made a wide curve between high banks, Grania caught a glimpse, through a gap, of a smart glittering trap drawn by a large bay horse. For a moment startled faces gazed towards them. Then they moved out of sight.

"They have to cross by the ferry and they haven't a proper road," explained Desmond. "Wait! I meant to show you – there's Kilvaragh. But we can't stop now!"

As Grania followed she had glimpses of a harbour, fishing boats drawn up to the quays, huddled houses, wet roofs glistening. The sea was grey, the houses, the quays – but the furled sails of the boats were red and brown, some of the women coming from the houses wore red petticoats, girls and children were like dancing flowers in their gay scarves and tammies. Over all, a bell was ringing, drawing them out, through the cold drizzle and driving wind to the chapel at the top of the town.

Grania and Desmond reached the gate as Bogtrotter came clattering along the main street. Mrs O'Hara's fur coat was so wet she looked like a seal. But, as Phil lifted her down, she was chuckling.

"Forty years I've had this coat an it kept me dry the whole time. Is it yerselves, childer? Run along into the chapel, Grania, out of the rain. Weren't ye very sensible to walk. Des, will ye tie up the cart an let Phil into Mass while he's in a fit condition of mind?"

Eily and Grania kept with the old woman. She led the way to the front seat. But it was already filled, so was the second. A girl at the end of the third stood up to let them pass, but Mrs O'Hara pushed her along, motioned Eily and Grania in and, sitting down, propped herself sideways.

Grania had her own little prayer book in her pocket, together with the pearl rosary beads Aunt Bridgie had given her. She tried to keep her mind on following the

Mass, but her thoughts strayed to the harbour and the fishing boats.

Outside the last window, near the altar, a wind-beaten leafless tree streamed in the wind. An old man and boy knelt in front of her. Both wore blue jerseys smelling of brine, their faces were dark brown, the boy's hair fair, the man's white. When they moved their heads Grania saw in the boy's face what the man had been: in the man's what the boy would be.

"If I could paint them!" she thought.

At once she closed her eyes, determined not to let her mind wander. There was so much to see – faces all around her: the tree at the window: the queer stains on the damp walls: the arched roof with brown wood lining.

She looked again and there were the Farrellys – six of them filling a whole bench. They were the enemy, but there was kindness in every face. Her resentment against Big Bill for chasing her with a pitchfork vanished. He reminded her of Uncle Christie, yet he was a big, heavy man. The woman was smiling, even though she was serious and reverent. The girl was pretty and freckled. Grania like the way her long, light-brown plaits were twisted round her head. She couldn't see the young men properly. They were hidden by their father.

"The world's full of pictures and I've hardly started," Grania reflected. "Oh, God! Make me work hard and be a good artist!"

Coming out from Mass she noticed how every one greeted the Farrellys and her mother. "How are ye, Big Bill?" "Is it yerself, Mrs Farrelly, and the family?" "Ye're lookin gran, Eily O'Hara! Ye have the little gerrul wid ye now? Isn't that great!"

There were smiles and nods for Grania as she kept close to her mother. People stepped back to let the O'Hara's go by. But no one had a friendly word for them, not even for Desmond!

"And he's not an O'Hara!" thought the girl indignantly.

As they reached the gate the pressure of the crowd forced O'Haras and Farrellys together. The O'Haras glared, the Farrellys looked blank as though their enemies were invisible.

But Jer tittered and Big Bill Farrelly scowled.

"Tinkers!" he said loudly.

His sons pushed him on.

"Are we to take impudence from paupers?" demanded Judy.

Phil swung towards them. His mother pulled him away.

"Are ye mad?" she asked. "Do ye want us to be called from the altar?"

Judy seized Grania by the arm.

"Let's away to the Widda Dooley's and buy the paper pattern. There'll be no fight here this morning!"

She looked scornfully at her brothers, then swept off with Grania.

Widow Dooley's was the newspaper shop nearest the chapel. The widow did most of her trade on Sunday mornings. Judy, with Grania at her elbow, thrust her way down the three crowded steps from the pavement to the door. There they stopped, for the tiny shop was packed between its two counters. Martin Dooley, the widow's son, sold newspapers in a pleasant leisurely way, reading out the headlines as he handed them over.

His mother sold tobacco, sweets, and toys at the other counter. She was as quick as Martin was slow, but she gossiped even more. Dooley's was the place for news, not only in the papers.

Judy dug her elbows into the backs and ribs of those near her. They edged away but still hemmed her in.

"Squeeze along in there to the widda," she ordered Grania. "Tis she has the pattern papers. Here's two shillings, you can keep the change."

Grania was small and thin. She soon reached the counter.

Mrs Dooley looked at her intently.

"Ye're a stranger!" she declared, screwing her face into so many wrinkles, Grania was fascinated. "Now where do ye belong?" she blinked rapidly. "I have it! Ye're Eily O'Hara's little gerrul, that was being reared be the Hanlons over at Dromard. Tis a terrible change for ye!" She leaned across the counter and whispered, "How d'ye like it? Do they beat ye?"

Grania could feel her cheeks growing redder and redder. Her eyes flashed. A look of Judy passed over her face. But the proud way she pressed her lips and gazed straight into the widow's eyes was all Eily's.

"I'm very happy, thank you!" she said. "Could I have a pattern for a lady's frock and four ounces of mixed sweets, please?"

Mrs Dooley reached up to the shelf and flopped a bundle of fashion magazines on the counter.

"Is it for yer mammy, pet? Help yourself. I'll get the sweeties."

Grania turned over the magazines. She was conscious of curious looks, but her whole interest was on the frock for Judy. She judged by the pictures on the covers and, when she saw a red-haired woman in a flowing brown frock, she looked no more.

"I'll have this, please!" she said, putting the two-shilling piece beside the bag of sweets.

The widow Dooley stared at the red-haired woman.

"Bless an save us, child! Yer mammy couldn't wear a dress that long. I'll pick ye one!"

"This is the one I'm taking!" declared Grania.

Mrs Dooley picked up the money, paid out the change, and didn't say another word. Grania backed through the shop to Judy.

"Aisy to tell that young one's an O'Hara!" she heard. "The spit of her Aunt Judy!" "God help poor Eily O'Hara!" "That's a bold young strap!"

Judy was grinning when Grania reached her.

"You've made your bow to Kilvaragh!" she told her niece. "Is it a good frock you've chosen?"

"A beauty!" Grania assured her. "A bit long but we can alter that."

"Why shouldn't I have a long dress?" demanded Judy. "All my life I've wanted one with a train. I wonder would the green stuff run to it?"

They wandered down the windswept quays. The rain had ceased, but the sky was so low and heavy it seemed to rest on the grey roofs. Every few yards Grania stopped to look at the steps going down to the river, a ferry-boat deep in the water, a dirty little coasting steamer at anchor, with a sailor sitting on deck smoking a big pipe with a shiny lid and nursing a huge tabby cat. She saw a tower – all glass at the top – at the end of a line of rocks over which the sea was breaking.

"A round tower! I've never seen one before!" she exclaimed.

Judy looked without interest.

"That's Kilvaragh lighthouse. Yonder's the boat from Abbey Strand, a god-forsaken place. They have no chapel of their own but must come in to Kilvaragh."

"Judy! Did you never go to Dublin, or Cork, or Waterford?" asked Grania.

"Mind your business!" snapped Judy. "There's Des. You can keep with him. Give me the pattern book."

Grania handed her the gaily-coloured magazine and Judy turned from the quays, going by the post office, up the main street, studying the red-haired woman in the flowing brown frock.

"How do you like Kilvaragh?" asked Desmond.

His hair was plastered wetly to his forehead, but at the back a fair lock was standing up stiff and erect.

"I love it!" declared Grania. "I love the boats and the smell and the people! No, I don't like the people! They're not friendly!"

"If you came alone, they'd be friendly!" the boy told her. "They were kind to me at first, because every one liked Kevin and twas he brought me to the castle."

"Kevin! My father? asked Grania.

Desmond nodded.

"He was good to me. I was happy while he lived. I remember Eily running away with you. I was only a little chap. But I was sorry for her when she came back alone. Twas of her I was thinking that day I came to Dromard. Maybe I should be sorry for you now?"

"Not for me!" declared Grania. "If I'd stayed with Aunt Bridgie I'd never be an artist."

"So I've done Eily good and you no harm," said Desmond, and he whistled skilfully as they went through the town.

14

What's the News?

There were many shops in Kilvaragh, small and dark. One of them was a picture shop.

Grania had never before seen so many pictures together.

"What a lovely shop!" she said.

She moved slowly along.

"They're not so good. The one in the corner – but that's just a copy. I could do better."

"We must be going!" Desmond urged her. "You'll be in Kilvaragh again."

A horse neighed shrilly.

"That's Bogtrotter," said the boy. "They're on the way. Run!"

Rain began to fall as they saw the cart bumping its way out of Kilvaragh.

"We needn't hurry if we have to walk!" grumbled Grania, who was cold and tired.

"What's the news?" the old woman was asking as they came up.

The cart sheltered them from wind but not from the rain. Grania felt her shoulders wet and her hair glittered with raindrops. Her town shoes squelched at every step and she was thankful Desmond did not suggest the short cut.

He, too, wanted to hear the news.

"Tis true enough," said Phil. "The Farrellys have a grant to help them build a road. They'll have the laugh of us after all."

"We might have had that grant for the old road," murmured Eily.

She looked pale and discouraged.

"If I learn to paint really well she shall have a road and electric light better than the Farrellys'," thought Grania.

"Wisha! Them an their road!" muttered Mrs O'Hara. "They'll still have to cross be the town ferry and lave their gran trap on the other side, when all's said an done."

"There's talk of a bridge above the ferry," put in Jer. "The plans is up at the town hall."

Desmond was listening eagerly.

"We could fix up our bridge and use their road," he said. "It will be for everyone surely!"

"And own ourselves in the wrong?" asked Phil, looking down at him sourly.

"I never thought of that," confessed Desmond.

"I do wish we'd never quarrelled with the Farrellys!" declared Eily. "I don't mind the road. But since that quarrel we've had no luck!"

"You've no spirit!" retorted Judy.

Desmond nudged Grania.

"Another short cut!" he said. "We'll be home before them!"

Grania was so wet she was sure she couldn't be any wetter, and her mother's dejected face made her sad. But she couldn't climb rocks in a downpour of rain.

She opened her mouth to say "No!" when Phil reached out his hand.

"Come up out of that!" he ordered.

Bogtrotter was having a desperate struggle with a heavy cart and Phil clearly had no intention of walking. Grania determined not to be ordered.

"I'm staying with Desmond," she said.

Slipping and stumbling, she followed him along a path which turned suddenly, leaving them hemmed in by rocks. Desmond squeezed through a narrow gap, scrambled up a natural staircase pulling Grania after him, and they were ahead of the others and in sight of the castle.

"Those young ones could do with a hammering!" Phil's cold, ill-tempered voice was blown to them on the wind.

"Let him try hammering me!" exclaimed Grania. "And yet, I suppose he was trying to be friendly."

"Will you look who's there!" shouted Desmond.

"Where?"

"On the stone bench at the door! Hi! Hi! Travelling Finn!" he called.

Grania's eyes weren't as sharp as Desmond's, but now she could see a battered old man sitting on the stone bench. He had a small black-and-white dog sprawling across his knees, Timmy Fuzz perched on his shoulder, and the O'Hara dogs crowded as close to him as they could squeeze. A bulging sack, tied at the neck with rope, lay against the door.

Desmond rushed over the causeway and stood before the stranger. Grania, tired and shivering, came slowly and stood beside him. The wide eaves and the projecting wall sheltered the seat from rain and wind. But she longed to be indoors.

Timmy Fuzz looked at her and blinked, but would not budge.

"Is this yer kitten, girleen?" asked the old man. "Don't mind his contrairy ways. Tis meself's to blame. There isn't a four-legged crature can stand out agin me. No, nor a bird, nayther. The only one I ever met to aquil me that way, was Red Sarah O'Hara, God bless her! Are ye a neighbour's child?"

"She's Grania O'Hara," explained Desmond. "You remember the one that was with the O'Hanlons over at Dromard."

Travelling Finn looked up at her.

"I never saw you before," she told him.

"Sure you wouldn't remember me! I'm Travelling Finn, a poor man widout a story and widout a home – an but one friend – me little Pegeen!"

The dog he was nursing stood on his hind legs and licked his face frantically.

"That's not true!" declared Desmond. "I'm your friend!"

"Thank ye, lad," said the travelling man. "I'll not forget that."

"So ye've come back to yer own people," he went on, talking to Grania. "I might have known ye were an O'Hara. Ye have a look of Judy, but more of poor Kevin – God rest his soul! There's not much of Eily in ye, allanna!"

"The others are coming up," said Desmond. "They're raging! The Farrellys have a grant for a road and we'll not have the laugh of them any more."

"A road's a road," said the old man, "no matter how tis made. But here's themselves!"

Even Phil and Judy were glad to see Travelling Finn. He sat beside the fire opposite the old woman with the dogs clustered at his feet and the kitten still on his shoulder.

"Have you any new songs?" asked Judy eagerly.

"I have, Judy, gerrul. I'd sing them all for ye but I must be on me way."

"Ye'll not stir from this house till the mornin!" declared Mrs O'Hara.

"Thank ye, ma'am, thank ye! But tis this way. I had a drame, an a quare drame it was, late on Wednesday night. I was down in Arklow where there's a very dacent lodging house kept by a poor widda woman be the name of Ryan. Between her family of childer an the lodgers, the place was full up. But she gave me the stretchin of me bones in the shed. Well, as I was saying, I had a quare drame. I thought I was on me way across the High Bog –"

He stopped. Eily was taking the lids from two pot ovens. One was half-filled with white cabbage and peeled potatoes piled on top. In the other a large fowl and a piece of lean bacon steamed side by side.

"Bedad! That's a lovely sight!" said Travelling Finn. "I don't know when I seen anything to better it. Wasn't I the lucky man to sit in here on me way down to Kilvaragh!"

Eily smiled at him through the delicious mist rising before her face.

"The dream can wait, the food can't. Sit up to the table now!"

Grania had changed her wet clothes and put on dry shoes. No one else had bothered.

Down at Dromard, in spite of Aunt Bridgie's good cooking, clean tablecloths, polished cutlery, and gleaming delph, Grania had never eaten enough to please her aunt. Now she waited impatiently for her plate to be filled, and, because she was the youngest, she had to wait till the last.

Her mother sat beside her, prepared to coax her to eat a good dinner. But Grania needed no coaxing.

Timmy Fuzz, digging his claws into her frock, scrambled to her lap. She cut up bits and put them at the side. Soon his purring added to her comfort.

"You only want me when you're hungry," she reproached him.

The kitten gave her finger a friendly bite and went on eating. The dogs had a tray of bread, cabbage, and bones all mixed up, and it was a marvel how the wild O'Hara dogs allowed Pegeen to eat with them.

"When I'm tired of stravagin the country I'll settle down wid a few horses an go in for buyin an sellin. That's the way to make a purse of money nowadays," declared Travelling Finn, feeling for his pipe.

Eily touched his arm.

"Wait now! There's tea and boiled jam pudding."

The old wanderer rubbed his hands.

"Tis a hotel for the gentry ye should be kapin, Eily! Ye're wasted here!"

"Ye didn't finish the telling of the drame," Mrs O'Hara reminded him.

"Let the man drink his tea and eat a saucer of pudding," protested Eily.

"Can't he tell a dream and eat too?" demanded Judy impatiently. "Listen now, Grania, weren't you boasting you could explain dreams?"

"I don't like dream-telling, nor fortune-telling, either!" declared Eily. "It isn't good for the child."

"Child, moryah! A great lump of a girl, fourteen years old!" exclaimed Judy.

"I'm not a great lump of a girl!" cried Grania, her face as angry and red as Judy's.

Travelling Finn shook his head, half-amused, half-bewildered.

"Well, I always did say, where there's O'Haras there's argyin an quarrelin. Now I'll finish me drame!"

Judy snatched the pack of cards from the mantelpiece and flung them on the table.

"You can keep the dream!" she exclaimed. "Eily! Will you pour the tea or won't you?"

Finn chuckled.

"The tantrums of that one!" he murmured.

Eily finished pouring the tea and leaned back in her chair, half-smiling as she looked into the fire.

"Am I very like Judy?" Grania asked her anxiously, speaking in a whisper.

Eily looked at her silently. She laughed softly.

"Don't forget, Grania, your father was an O'Hara too! And Judy isn't always in a temper."

Mrs O'Hara held up a spoonful of the pudding.

"Pon me sowl, isn't it gran to be me, wid Eily feedin me up on the best in the land! Now, Finn! When the jam puddin's finished – did ye hear any news? I'd always sooner hear news than drames. Tell me all that's happenin in the great world beyond the mountains. What fairs were ye at lately? Is there many tinkers goin the roads? Who's dead an who's livin? An have ye any word from me own people an the place where I was born an reared?"

Travelling Finn pushed back his chair and filled his pipe before answering.

"I was in at yer own home, ma'am. But those who knew Red Sarah, an she a wild young one, are all gone. There's strangers in the house, ma'am!"

"What of it?" muttered the old woman. "Still an all 'tis hard to be forgot, an I alive an in the world!"

"Were you Red Sarah?" asked Grania, drawing a stool close to her grandmother.

"I was indade. An one day I'll tell ye the whole story. But listen now to Finn – tis he's the one that gets about. Tell me, how did ye find the house, Finn? Is it in ruins it is, not one stone left on another?"

Finn took his clay pipe from his mouth and held it at arm's length.

"The colour of it!" he said admiringly. "Ah, ma'am, if ye were put down at the gate of yer old home ye wouldn't know it."

Mrs O'Hara groaned.

"Wisha, if the people is gone, why wouldn't the house be gone wid them! Isn't that sinse?"

Travelling Finn laughed.

"Did I say the house was gone? Ma'am, ye misunderstood me! I said ye wouldn't know it. The people that's in it now has the lectric light. They pull down a wee fairy handle an a light springs up in the ceilin. But I'm goin to tell ye something ye'll find it hard to credit – they have a lectric light in the cowshed!"

He looked round triumphantly. Even Judy was listening now. The cards lay unheeded.

"Electric light in the cowshed!" jeered Phil. "Electric light in the cowshed! And in the pigsty too, I suppose?"

The old man looked offended.

"Ye suppose wrong," he said. "But let me tell ye,

there's lectric light goin up all over Ireland. I hear tell that where there's flowing water there's lectric light for them that has the larnin an the understandin!"

Terry beat his hands together. Jer laid his head on the table giggling.

"Where there's water there's electric light, so ye say?" asked Phil.

"If Travelling Finn says so, I believe him!" declared Eily.

"Mind yer manners, lads!" said Mrs O'Hara. "I'll not have a visitor mocked in this house."

"There's electric light in Dromard!" put in Grania. "Aunt Bridgie is having it for the shop."

"There's electric light in Kilvaragh!" snapped Phil. "Who says there isn't? But when Travelling Finn come talking about if you've water you can have electricity – I suppose when we're flooded in the winter, we can just strike a match and light up!"

His face was white, his eyes flashed. Grania was amazed at such anger. Finn shook his head and smoked silently.

"Is the castle really flooded?" Grania asked Desmond.

He nodded.

"See over there where the box is against the wall. The stones are loose. When the river rises, the water pours down against the castle. It comes in there and goes out at the door. Everything is damp for weeks after."

"Can't you do anything to stop it?" asked Grania, who hated damp as much as cold.

"Of course I could stop the flooding. But Phil tried to do it once and didn't succeed, so he won't let anyone else have a try."

They spoke in whispers. Phil turned in his chair and looked at them. Grania smiled at him, but Desmond turned away.

"Are you asleep, Phil?" demanded Judy. "Cut the cards!"

"Please finish your dream," Grania coaxed Travelling Finn.

He glanced sideways at Phil.

"I wouldn't want to be makin a vexatious old torment of meself. Mebbe I should be makin for the road!"

Phil laid down the cards.

"Time enough, time enough for the road!" said Mrs O'Hara. "Ye'll have me heart scalded if ye don't give us drames an a song or two. Ye know what Judy is for the drames."

"Pull round the settle!" Phil ordered his brothers. "Judy! I'll fix your chair nearer the fire."

Then he turned to Finn.

"You surely wouldn't leave Castle O'Hara without giving us a song or a story. That's not like you, Finn Hegarty!"

The old man was pleased. Not many called him by his full name: few knew it.

"There's no doubt, Phil O'Hara, ye have a way wid ye, when ye like," he said. "Though dear knows, ye have the devil's own temper too!"

"True enough," agreed Phil. "Now for a song!"

Travelling Finn puffed his pipe then put it aside.

"Tisn't lucky to lave a drame half-told," said Mrs O'Hara. "The song can folly after. Phil won't complain!"

"You were on your way across the High Bog," prompted Grania.

Finn rubbed his hands.

"I was indade, halfway across I was, when I seen a quare kind of a horse gallopin before me. It looked to be gallopin, but it never went out of sight an, thinks I, that's mighty strange. Then Pegeen wasn't takin any notice at all. She trotted at me side as if there wasn't a crature widin miles. An you know the way she is wid a strange horse.

"'Pegeen!' says I. 'D'ye not want to make friends wid that horse that's away there?'

"Then Pegeen gave a kind of a whimper an slunk behind me, while the horse looked over its shoulder.

"'There's money for ye at the Dromard Fair if you reach it before the stroke of noon,' ses the horse.

"An widout another word it shook out a great pair of wings and went flapping off towards the mountains like an old crow!"

Pegeen had been listening as intently as any of them. Now she stood on her hind legs, put her paws on Travelling Finn's knees, and barked.

"That baste knows more than we think!" declared Mrs O'Hara.

"Would that be a lucky dream?" asked Judy. "Grania! Can you tell the meaning?"

"There's no need to ax Grania," said Finn. "Sure, I can tell me own drames. An a drame like that's as plain as the nose on yer face – I'm to be at the horse fair before noon, an I'll be there. I'll not lose the good money by comin late!"

"Good luck to ye!" said Mrs O'Hara. "Now for a song! Have ye any new ones?"

"I have not. Well – listen to this bit of a tune:

"Young Rory was a farmer bold:
A farmer bold, a farmer bold.
He had a horse, a dog, a cat,
He would not sell for gold:
He would not sell for gold.

Young Rory to the market went,
Six calves to buy: six calves to buy.
Now on the road he heard a lad
Sing loud an high:
Sing loud an high.

The young lad had a strange wild look,
But farmer Rory liked him well,
For on that road from morn till noon
The lonesomeness was like a spell:
The lonesomeness was like a spell.

In front the young lad drove six calves,
Two black, one white, three red.
And Rory longed for those six calves.
'I'll pay ye well for them,' he said.
'I'll pay ye well,' he said.

'Me master's rich an very proud,
He needs no gold,' the young lad said.
'He needs no gold, or silver fine,
For his calves, black and white an red,
For his calves, white and red.'

On went the lad: on went the calves.
On went Young Rory bold,

Until the shadows walked the road
An the West had turned to gold:
An the West had turned to gold.

'Sell me those calves. I'll give me cat,
The best in all the land.
Her fur is long, her eyes are blue,
She'll eat from out yer hand:
She'll eat from out yer hand.

'I'll give me cat. I'll give me dog,
Me old friend, wise and true.
While he mounts guard, no enemy
Shall e'er lay hand on you:
Shall e'er lay hand on you.

'I'll give me horse – the swiftest,
With longest tail and mane,
The gentlest an the friendliest,
That scarcely needs a rein:
That scarcely needs a rein.

'I'll give me house. I'll give me land.'
Cried Rory bold, cried Rory bold.
He followed on until the night
Was dark an cold:
Was dark an cold.

An yet he journeyed till the moon
Rose over bog an mountain high,
An every bush, an tree an rock
Was silvered like the untrodden sky:
Was silvered like the untrodden sky.

He rode till day an night were done:
And followed on the path that strays
Beyond the borders of the world,
Where days are nights an nights are days:
Where days are nights an nights are days.

Young Rory he came home no more.
His cat, his dog, they watch for him.
He rides a mare, that silent treads
The path that tops the ocean's rim:
The path that tops the ocean's rim.

The calves he followed – where are they?
The white, the black, the lovely red?
He rides an seeks, but never finds;
For who can find a dream that's fled?
For who can find a dream that's fled?"

Then he sang *Three Lovely Lasses* and *Let Him Go, Let Him Tarry* and they all sang with him.

Travelling Finn drank tea while Judy gave them *Och! Johnny, I Hardly Knew Ye* and Grania wondered at her aunt's clear, strong voice.

While they ate thick slices of buttered toast, Finn told them about the man who built a three-cornered cabin on the road from Killorglin to Bantry for a bet and learned to his sorrow that it was where three fairy paths crossed one another.

"A three-cornered cabin!" chuckled Mrs O'Hara. "Wisha! That chap had said good-bye to any sinse he had, the poor gorsoon!"

"There are times when I think the castle is built across a fairy path!" said Phil. "There's little luck comes this way. Tell about the Whisperer, the chap that could charm the wildest stallion ever shod!"

Travelling Finn told that story and another and another, until Grania's eyes were closing and she couldn't be sure if she was in bed dreaming, or still sitting by the fire.

"Go up, child!" whispered her mother. "Leave your door open and you'll hear the singing."

Grania took the lighted candle her mother held out to her and groped her way upstairs. Even the cold air in the little stone room did not rouse her. And although she had propped her door open she did not hear her mother singing *The Snowy-breasted Pearl.* And she could not see the tears in Phil's eyes as he listened.

"I wonder," muttered old Mrs O'Hara to herself. "Could it be the old happy times is comin back?"

15

The Green Dress

Grania lay in bed, her eyes half-closed.

"I'll go down first and build up the fire," she thought. "Then I'll make a pot of tea and some big slices of toast and I'll take some in to my mother to surprise her."

She sat up suddenly before she could change her mind.

Grania groped for the matches and tried to strike one. It spluttered and went out, a second snapped and the third had no head. The box was empty.

"I'll have to get up in the dark," she sighed, lying back.

The castle was so quiet maybe it was still night. But Grania knew the day had come.

"Why did I promise to make Judy's frock?" she asked herself mournfully. "I'll have to sew all day and all night. I'll never finish it!"

The door opened. Her mother stood there, her face outlined against the darkness by the light of the candle stuck on the tray she carried.

Timmy Fuzz walked in front. He leapt to the bed, dived under the clothes, and snuggled against Grania.

"I meant to be down first," she murmured. "I was going to give you breakfast in bed."

Eily smiled at her.

"How would you know the time? Besides, sleep is good for you and I like to be here, the two of us alone."

She wrapped a shawl round Grania and buttoned up the heavy coat she wore.

"This is a cold dark room," said Eily. "Don't you miss Bridgie's lovely, bright, clean house?"

"I hadn't a room to myself till I came here," Grania reminded her.

She ate the fingers of toast and sipped her tea. The black kitten poked out his head and purred loudly.

Eily broke a piece of toast for him on the floor. He refused to leave the comfortable bed and had his breakfast on the tray.

"I'm going to work very hard!" declared Grania. "I'll start on Judy's frock this morning and I'll draw all the rest of the day. And I'll help you!" she added.

"I wonder would you begin by writing a letter?" suggested Eily. "To your Aunt Bridgie. She deserves that. She knows you're safe, no more!"

Grania wrote the letter sitting in Phil's place at the table. The lantern was alight and a reflector lamp, nailed to the wall near the staircase, was also lit. Yet the room was so large the greater part of it was in shadow.

When Desmond opened the door to go for water, Grania saw thick mist like a wet, grey blanket.

"I'll come," she said, running to the door.

"Finish the letter!" her mother told her. "Then you can bring in the turf. The evening may be fine and you could go down to Kilvaragh with Desmond and post the letter."

Grania told Aunt Bridgie a great deal of what had happened to her – not all. Every few sentences she drew a sketch – the kitchen with Mrs O'Hara at the fire; Travelling Finn, his sack and his dog; the settle and the three brothers sitting on it, side by side; a drawing of Judy half-filled a page.

Eily looked over her shoulder.

"Wouldn't you put me in it?" she asked wistfully.

Grania glanced up.

"You're on the next page, looking over the door. It's not done yet. One day I'm going to paint a big picture of you, as big as yourself. Maybe it will hang in a picture gallery in a city and both our names will be on it!"

Eily laughed so happily, Mrs O'Hara, hobbling into the kitchen on her stick, stopped to stare at her.

"Bedad, me gerrul," she said. "Ye haven't laughed like that since poor Kevin died!"

Eily flushed.

"I've been lonely. Tis wonderful to have Grania and Kevin looking at me out of her eyes. But I'd never have brought her back."

"A daughter has a right to make her mother happy, and sons too!" grumbled the old woman. "Will ye look at me own treasures!"

She chuckled and winked at Grania.

"Divils, that's what they are! Where's Desmond? Ah, lad, there y'are! Fill up the kettle, like a good child. I'm parched wid the drought!"

Grania thought it great fun going with Desmond to the turf pile and bringing in creels of sods. She kept close behind him for the mist was in their eyes, so that rocks and bushes were blurred and, until they came to the lighted window, the castle was only a dark mass.

All sounds were muffled, even the waterfall sounded

strange and melancholy. Through the mist a sorrowful wail came at regular intervals.

"That's a queer noise! Is it a bull bellowing?" asked Grania.

"Dooneen lightship," Desmond told her.

The glowing fire, the bubbling stirabout, her grandmother by the hearth made a picture which brought Grania to a halt.

"No one could get that on paper!" she thought.

Grania was scraping the last of a bowl of stirabout when Phil, looking half asleep, came down the stairs, followed by Jer and Terry. They shivered as they seated themselves on the settle and, when Judy came in, her face was pinched with cold.

"Pull up to the fire!" urged Mrs O'Hara. "Phil! Why wouldn't ye lave the settle where a settle should be an not island it out in the middle of the floor?"

He shook his head without speaking.

"The tea's grand and strong," said Eily. "Or would you have the stirabout first?"

"Tea," said Judy.

Grania laid the table.

"I'm beginning your frock after breakfast," she told Judy, wondering when breakfast would be finished.

Her aunt frowned.

"Do you think I'd let a young one like you run a scissors through me good stuff?" she demanded. "I was only letting on!"

Grania looked away. She didn't want Judy to see how glad she was. Yet at the same moment she thought how contrary her aunt could be.

"I'll show her!" she determined.

"I'm just as glad," she said. "I'll have more time for my drawing."

Phil grinned.

"She has you there, Judy. You'll have to give the lovely bit of green stuff to Miss Janie O'Toole after all. The poor little wretch will be scared stiff when she sees you coming!"

Judy looked from him to Grania as if she longed to knock their heads together.

"I might have known you'd never tackle a job of work!" she declared scornfully. "You'd spoil all the paper in creation with your scribbles, but thread a needle – oh dear, no! You, to make a frock! You little boaster!"

Mrs O'Hara chuckled. Desmond laughed into his hand and the dogs barked.

"If you want me to make the frock, I'll do my best!" said Grania. "If you don't want me to – I'm just as pleased!"

Judy glared at her and swept from the room. Phil stirred his tea round and round. Terry grinned, his eyebrows bobbing up and down.

"Can ye really make a dress, Grania?" Jer asked, leaning across the table, his fat face very solemn. "Because, if ye can't, don't try to larn on Judy's stuff. Twould be better for ye to leg it back to Dromard. I'm tellin ye!"

"As if Grania wouldn't make a frock better than Janie O'Toole!" exclaimed Eily. "Wasn't she so good, Bridgie was goin to prentice her to the best dressmaker in all Dromard?"

She looked at Grania proudly.

"I'll do my very best!" promised the girl.

"Jer, help Desmond bring down that trestle from the

corner room!" pleaded Eily. "Grania will need a long table for her work."

Jer looked vacant but didn't move. Terry stood up and pulled his brother with him.

"Let Desmond mind his business. Stir yerself, Jer! We'll have the table fixed before Judy brings the stuff."

As they tramped up the stairs Eily turned to Grania.

"We'll all help," she said. "Grania, if you do this well, Judy will be pleased."

"I'd sooner be making a frock for you!" declared Grania.

"Better not let Judy hear you," said Phil with a grin.

"Sure, she'll be making frocks for all of us!" cried Mrs O'Hara. "We'll be the most stylish family in Kilvaragh yet, so we will!"

"I must have some chalk, white chalk," murmured Grania.

"There's a bit in the shed!" and off went Desmond.

Terry appeared at the foot of the stairs with one end of the trestle table on his shoulder.

"Let go!" he shouted.

"Let go yerself!" roared Jer. "Ye have me transfixed in the corner an I can't stir a step!"

"Go up to him, Grania, and knock some sense into his silly head!" ordered Terry.

But the boards were wide and left no room for any one to go up or down.

"Why wouldn't ye turn it sideways?" asked Mrs O'Hara.

"Judy!" called Jer. "Judy! Will ye come out an see what Terry is doing at me."

"Get along out of that!" they could hear. "Do you want to be delaying my frock?"

The table gave a sudden jerk that sent Terry sprawling and clattered down on top of him.

"You numbskull!" cried Judy. "You've killed Terry!"

"Lift up the board, Des!" said Phil.

He made no attempt to help, but watched with amused interest while Grania pushed the table to one side and Desmond pulled Terry to his feet. Jer stayed at the turn of the stairs, too frightened to move.

"Me skull's split: I'm finished!" groaned Terry.

"What harm? You've no brains to lose," drawled Phil.

"That's no way to talk to yer brother an he overtaken wid misfortune!" Mrs O'Hara exclaimed indignantly.

"Sit down, Terry!" urged Eily. "Let me see the hurt!"

"Will one of you omadhauns clear the stairs?" called Judy. "What's going on down below?"

Desmond pulled gently at the table and leaned it against the wall. Judy pushed Jer and came down carrying a pile of green stuff.

"I'll get the trestle legs!" said the boy, running up the stairs.

Unluckily Jer darted suddenly from the corner and nearly flung Desmond down. He cried out in alarm and retreated.

Mrs O'Hara thumped the floor with her stick.

"Phil! Bring Jer down out of that before he does himself an injury!" she said.

Phil always obeyed his mother and Jer obeyed Phil.

"Jer! You're wanted at once!" called Phil.

And down came Jer, still agitated, but grinning.

Desmond and Terry fixed the trestle table. Eily rubbed it clean and Grania opened out her paper pattern.

It looked terribly complicated and, when Judy piled the green stuff at one end of the table, Grania was so nervous she had to read the instructions three times before she could understand them.

"I must measure you," she told her aunt.

Judy stood in the middle of the room, her head raised proudly, while Grania held the tape measure round her waist, along her arm, from waist to ankle and from neck to waist.

She had to stand on tiptoe and, as she called out the measurements, Desmond wrote them on a piece of paper.

Eily watched the brothers, expecting them to laugh, or mock. But they were as interested as Mrs O'Hara.

Grania compared the figures Desmond had taken down with those on the pattern.

"Judy! You're exactly right!" she declared.

"Exactly right!" echoed Mrs O'Hara. "Didn't I always say she was a fine lump of a gerrul?"

Phil stared at Judy as if he had never seen her before. But Jer was laying out the cards, and Terry, his elbows on the big square table, was impatient for the first game of the day.

Judy sat bolt upright in her chair, watching Grania as she opened the cloth and fastened the thin sheets of brown tissue paper to it with pins.

"Give the child a hand, Eily, and lave the dinner to me," said the old woman. "I'll fix the praties an sure the bacon's on the boil."

"I'll get some heads of cabbage," offered Desmond.

"The mist is lifting," he reported as he came in.

"There'll be a heavy frost tonight, mist or no mist, I'm thinking," muttered Mrs O'Hara, washing the potatoes in a bowl of water. "Isn't it the world's pity we're so far from the town. I've a great wish for a Peggy's Leg!"

Grania heard her, as she chalked the outline of the pattern in the way she had seen Mrs Fogarty marking stuff one day when she was at the dressmaker's with Aunt Bridgie. She wasn't nervous now. This was only a kind of drawing.

"First the skirt," Mrs Fogarty had chanted. "Then the sleeves, and last of all, the top!"

"That's the skirt!" declared Grania. "Where's the scissors? I'll need long sharp ones like Mrs Fogarty."

"Cocking yourself up!" muttered Judy.

"Keep quiet!" snapped Phil. "D'you want to destroy your own frock?"

Judy leaned back, amused, her eyes dancing.

"There's my little scissors," faltered Eily. "But they'd never cut that lovely thick cloth!"

"Sure I lent mine to Judy an she has it blunted on me!" wailed Mrs O'Hara.

"Would the shears do?" asked Desmond anxiously.

"Hark at them!" jeered Phil. "Let me to the table. I'll cut the stuff!"

He pulled open a drawer in the dresser and took out an old-fashioned razor. Running his finger along the edge, he stood beside Grania.

"Will you trust me?" he asked.

She nodded.

"Outside the line," she whispered.

He drew the blade lightly along the cloth and Grania sighed, for there wasn't the sign of a cut. Down the sides, top and bottom. Laying the razor on the table he lifted up the largest piece, so cleanly cut Grania was delighted.

"Go ahead!" said Phil. "We'll finish the lot!"

Eily went back to her cooking. She raised her eyebrows at Mrs O'Hara and the old woman wagged her head happily, for Phil was smiling without bitterness.

When Eily said in her soft voice, "Dinner's on the table," the cutting was finished, each piece folded and ready for pinning.

The moment Phil put away the razor his face was sour again.

"That's a good blade destroyed!" he said. "Was it worth it?"

"You grudge me a decent frock?" asked Judy, leaning across so that her face was close to his.

He glared at her, then looked away.

"I grudge you nothing!" he said. "You're as foolish as I am and I can sharpen up the razor!"

As they sat eating the mist lifted, though when Timmy Fuzz came crying at the door and Grania let him in, his fur was glistening with drops of moisture. She left her dinner to rub him dry, and when he sat on her knee purring and digging his claws into her frock, she wondered at her own happiness.

Was it because she felt sure the green frock would be a success, or that Uncle Phil had been friendly, or that she was pleasing her mother?

"I'll be down to Kilvaragh after dinner," said Phil. "I'm getting two colts to train. The young ones can come in the cart."

The old woman roused herself.

"Aren't we all goin? I'm for Confession, so is Eily. How about yerself, Judy?"

"I'll be coming!" Judy answered.

Phil stood up.

"If you're all going, the young ones can wait for the others."

"Couldn't we come with you?" asked Grania. "I'd love to be out now." She looked at him coaxingly.

"You've a great look of Kevin!" he muttered. "Sure you can come!"

"I'll harness Bogtrotter first!" Desmond told the old woman. "I can easily catch them up!"

Phil strode across the causeway and Grania ran after him.

16

We Were Always the Mad O'Haras!

Mist filled every hollow and the air was bitter. Grania pulled on her coat as she came out, tugged her tammy over her ears, and dug her hands into the deep pockets. Phil was capless and he never wore a top-coat. She could see the wind ruffling his hair as he swung down the road, walking as if he were on springs.

Grania was dreaming as she followed, content to keep him in sight. At first every time she came out of the castle she had looked over the bog. It was her link with Dromard. But each day seemed to make the distance greater. Hanlon's was no longer her home!

Yet she was thinking of Aunt Bridgie now, seeing her as she leaned across the counter, measuring lace or ribbons – big, clean, confident – mixing dumplings in the kitchen, walking down to the town, scolding, praising. "A credit!" Uncle Christie called her. And there was the little man himself – rumpled, silky grey hair, smiling, wandering eyes, his pockets bulging, his clothes daubed with paint. There was a clack of high heels – Norrie, pretty, a town girl; Sally, with the neat swagger of a jockey. Queer how Phil reminded her of Sally.

"She loves horses, too!" said Grania, speaking aloud.

"Another Mad O'Hara!" came from the mist.

Grania blinked. The road lay empty before her. She glanced back. Desmond hadn't caught up yet.

"Look up, you little bosthoon!" commanded the mocking voice.

She obeyed and there was Phil, grinning down at her from a gap in the rocks. Grania could see only his chin resting on his hands, the thin brown face and restless light grey eyes.

"Were you seeing ghosts?" he asked. "Look at the two big eyes and the solemn face – and you talking to yourself! Ah, if only Aunt Bridgie could see you now! Hair wild, a hole in the knee of your stocking, shoes thick with mud! You'd shock nice decent Aunt Bridgie!"

Seeing him perched up there, Grania no longer found Phil alarming.

"I was seeing them in the mist," she told him. "Isn't it strange, now! There's Sally working at the hairdresser's and she dotes on horses. She wants to ride races."

"Quit talking about those Hanlons or I'll send a rock down!" said Phil impatiently. "Can you climb?"

"I think so," replied Grania.

"See that rock sticking out? There's one low down. Then to the left, then straight up. For pity's sake – use your eyes!"

The rock rose straight and she wondered if Phil were playing a trick. But there was a jutting point she could reach and another a few feet above. Slowly she scrambled up and, while she was wondering if it would be better to drop back to the road, Phil stretched down his hands and, catching her wrists, heaved her to the ledge beside him.

"If twasn't for this," he said, "I'd never have stuck the

place. A man could live here and no one be a penny the wiser."

They were at the entrance to a dry cave, a stream trickled beside it, the sun shone in all day long, and a crack high up at the back served as a window.

"When I'm away, I'll make you a present of it," Phil told her, with a jerk of his chin. "Only don't be bringing that farmer's brat, Desmond, here!"

"Desmond! What's wrong with Desmond?"

Phil sneered.

"Did you think he was an O'Hara? Him, with his good nature and his love of work, and all the old plamaus of him! Kevin picked him up at the back of beyond and brought him in on his saddle one wild night. There he comes! Wait till he passes, then follow!"

Desmond came whistling down the road, his hands in his pockets, his head flung back.

"He was like a little dog with Kevin," said Phil, his jealous eyes following the boy.

Grania found the return harder. She missed her footing and fell on hands and knees in the roadway.

"Clumsy young eejit!" called Phil.

She scrambled up. The knees of her stockings were plastered with mud.

She had torn one and scraped her leg. When she looked up there was no sign of her uncle. But away in front, a dim shadow in the mist, was Desmond, going steadily, still whistling.

She ran after him. As her footsteps came near, he stopped without turning round.

"Oh!" exclaimed Grania, as she stumbled over a stone.

He turned then and saw she was limping.

"You've hurt that knee! You'll have to wash out the dirt. That's a clean pool over yonder."

Grania was thankful to sit on a rock while he washed his own handkerchief. He wrung it tightly, then spread it on a bush to dry while he dabbed the dirt from her knee.

The cold water stung, but when Desmond had bound up the cut she was able to walk easily.

"You'll be stiff tomorrow," he said. "But Phil won't mind. He never minds if he hurts any one."

They walked on in silence. Grania stepped in a puddle and shivered.

"It's terrible cold out here," she grumbled. "I thought Phil was going to take us into Kilvaragh."

It wasn't only the cold that bothered Grania. She glanced sideways at her companion.

"Desmond! What do you do when you want money?"

He stopped and faced her.

"Now what are you hinting at, Grania?"

"It's this way," she began. "I want a new drawing-book and paper. I want pencils and I want a new pair of shoes. Who buys them? Who pays for them?"

He looked at her feet and whistled.

"You need a good thick pair of boots! Those dolly's shoes are cut to pieces on the rocks."

"I'd hate to ask Eily!" said Grania. "She never seems to have any money. How do the O'Haras earn their living, Desmond? Or are they rich?"

Desmond laughed.

"How would they be rich? They just scramble along. Sometimes Phil will come home with a bunch of colts. He'll train them – one for jumping: one, mebbe, for running: and the rest to pull carts or just to carry creels.

Then there'll be money for everything. But it never lasts long. He bets on races and cards and he only wins when he hasn't the money to lose."

"You think the world of Phil!" said Grania slowly.

Desmond looked startled.

"I hate him!" exclaimed the boy. "Do you hear me! I hate him!"

"And what do you want to do?" asked Grania.

"I'm like Kevin. I want to grow things. He had great plans. He'd started a wonderful garden and he was going to build glasshouses. He had books about it. He was always reading them."

"Couldn't you go on with the garden?" asked Grania.

Desmond kicked a stone along the road.

"I wouldn't get the chance. You know, Phil went crazy when Kevin died. He just smashed everything up. Jer and Terry thought it fun. But Phil did it because he was unhappy. I understand now!"

"If Phil would only be friends with Desmond and my mother!" thought Grania.

They were in sight of Kilvaragh before she spoke.

"Listen, Desmond," she said. "We'll have that garden yet."

He looked at her and shook his head.

"Phil never changes his mind."

"You'll see!" she told him confidently.

He laughed, and catching her hand swung her along with him. As they raced down towards the harbour she didn't notice the puddles, but splashed gaily through them, her coat spattered, her hair flying, until she looked like the tinker her mother feared she would become.

17

Pictures and People

Grania was humming a song Travelling Finn had taught her before he shouldered his sack and went off with Pegeen.

I went one morning to the Fair,
One morning, one morning,
I went one morning to the Fair
With a horse to sell and a cow to buy,
One morning, one morning.

She sat on a rock, her drawing-board on her knee, smiling, then frowning, as she drew or as she thought. Mrs O'Hara sat in the corner mending her red petticoat. There were so many patches that scarcely any of the original flannel remained. Beside her sat Eily sewing the long seams of Judy's green dress. It was flung over a clean sheet spread over the ground at her feet.

Beyond – just in sight – was Desmond, forking a strip he had cleared of cabbages. Judy was down in Kilvaragh, the brothers and the dogs were away on the bog.

The days were growing shorter. Early darkness and bitter cold winds told them that winter had come. Still

Eily had not decided whether to send Grania back to Dromard and she grew more and more into the life of the castle.

Grania was thinking about money.

At Dromard, Aunt Bridgie had given her sixpence a week. She could always coax pennies from Uncle Christie. He never went above threepence, but he never remembered when he had given her the last. Now she hated asking for money.

"And I want so much," she thought, "shillings and shillings, maybe pounds."

Desmond laid down his fork, strolled over, and stood behind her singing:

I went a-roaming from the Fair,
One gloaming, one gloaming.
I went a-roaming from the Fair
And I rode the horse that I wouldn't sell,
And I'm roaming, still roaming.

"You could paint grand flowers," he said. "If I were a painter I'd paint roses."

"Sure, child – ye're goin to do better – ye'll grow em!" Mrs O'Hara told him.

She chuckled at Grania's horrified expression.

"Don't ate me, love! Tis right for yerself to draw gran pictures. But wouldn't Desmond look quare trying to do the same when growin's his job."

"Wish I knew more about gardening," sighed Desmond.

"I wish I knew more about painting!" echoed Grania.

She looked at the three friendly faces smiling at her.

Desmond leaned against the wall where the sun struck the stone and sang to himself.

"That's a lovely painting!" said Eily, biting the green thread and twisting a knot.

Grania shook her head.

"I get the colours wrong. When I draw people, the arms and legs aren't right – I know they're not!"

"Didn't you learn drawing at school?" asked Eily reproachfully. "Bridgie told me you did and she was so proud."

"And then she wasn't pleased at all!" declared Grania.

"She didn't understand. I do!" said Eily. "There's a drawing class at the tech school down in Kilvaragh. Why wouldn't you go there, if you stay? – If you stay!"

Grania stared at her mother in amazement. Eily had wanted her to be a dressmaker, she dreamed of her being a lady, someone she could be proud of.

"And now she's trying to give me just what I want!" thought Grania.

"One day you'll be proud of me!" she stammered. "I promise, I'll work so hard!"

Eily smiled at her across the pile of green stuff.

"It's terrible to be discontented!" she said.

"If I could only paint you sitting there!" exclaimed Grania. "You with Judy's green frock and Grannie with all the different reds in her petticoat, and Desmond in his old blue shirt against the wall, with Timmy Fuzz on the half-door. But this is all wrong! I can see the picture but I can't get it down!"

She tore the sheet of paper from her drawing board and flung it on the ground.

Desmond rushed forward and lifted it up. Luckily the

painted side lay upward and the colours were almost dry.

"Give it here!" said Eily. "I'll put it up in my own room."

"I'll frame it!" declared Desmond. "I have a piece of glass and some strips of smooth wood."

Old Mrs O'Hara peered over Eily's shoulder at the painting.

"Bedad, is that meself?" she asked. "I look a gallus old woman and it serves me right! But the red petticoat's gran! Indade, if ye larn to do better there'll be no holdin ye!"

Grania was still worried.

"If I go to the tech it will cost money," she told her mother. "It isn't only for the classes. If I learn to use oils they cost a lot, and there's canvas."

Eily stitched away.

"We'll find the money!" she murmured.

"She needs a pair of boots she can walk in!" said Mrs O'Hara.

"This weather won't hold!" said Desmond.

He looked at the sky overhead, then his eyes travelled to the horizon.

"There's wind comin, and rain, maybe snow!"

"Snow!" cried Grania. "With the sun shining? Will there be snow and frost and ice?"

Mrs O'Hara wetted her finger in her mouth and held it up.

"There'll be no frost while the wind holds the way it is, up from Spain and the inland ocean. But the wind will change an I wouldn't say but Des is right – we'll have snow. Last night there was a whisper of snow on the wind."

"I love snow!" said Grania. "Will there be ice on the pools? Can you skate, Desmond?"

He shook his head.

"I never had the skates. But Phil can. Last year, I remember, he skated the whole of one moonlight night!"

Eily stood up.

"Help me fold this dress, Grania. Another good sit down and I'll have it finished!"

Grania held an armful of the stuff and gazed at it in wonder. The pale winter sunlight threaded the green with silver.

"Quick, now!" said her mother. "I want you to help me. Tomorrow you and I and Des are going to Dromard."

"Dromard!" echoed Grania, half-frightened.

"Across the High Bog?" asked Desmond.

"Indeed no! Poor little Bogtrotter couldn't carry the three of us. We'll go down in the cart to Kilvaragh and take the bus along the shore road to Barnakeel. Andy Mahon's brother will give us a lift up to Dromard. Andy is going for a load of hides and he has a pair of boots that will fit Grania. I tried them on. We take the same size."

"Tis time Des had a new rig," said Mrs O'Hara. "He's growing so tall he'll be looking down on Phil soon. I'll talk to Phil about it meself tonight!"

"If I could earn some money," muttered Desmond.

Mrs O'Hara held up the red petticoat.

"Twill surely last me time out. What's that ye're sayin, lad? Ye wish ye could earn money! If ye had yer rights, there should be a good job here for ye. Don't ye grow all that is grown and cut the turf an dear knows what? When I've finished wid Phil on yer clothes, I'll set about him to give ye a few shillings in yer pocket. Come along in! I hear them lads comin to their dinner."

Eily held Grania back.

"I want you to realise what you are giving up. That's why we're going to Dromard."

Only Terry and Jer arrived with the dogs. Phil had cut through the glen to go down to Kilvaragh and meet Judy.

"They'll not be back till nightfall," said Terry. "An I wish they'd never come back. I'm sick to death of bullyin an the divil's own temper that's in Phil!"

He flung himself lengthways on the settle, so that there was no room for Jer, who sat mournfully on the creepy beside his mother.

"Set the dogs on me, he did!" grumbled Jer, aiming a kick at Bran, who showed his teeth.

"What made Phil that mad?" asked the old woman.

"I said why didn't we take to the roads instead of prisonin ourselves here? That's all I said. You'll bear me out, Terry?"

"Ye're a ravin eejit!" said Terry.

"Judy's dress will be ready for the Christmas ceilidh and we could all go," suggested Eily.

"The O'Haras at a ceilidh! God give ye sinse!" cried Terry.

He and Jer spluttered with laughter.

"Why shouldn't the O'Haras be at a ceilidh?" demanded Mrs O'Hara. "Aren't we as good as the Malleys and the Devines and the rest of the poor trash in Kilvaragh? An is there two better dancers in the whole country than Phil and Judy?"

Grania laid the table. Desmond had sharpened the knives and she had polished them. The forks and spoons, washed in the hot soapy water, glittered in the firelight. Some of the plates were good – the rest, cheap delph bought in the market.

"When we've whitewashed the walls, I'll paint pictures all round," she said. "We can have blue curtains and a blue tablecloth. We'll make this place lovely!"

"Is it ruinate the castle ye would?" demanded Jer, indignantly.

"I never heard such talk!" said Terry. "Ye're an impident little strap, but ye have spirit!"

"Why wouldn't she?" asked Jer. "Isn't she an O'Hara?"

And Grania was pleased, though she tried to be offended.

"I'm every bit as mad as they are!" she thought.

Tea was almost ended when the dogs rushed barking to the half-door and leaped over. Timmy Fuzz sprang to Grania's shoulder, almost as excited, his fur fluffed out, his tail on end.

"Silly kitten!" said Grania, rubbing her head against Timmy's. "It's only Phil and Judy!"

They came in looking so pleased everyone stopped eating and drinking to stare.

"If only they'd look happy always!" thought Grania.

Judy flung her hat and coat on the floor and Desmond, picking them up, hung the coat on one of the hooks beside the stairs with the hat on top.

"Here's something for yourself, lad!" said Judy, tossing two half-crowns on the table.

Desmond took them one at a time, his eyes startled.

"Had ye good luck, Judy girl?" asked Mrs O'Hara, as puzzled as the rest.

Judy laughed.

"We've made the old ones in Kilvaragh sit up," she said, seating herself beside Grania, her elbows on the table. "Phil has paid every penny we owe, every penny!"

"That's something to be proud of!" said Eily approvingly.

"And what's better," added Phil. "I made them pay themselves!"

The old woman clapped her hands.

"Good lad! Good lad!" she cried.

"How could you?" asked Eily. "It sounds queer!"

Phil's good temper vanished.

"Say it out!" he exclaimed. "Say you think I've been cheating and twisting – say it!"

Eily looked at him calmly.

"How did you do it? That's all I'm wanting to know!"

"You're always fretting and fuming because of the bills. Well – the bills are paid, every one of them, that's all you need to know!"

Judy thumped the table impatiently.

"You make me tired, the two of you! Why shouldn't she know? Twas clever – real clever! Listen, Eily! You know those colts he was talking of? He sold them before he bought them, and paid the buying money with the selling price."

Eily shook her head.

"I don't understand. I hope it's a right way of doing business."

"Why wouldn't it be right?" demanded Phil. "I knew the colts were good. I gave my word they were good. And my word is good enough for them that know me, even if it isn't for you! I sold the colts for sixty pounds and another ten horses for a hundred and fifty. I paid thirty for the first lot and a hundred for the second, after I'd sold them. Judy coaxed me to pay the bills before I'd lose all I had. She's like you, Eily, she has no faith in me!"

"Not in your luck, Phil!" laughed Judy. "But you can buy and sell horses with any one!"

Grania looked at Phil in amazement.

"You're wonderful!" she exclaimed. "Oh, I wish I could draw horses!"

He smiled back at her.

"I'll teach you to ride a horse," he said. "That's better than drawing!"

He did not speak again and, while they were still eating the hot potato cake and drinking the fresh tea Eily made, Terry brought out the cards. Mrs O'Hara said the rosary to herself, Eily mended socks and stockings, Desmond fitted the frame for the picture Grania had painted, and Grania played with Timmy Fuzz.

It was like all the other evenings, thought Grania. The difference was every one looked happy – even Eily, though she was still puzzling about Phil's way of selling horses.

18

Going to Hanlon's

"Hurry, Grania! Hurry, Des!" said Eily.

Desmond polished his boots, Grania was trying to put on her coat.

"What ails you?" exclaimed Judy. "I'm sick to death seeing you put the thing on back to front. Pon me word – she's all so moidhered because she's going to see Bridgie Hanlon and that old gommie, Christie! Come here!"

She thrust the coat on Grania, laughing maliciously.

"I'd never be moidhered because I was seeing you!" retorted Grania.

"Grania, I'm ashamed of you!" exclaimed Eily. "What's come into you at all!"

Judy's eyes flashed.

"Leave the girl alone! If I don't mind her impudence, why should you? Are you still trying to make a lady of her?"

"You're right!" said Grania to her mother. "I should remember my manners even if Judy forgets hers!"

Eily tried not to laugh, but Grania saw Judy's ill temper vanish.

"Judy likes me when I'm rude," she thought, following Desmond out to the stable. "It's very queer, but I just won't be rude!"

She had learned to harness Bogtrotter and drive him too, but she was still nervous of riding. Now she wished she could ride over the High Bog as Desmond had done and arrive alone in Dromard.

Eily was dressed in the best clothes she had cherished for years. She climbed into the cart and Desmond tucked a bundle of hay round her feet. He brought out a red blanket and wrapped it about her shoulders.

"Sure, you're spoiling me!" she told him.

"Give me best respects to odd-job Christie!" called Phil, lounging against the door.

The icy wind blew his hair straight up and he wore no coat. But Grania had never seen him sitting near the fire. She hated cold and wind. To her a glowing turf fire was one of the loveliest pictures in the world!

"I'm not so much of an O'Hara after all," she thought.

She ran to the cart and scrambled in. Her mother wrapped a corner of the blanket round her and she snuggled her feet in under the hay.

"We'll drop in for the new boots if there's time," said Eily.

Desmond walked at Bogtrotter's head, kicking every stone or piece of rock he could reach into a hole.

"The Farrellys are great people for road-making!" declared Eily. "Isn't it a terrible pity we can't be friends with them?"

Grania didn't want to talk about the Farrellys.

"Isn't it grand for the three of us to be going off together?" she said. "This is a real holiday. Will we be at Aunt Bridgie's in time for dinner?"

"I hope we will," answered Eily, laughing, "or you two

poor children will be starved. Though Bridgie's not the one to let us go hungry!"

The mist which had covered the bog all night had blown before the wind, but glistening tatters still clung to the bushes. Grania reached out and snatched a handful. When she opened her fingers there was only a wet patch.

The shining roofs of Kilvaragh lay below them. Blue turf smoke rose from the chimneys, streaming in long thin banners. Beyond the harbour the fishing fleet tossed its way towards the horizon, the red and brown sails glowing against the grey waves. Captain Scully's steamship lay up at the quay, a gull, like a silver toy, perched on its mast.

The streets of Kilvaragh were crowded but the bootmaker's shop was still closed.

"Will I see to Bogtrotter and come back for you?" asked Desmond.

Eily stepped to the ground.

"No! Meet us at the bus stop. Then we'll be sure of a seat."

The shops of Kilvaragh were small and dark. But Andy Mahon's bootshop was the smallest and darkest in the town. It was perched at the top of a long stone parapet, and a heap of leather, cut into rough pieces, ornamented the window. The panes were dirty and, from the top corners, thick cobwebs hung halfway down. Above, two small windows had ragged lace curtains and Grania frowned.

"I don't like this shop." she said. "Why can't we go to the shop at the corner? They have all kinds of boots. We can see what we're buying and – it's open!"

Eily laughed.

"The O'Haras always have their boots made by Mahon.

There's no better bootmaker in the country. Besides, when there's no money, he'll hand them out and wait for Phil to pay. Knock at the door, like a good child! Andy's coming with us and we shouldn't be too long!"

Grania thumped on the dingy door.

"If this was Uncle Christie's shop, he'd have the door shining with paint. He'd have the windows clean, too!" she added scornfully.

"Knock again! Maybe he didn't hear!" Eily told her.

Grania thumped, then she kicked. At last she picked up a stone and hammered on the door.

It opened so suddenly she fell in against an angry wizened little man only half-dressed, his hair tousled, and his feet bare.

He caught her by the arm.

"I have ye, me lassie-o! An this time ye'll come along to the barracks. I've told the gardaí all about yer tricks and they'll skelp ye!"

"Don't be foolish! Leave the child be, Andy Mahon!" exclaimed Eily. "If you won't open your shop, what can people do? I told her to knock."

The little man stood back.

"Tis yerself, is it, Eily O'Hara? What are ye wantin?"

"The boots, Andy, the boots! And aren't you coming to Dromard? You'll be late! The bus won't wait for you or me!"

"Heaven help me!" groaned Andy, tugging his long hair. "I clane forgot. Let the pair of yez find the boots while I fix meself!"

He scuttled up the dark staircase. Eily pushed a door with broken glass panels and they entered the shop.

There were shelves from floor to ceiling, all along one

side, facing the window. Against the far wall a long wooden bench was piled with boots nearly finished, half-made, soles and uppers, rolls of soft leather for tongues, insoles, boxes of sprigs, hard thick leather for heels.

Grania forgot the dirt and disorder. She wanted to paint a picture of the cobbler's shop.

Eily set down her basket and hunted on the shelves.

"Help me look, Grania. Tis a pair of high, brown lace boots. We musn't delay!"

"High brown boots!" Grania was delighted.

"Here they are – on the floor!"

She sat on a box, kicked off her old muddy shoes, and drew on the new brown boots. They came halfway up her leg and she felt she could dance in them from Kilvaragh to Dromard.

"I've never had such boots in all my life!" she cried, standing on tiptoe.

"Because they're made be a bootmaker, not a machine!" growled Andy from the doorway.

He was fully dressed but he was no tidier. He hadn't even bothered to comb his hair, and he was biting at half a loaf of stale baker's bread.

"The day will come when people will larn sense an destroy the machines!" he declared. "The only boots worn will be handmade, sewn, not a nail in em, barrin the heels!"

"But aren't they very dear?" asked Grania.

"An if they are, why shouldn't they be?" he demanded, darting his head forward. "A bootmaker is a tradesman an entitled to his money. If they can't pay for dacent boots an shoes, let em go barefoot as they did in the olden days."

"Why should people go barefoot because they're

poor?" cried Grania. "I never had handmade boots before and I don't want them now!"

"Grania!" pleaded Eily.

"Hold yer whisht, ye young strap! Ye're only annoyin yer mother! I've never minded an O'Hara in me life an I'm not goin to begin now!"

Andy motioned them to follow him out into the street.

Over his shoulder he carried a sack, his hat was so big it rested on his back, and the brim in front was caught up with a safety pin.

"I hope he won't stay with us when we get to Dromard," thought Grania. "He's a show!"

A group of people waited against the wall at the end of the fish market. The stalls had not yet been mounted on their trestles, but lay in heaps waiting for the return of the boats.

"I can go on painting for years and years," thought Grania. "There are pictures everywhere!"

Her new boots made walking so pleasant she couldn't feel angry with Andy. But he paid no attention to her or to any one else, until the big motor bus came along the quay and drew up with a crash.

Then he thrust his way through the crowd and climbed the steps, pushing aside the conductor who was coming out.

"I might have known the ignorant bosthoon who'd push by a conductor on his own bus would be Andy Mahon!" said the man indignantly. "Ye should wait yer turn!"

"He'll take the front seat, I know he will!" murmured Grania, talking to herself. "Why doesn't Desmond come?"

But Andy Mahon had no interest in front seats. He

liked the end of the bus where he had room to stretch out his feet and put down his sack.

Desmond came racing down the quay, his coat open, splashing through puddles, dodging women with baskets, children hopping from kerb to gutter and back again, along by the stalls, pausing only when his foot was on the step.

"I was terrified we'd lose the front seat!" he gasped, squeezing in beside Grania so that Eily had room enough, for there were so many passengers they were sitting three instead of two on a seat.

"Isn't it well you're small and I'm thin?" said Eily, smiling across him at Grania.

"I'm selfish to keep the corner seat," though Grania.

"You can have a turn at sitting next the window," she told Desmond.

"I'd as soon sit here," he said indifferently. "I like to look straight ahead. Wish I could drive a bus!"

Grania settled down happily.

The road lay between sea and sandhills, mottled with coarse scanty grass with the cliffs rising beyond. The waves, torn and beaten by the wind, foamed over the strand, and surging between rocks dashed against the low sea wall.

The windows of the bus were splashed with sliding drops. Was it rain or spray? Grania couldn't be sure. But it was grand to sit there, warm and comfortable, while the seagulls soared and dived just ahead.

The coast was broken by rocky inlets and the road cut across, now driving straight to the mass of grey water then swerving inland.

A rattle on the panes startled her.

"That's hail!" said Desmond. "We'll have snow before night. There's Barnakeel. We're coming in!"

"I wish we could go on like this for ever," sighed Grania.

Barnakeel had one street facing the sea, one shop which was post office as well as village stores, and the ruins of a police barracks.

The bus pulled up in the shelter of the barracks wall and the passengers clambered out.

Some lived in Barnakeel, others along the river. Only the bootmaker and the three from Castle O'Hara were bound for Dromard.

Grania was shivering in the blast which swept over the crouching houses, when a low-hung trap, drawn by a shaggy, brown pony, swung out from beyond the barracks yard and drew up beside the bus.

The driver was so like Andy, Grania looked round for the bootmaker. He was huddled against the wall but darted across to the trap.

"I was afeard ye'd forgotten us, Liam!" he complained.

Liam laughed and at once he wasn't the least bit like his brother. His blue eyes were smiling. Andy's were grim. Liam's mouth was full and generous, Andy's lips were thin and peevish.

Yet Grania could see they were very fond of one another. As Andy scrambled to the seat beside Liam, he touched his shoulder and Liam looked at his brother so kindly, Grania warmed to them both.

"How's yerself, Mrs O'Hara?" asked Liam. "Tis a long time since I seen ye or the young lad! And this is Kevin's little gerrul! Isn't it grand she's with ye now!"

Eily smiled without speaking.

"Pull up the rug and tuck the hay round your feet," said Liam. "We'll be on our way."

When Grania first went to the castle she thought it strange to hear her mother called Eily. Now it seemed stranger that she should be Mrs O'Hara. Surely the only Mrs O'Hara was the old woman up at the castle!

The road beside the Barna river was no better than a boreen. Liam had to drive so carefully he had no time to talk. They passed by Mr Donnelan's house where Grania had painted the golden apple-tree, so long ago it seemed; drove over the railway lines at the level-crossing and there was Dromard.

"We'll get down here, Liam!" said Eily. "Thank you kindly for the lift. What time would you be going back?"

"We'll be outside the chapel as the Angelus rings," Liam told her. "That will give you plenty of time to catch the bus at Barnakeel."

"Why couldn't we drive the whole way?" asked Grania.

"Don't you long to see every street and house in the town?" was her mother's answer.

Grania was silent. The pavement was narrow and she walked behind Eily and Desmond, thinking.

The shops were decorated for Christmas and, in spite of wind and rain, women with bags and baskets went in and out, children stood as close to the windows as they could, and men carried so many parcels and bundles they were almost hidden.

They went by Mrs Fogarty's. A green dress with silver trimming hung in the window and Eily glanced over her shoulder with a pleased smile.

"Judy's dress beats that, Grania!"

They came out on the market square. There were a

few bullocks and sheep, but most of the space was given over to hens and geese and a flock of turkeys. Grania liked the fruit and vegetable stalls for their colours, and Desmond, seeing a square, glistening block of dates, began feeling in his pockets for the money Judy had given him.

"We'll go into the chapel – just for a moment," suggested Eily.

After the small bare chapel at Kilvaragh this seemed grand and lofty with chains of ivy and every Station of the Cross was festooned with holly. The choir gallery and the organ were banked with green, and the Crib was better than Grania had ever seen it.

"We used to make the ivy chains at school," whispered Grania as they came out.

They peeped in at Murphy's sweet-shop, but another girl was in Norrie's place.

"She's home for her dinner," explained Grania.

"If I'd ridden in this end of the town that first day," thought Desmond, "I'd never have dared go near Hanlon's!"

As they climbed the cobbles the pleasant smells of dinner climbed with them. Grania hung back. She was going to see Norrie and Sally, Aunt Bridgie and Uncle Christie again. Would they seem very strange?

"I wish I hadn't come!" she thought, going on past the window Aunt Bridgie had made so gay.

"Here we are, child!" called her mother, pulling her back, and pushing her in at the door. "We're here, Bridgie!"

"Oh, I'm glad to be back!" said Grania, as two friendly arms hugged her and Aunt Bridgie's eyes beamed down.

"I knew you'd bring her," cried Bridgie Hanlon. "I knew it before I caught a glimpse of the letter!"

19

Will You Stay or Will You Go?

There were no customers in the shop. All the morning it had been crowded and, when dinner was over, Aunt Bridgie would be taking down new boxes, bringing out lace collars and pinafores, and displaying her special stocks of dresses.

"The girls are upstairs," she said. "They're run off their feet these days and they're bursting with pride, God help them! The pair of them had a rise this week and you'd think they were American millionaires!"

"Where's Uncle Christie?" asked Grania, looking at the coloured paper chains, the silver balls, the strings of cotton wool snow, and the holly.

"It's lovely!" she said. "I'd forgotten what Christmas was like. Did Uncle Christie do it all?"

"He did, the poor man!" Aunt Bridgie told her. "And wasn't he wishing for his little Grania to bring him the drawing-pins and hold the ladder and tell him what a grand fellow he is. Go in to him now! He's listening to the pudden!"

Desmond kept close to Grania, he ducked under the flap in the counter as she did, but bumped his head. He was uneasy because Aunt Bridgie hadn't spoken to him, only given him a reproachful look. Now in the dark passage he stumbled and, as Grania pushed open the kitchen door, he was wishing he had stayed behind with Mrs O'Hara.

Uncle Christie was sitting on the form clasping his knees. Before he knew who had entered, Grania was sitting beside him and Desmond had perched on the corner of the high fender.

"I'm back!" said Grania.

"An I never heard ye!" exclaimed the little man. "Bedad, tis Christmas already to see ye sitting there. When Bridgie got the letter I set to work on the decorations. D'ye think they're as good as last year? How are ye, Desmond lad? Pon me soul, tis gran to have the two of yez here!"

Grania looked about her.

"You never whitewashed over my black kitten!" she cried. "Oh, Uncle Christie!"

He slapped his knees.

"Twas the divil's own job I had to clane the wall an let the kitten be. I used me smallest brush, but I done it. Yer aunt's proud of it!"

"Grania's painting real well up at the castle," declared Desmond. "There's one she did I'm making a frame for to hang in Eily's room."

"If that don't bate all!" muttered Christie.

He rattled the nails in his pockets.

"I wonder now, Grania, would you paint me a picture I could frame?" he asked.

"What would you like me to paint?"

"D'ye remember the golden apple-tree ye did for Mr Donnelan?"

Grania nodded. She'd never forget that tree!

"One day, when you've time – remember – a golden apple-tree," said Christie Hanlon.

"You never painted a golden apple-tree up at the castle!" said Desmond jealously.

"I painted an apple-tree, even if it wasn't all gold!" protested Grania.

"Did she paint a black kitten?" chuckled Christie.

The pudding was bubbling in the big saucepan on the stove. Farther back a kettle was singing. Sizzling and the smell of roast and stuffing came from the oven.

"I'm starving!" exclaimed Grania.

"Tis all ready the minute yer aunt gives the word," said Christie. "I'd start carvin now only she'd slaughter me!"

A clean stiff white cloth was on the table. The knives and forks glittered, the tumblers shone. Grania remembered the day Aunt Bridgie bought the salt and pepper boxes and how they had all admired them, for they were like tomatoes with corks stopping the holes in the bottom.

It was only now she understood the room was beautiful!

"Uncle Christie!" she began, when her mother and Aunt Bridgie came in from the shop, and Norrie and Sally rushed down the stairs.

"Grania! You look like a tinker!" cried Sally.

"Have you no manners?" cried Bridgie indignantly.

Sally screwed up her face.

"I meant she looks fine and healthy. Sure, there's no harm in that!"

"I'm as hungry as a tinker," declared Grania, so delighted to be with them all, she didn't mind what Sally said.

"That's the girl!" said Christie. "They haven't broke her spirit yet."

"Why should they?" demanded Eily. "Hasn't she a mother to care for her?"

"God help the mother!" muttered Christie, trying to look fierce.

"She has me to look after her," Grania told him, laughing.

"So ye're all as happy as Larry!" he joked.

"Tell us what's happened!" exclaimed Sally. "How do you like living with horses and dogs in a castle? What are the O'Haras really like? What neighbours have you? Is it fun up there on the High Bog? Did you have great times at Hallowe'en?"

"Don't mind her! You look grand, Grania!" said Norrie kindly. "And I'm terribly glad to see Aunt Eily after all this while!"

Christie cut up the roast chicken, Norrie sliced the boiled ham, while Sally drained the Brussels sprouts. Desmond, determined to show how helpful he could be, mashed the potatoes until they were in a creamy fluff.

He sat between the girls. Sally teased him. Norrie poked more on his plate as soon as he cleared a space. Grania was very quiet.

"This is a Christmas dinner!" she exclaimed, when Bridgie lifted a great round steaming pudding in a cloth from the pot on the stove.

"We'll have two Christmases this year!" explained Christie, cutting the string. "But the real one is now!"

There was a jug of cream to pour over the brown, fruity slices, and Desmond wished there was a cow up at the castle instead of the goats. He looked at Grania's thoughtful face.

"She's remembering she needn't come back!" he thought in a panic and shook his head when Bridgie offered him another slice of pudding.

"How is Mrs Fogarty?" asked Eily.

"Grand!" replied Bridgie. "Only her prentices have her destroyed. Yesterday she was wishing she had Grania!"

They all stared at Grania.

"If you changed your mind and stayed you could begin again," said Bridgie. "You know now what life is like at Castle O'Hara."

Grania looked at Eily.

"Do you want me to stay or to come back?" she asked.

Desmond was angry. It wasn't fair to bring Grania here with the place made so pretty and then ask her to choose all over again. Hadn't she chosen once?

"I want you to do what's best for yourself," whispered Eily. "But it would be hard to go back without you."

"After all, she is yer daughter!" muttered Christie. "An for all the old chat, tis up wid the O'Haras she'll get her chance to do what she wants an not down here!"

"Christie Hanlon!" cried Bridgie. "You should be ashamed."

Christie was so confused he dropped his pipe. Desmond picked it up for him. Their eyes met.

"I'm not ashamed!" declared Christie. "Lave Grania alone. She has a gift. Let her use it. She'll be happy that way. An the O'Haras are that quare they don't mind a girl spendin her time paintin. I'm like that meself. But why wouldn't Grania an Eily come a little oftener? Then we'd all be content."

"They're not going yet," said Bridgie. "Let Grania think it over while she has the chance."

The girls had to hurry back to their work and Bridgie to the shop. Christie began the washing-up, but Grania coaxed him away from the bowl of hot soapy water and he sat with Eily by the fire.

"I'd love to help Bridgie in the shop," she told him, slipping away like a shadow.

Christie moved up to the end of the bench.

"Now tell me about them O'Haras," he said. "Aren't ye a great lad at the dryin, Desmond Burke!"

Grania and Desmond were still telling him when Bridgie put her head in at the door to ask was tea ready.

"In two minutes, Bridgie!" promised Christie. "We're rushin it! Slap on the kettle, Grania. Glory be! We've let it dry out! Twill be destroyed on us!"

"There's a teeny drop of water!" announced Grania. "And heaps of steam."

"Let it cool off before you fill it," advised Desmond. "Then it won't take any harm."

"Ye've a head on your shoulders," said Christie admiringly. "Can ye cut bread – thin now? Tis the way herself likes it. I'll see to the toast. There's lashings of butter!"

He sat with his feet on the polished fender. The copper toasting fork glowed and each slice was the perfect golden brown. Grania buttered and piled them on a wide dish, where the toast would keep hot but not dry out. Desmond watched Grania. She wasn't looking about her now but staring into the fire. Hadn't she made up her mind yet?

Christie leaned forward to speak to Grania, when Bridgie came in followed by Eily.

"The people of Dromard is at their teas," said Bridgie. "And we'll hear the bell. But afterwards they'll be swarming!"

"Will we start without Norrie and Sally?" asked Grania, as her aunt began to pour the tea.

"We must, pet! Those poor childer will be lucky if they get a cup in their hands. Right up to Christmas Eve, sweets and hairdressing is just terrible!"

As she ate and drank Grania was thinking of the castle, so dark and bleak. Were real castles like that?

"But I couldn't live here again!" she told herself. "And yet I'm fonder of Aunt Bridgie and Uncle Christie than I used to be."

Bridgie switched on the electric light. She was still very proud of it and Desmond sat staring at the bulb.

"Wish we could have that!" he said enviously.

"Time we were going!" Eily reminded them.

She turned to Bridgie.

"I haven't been so happy in years!"

"You're quite sure, Grania?" asked Bridgie. "You won't stay?"

"I'm quite sure!" replied Grania. "I won't stay and yet I wish I could!"

20

Difficult Journey

As they went down the cobbled road to the market-place there were lights in shops and houses and all along the Mall. Under the leafless trees carol singers huddled together singing *Adeste Fideles.* As the wavering voices grew stronger, sleet, turning to snow, whirled by on the wind from the mountains. The Barna river, swollen by the flooding higher up, rushed from darkness into darkness, showing only where three big electric lamps on the bridge made an island of light.

Grania paused to watch the snowflakes dancing above the black water, then vanishing as they were drawn under.

"Hurry, child!" said Eily. "You wouldn't want to be keeping Liam Mahon waiting and he so kind to us. Besides, I'm longing to be home."

She laughed at Grania's amazement.

"It is home now. It used to seem a prison."

Grania couldn't think of anything to say, but slipped her hand in her mother's and squeezed it hard.

Desmond, walking just behind, drew a deep breath. In a few more years he'd show them what could be done with the castle. If only Phil would let him try!

Above their heads the Angelus rang as Liam Mahon drove his cart up to the chapel steps.

It was piled with sheets of leather wrapped in sacks, and they had to crowd at the back with their feet cocked up. Andy was squeezed in beside his brother.

"What a terrible smell!" exclaimed Grania.

"Sh! Sh!" whispered her mother.

"Terrible smell, moryah!" jeered Andy. "Tis the good wholesome smell of tanned leather. Ye're glad enough to wear the boots made from it, but too proud to sit alongside!"

"Listen to him!" said Liam, laughing over his shoulder at Grania. "Doesn't he know well there's not another man would haul his stuff! If he hadn't a brother that's foolish enough to put up wid him an his old hides he'd have to push a handcart from Dromard to Kilvaragh, God help him!"

"Ye unnatural blaggard, ye!" snapped Andy. "A brother to back up strangers! God forgive ye!"

Sitting up in the uncovered trap the wind beat the snow into their faces, into every fold and crevice of their clothes. The brown pony seemed to be feeling every step of the way and lifted each hoof so slowly and carefully, Grania wished they were walking.

But the splashing and plunging of hoofs and wheels told her how lucky they were not to be tramping on that uneven road in the snow.

Grania was shivering when she saw the lights of the bus shining on the coast road as it came steadily into the village street.

"Let a roar out of ye, Liam!" begged Andy. "For if the buzz goes an leaves us stannin, ye'll have to convey us into Kilvaragh yerself!"

"Have sense, man!" objected Liam. "How in the wide world could I do that?"

"Shout!" urged Eily. "Shout!"

Desmond put his hands to his mouth and made all the noise he could. Then he jumped down and ran, still calling out, towards the bus.

Andy and Liam argued until the horse, faced with the stream of light, backed suddenly.

"Stir yerselves!" shouted the conductor. "We've to rush! The sea's over the wall!"

"Me leather!" wailed Andy. "Are ye Christians to let a man's leather be left behind!"

He lugged one parcel over to the bus. Desmond and Grania carried another.

"There's just room!" said the conductor obligingly. "Stand them sideways."

Andy looked worried and darted off.

"He has a whole load," Desmond explained. "Couldn't you give us a hand with it?"

"I've me bus to mind!" said the conductor with great dignity. "And we can't wait. Will ye listen to the driver!"

The driver had poked his head out from the cabin in front and could be heard asking the reason for the delay.

"I'll help the poor chap!" said a young man with a suitcase on his knees. "Come along, Paddy Cassidy!"

He prodded his companion, who had fallen asleep. They groped their way out and two others followed, while the driver climbed down to discover what was happening.

Grania gazed at Paddy Cassidy's huge hands and broad shoulders as he shuffled towards the trap. She nudged Desmond.

"He's like a strong man at a fair," she whispered.

Paddy's friend heard her.

"Ye're a bright young one!" he said. "That's exactly what he is. We're on our way to a grand theatre up in Dublin. We'll make our fortunes before Paddy's finished. I take care of him."

"What'll I do, Hughie?" asked the strong man in a sleepy voice.

"Hold our yer arms, son, and we'll pile on the packages! Steady, now!"

Paddy Cassidy obediently held out his arms. Andy and Hughie laid the parcels of leather across, and when they reached his chin Hughie led him back to the bus.

Three times the strong man made the journey until at last the trap was empty and Liam drove away.

"Ye're a great pair!" Andy told the strong man and his friend. "If ever I'm up in Dublin, I'll come and give ye a clap. Mind now, I'm givin me word!"

"Tisn't much else that lad would give!" muttered Hughie to Desmond who was squeezed up against him.

Grania sat on the covered market basket at Eily's feet. She was out of the draught and so comfortable she was half asleep. Above her head the shoemaker wondered how he would get his leather to the shop, Hughie was boasting of his friend's strength, the conductor punched tickets and changed money, while passengers talked of high prices and the hardships of travel.

A fat little man with two small children on his knees sat beside Eily. Against the seat he had wedged a young Christmas tree. He told her how he had sold a dozen geese and six turkeys, and Eily praised his children.

Grania tried to listen, but the voices mingled with noises outside the bus – the thunder of waves on the rocks and a strange splashing which seemed to come closer and closer.

The bus lurched, slowed down, and stopped. Every voice ceased, and now the tumult of wind and sea was so great, Grania was amazed that she had heard any other sound. The conductor swung out from the step and whistled at what he saw. Desmond, Andy, and Hughie looked over his shoulders.

"What are ye stoppin for?" asked the little fat man.

"Sure, the sea's over the wall," Hughie told him. "We'll have to swim for it!"

The conductor shook his head doubtfully.

"The water's up to the step. Tis the high tide an the strong wind. In my opinion we should turn back while we can. But Conn Maguire – he's the lad that's drivin – he'd never turn back, if there was lions and tigers on the road!"

Grania knelt on the basket and tried to look out. But the lights were reflected back, and on each side she could see another shadowy bus.

"What'll I do at all!" gasped the man with the children. "Wasn't I very foolish to travel with two young ones!"

"We've bought our tickets to Cork an ye'll have to take us there, me bucko!" shouted Hughie. "We're expected in Dublin, let me tell you, an the train won't wait!"

All along the bus, passengers shouted and argued so that the sounds outside could no longer be heard.

Only the strong man slept, his mouth open.

The lights flickered. A faint red glow showed in each bulb. Voices dropped to whispers and the people looked at one another with startled eyes.

"Couldn't we get out and push?" asked Desmond.

"Here's another strong man!" jeered Andy, but his voice was shaking.

"Keep still, me boy!" said the conductor kindly. "If Conn wants us to help he'll let a roar out of him!"

As he spoke the bus shuddered, the lights came on, and slowly, quiveringly, they went a little way, a little way, quicker; the crashings continued, but the splashing on the roadway ceased and there were the dim lights of Kilvaragh before them!

"Only half an hour late!" announced the conductor proudly. "Who's leaving us at Kilvaragh?"

"Will that giant of a man help wid me leather?" Andy asked Hughie.

"He will not!" replied Hughie. "Can't ye see he's sleepin?"

The conductor grumbled but he began to push the sack-covered parcels over the step.

"Ye'll destroy me leather on me!" screamed Andy. "Hi, Mick! Leary! Give a chap a hand, will ye?"

Two men with a small handcart were coming along the quay. They looked at Andy with a grin and stopped beside the bus.

"Sixpence each parcel, Andy!" said the tall thin one.

"Sixpence the lot and that's robbery!" protested Andy.

"Will yer take ye old smelling bundles away from me bus?" demanded the conductor.

"Sixpence each!" cried the two men.

"Sixpence the lot!" repeated Andy.

"Could ye let me out, please?" asked the fat little man anxiously, pushing forward his Christmas tree.

The driver sounded his horn. Desmond began hauling one of the parcels.

"Are ye comin or are ye goin?" asked the conductor. "One minute more and ye'll have to pay the fare to Youghal!"

"Have it yer own way!" decided the tall man with the handcart.

Now the conductor helped, the strong man and his friend helped. Every one wanted to be rid of Andy.

"Put yer basket on top!" he told Eily. "Twill be a bit of a help to ye!"

"He's not so bad," thought Grania. "Still, he isn't doing the pushing!"

The wind was at their backs as they climbed Main Street. The shops had paraffin lamps and many of the houses had only a candle.

At Andy's, Desmond and Grania took the basket between them.

"I'll be glad to have Bogtrotter carry me to the castle tonight!" said Eily, as the bootmaker opened his door with a huge rusty key he kept under the doorstone.

21

The Way Home

Kilvaragh High Street was deserted as they toiled through the snow towards Rattigan's. Eily, anxious to be home, went on ahead, and they saw her standing in the gateway of the yard.

"What can be wrong?" muttered Desmond.

"Why should anything be wrong?" asked Grania, laughing.

She was excited by the journey on the bus and the beauty of the falling snow.

Desmond lengthened his stride and it was hard for her to keep up with him. The weight of the basket made her arm ache and she was thankful when they reached Eily and they could let it rest on the ground.

"That's strange!" exclaimed the boy. "Where's Bogtrotter?"

For the open shed where he had left the pony and the cart was empty.

They stood there with the snow muffling all sound, not knowing what to do until the wide door of Rattigan's swung back and Mrs Rattigan stared out at them, with the glow of fire and lamplight streaming past her on to the snow.

"Is it yerself, Eily O'Hara?" she called. "Judy went off with Bogtrotter an hour back. She took nearly all the parcels. Come in, the three of ye, and have a sup of tay. We're havin a bit of a ceilidh."

Silently they followed her into the kitchen where children's clothes hung drying before the fire. There were benches against the walls and they were crowded. An old man with an accordion leaned against the dresser and drank thirstily from a big milk jug.

"God save all here!" said Eily.

"God save ye kindly!" came a chorus of answers.

A man pushed a chair forward for her and those on the bench nearest the fire squeezed closer to make room for Grania and Desmond.

"Ye're very welcome, ma'am!" said a big, red-faced man, who was flinging fresh sods on the fire. "I'm afeard Judy's done ye a bad turn!"

"Did she leave much for us to take up, Mr Rattigan?" Eily asked.

Still bending, he pointed to a heap at the back of the door.

"There's a half-sack of meal and a can of oil. There's a box of dear knows what and a packet of candles."

"Tis a great shame for Judy to be leavin ye a load!" said Mrs Rattigan. "Though mebbe she didn't know ye'd have the heavy basket."

"Maybe she didn't!" agreed Eily.

"She did know!" exclaimed Desmond. "Isn't that the way Judy always behaves?"

"We can't carry that load uphill in the snow!" thought Grania.

Mr Rattigan patted Eily's hand.

"Don't worry, ma'am! Weren't Patsy and Sean saying only this minute how they'd give ye a hand up to the castle! An if they couldn't, there's half a dozen others here who'd see ye righted. The kettle's on the boil – Maggie!"

Mrs Rattigan emptied a cupful of tea into the kettle. Mr Rattigan unhooked it and went round the room filling the cups, mugs, and jars held out to him. He served Eily first, then Grania and Desmond. Mrs Rattigan followed with a great dish of hot bacon sandwiches.

"How are ye likin yer new home, girleen?" she asked Grania.

"I love it!" replied the girl, smiling up at her.

"I wonder would ye give us a bit of a song before ye go, Eily?" asked Mr Rattigan.

Eily shook her head, but every one in the room began to clap and stamp until she nodded. Then there was silence.

"What shall I sing?" she asked, looking up at Mrs Rattigan.

"My Mary with the Curling Hair," answered the dark, serious woman promptly. "I'll never forget the first time I heard ye sing it."

The old man took up his accordion and swung it gently.

"I'm always getting surprises!" thought Grania, as she heard a sweet, silvery voice rise in that smoky, steaming room. Most of the crowd were half-grown boys and girls who came there for a dance, but they listened so intently that, as Eily finished the song, they seemed to catch their breath.

"Arish! Arish! cried Mr Rattigan.

"Arish!" they echoed.

Eily laughed and began at once:

"We Were Sitting on the Wall upon a Sunday."

Grania, Desmond, and all of them joined in about the darling girl from Clare.

Then Eily stood up.

"Tis a good step to the castle," she said, though only those close to her could hear above the clapping and stamping. "We should be on our way!"

Grania sat staring at her.

"Ye'll sing at the Christmas ceilidh?" demanded Mr Rattigan.

"No!" replied Eily. "I've finished with such nonsense. Only when I'm with a few dear friends –" she broke off and looked around at the smiling faces.

Then abruptly she made for the door. Patsy and Sean, two round-faced, clumsy lads, were before her.

"We'll be bringing the handcart, ma'am," said Sean, the younger one. "All ye have to do is folly us up."

They brought the handcart into the room and Grania was glad to see there was room even for the basket.

The whole company crowded round the door, calling out "Safe home!" "Slán liv!" and Mr Rattigan ran after them with a lighted lantern.

"Let ye carry that!" the told Desmond. "An watch out, for the holes in the road is hidden wid the snow!"

The air was still, yet the snow fell in slanting lines. As they crossed the yard it beat in their faces so that their eyelashes were clogged with flakes, soft and persistent, and they could hardly breathe. As they reached the gate and turned to go away from the town the snow drove with them.

Glancing over her shoulder Grania saw the veiled

lights in the streets, and above, like gleaming swords, strong, unyielding rays from the lighthouse.

"How could I paint that?" she thought. "Snow and light and the blackness on the sea?"

The road rose steeply. Only the swinging, flickering light of the lantern showed the way and, with the ceaseless, downward dance of the snowflakes, it added confusion. Grania stumbled.

"You're dreaming!" said her mother. "That's dangerous now! Remember the holes and the rocks."

"Keep close to the cart!" called Sean.

He sounded breathless. He was pulling, his brother pushing.

"You take the lantern!" said Desmond, thrusting it towards Grania. "I'll help with the cart."

"I'll carry it!" declared Eily. "I wouldn't trust that one. She's painting pictures in her mind!"

There was laughter in her voice and Grania forgot the snow in thinking of her mother.

Her toes kicked a rock and her half-frozen feet tingled with pain. She slipped and tumbled against Eily, who dropped the lantern. Before it could roll over, Desmond grabbed it.

"Can't you look where you're going!" he snapped at Grania.

"Sure, twas me dropped the lantern!" protested Eily.

Grania was ashamed.

"I'll push with Patsy!" she said.

The moment she laid her hand on the cart one wheel went into a hole with a lurch that flung the basket against the precious can of oil. They heard an ominous crack.

"Thank God the oil is safe!" murmured Eily.

"The wheel's gone!" groaned Sean. "We can't hoist the cart up this desprit track with only one wheel!"

"Give me the lantern and wait here!" ordered Desmond. "It isn't the wheel! Don't let one of ye stir!"

"What's he up to?" asked Sean. "Is it hunting for a new wheel he is?"

Desmond set the lantern in the snow in the shelter of a straight-stemmed young ash. They saw him hacking and cutting with the knife he always carried. Soon he returned with two stout stakes which he threw beside the cart.

"You'll all have to lift!" he explained. "When we have the wheel out, still hold on while I strengthen the axle. Tisn't broken, only cracked."

His pockets were stuffed with string and wire.

"He'd have a great time with Uncle Christie," thought Grania, as they tugged and heaved, obeying every order from Desmond, until the cart stood upright and steady.

He handed the second stake to Grania.

"Go ahead with Eily and *feel* the way! We can't spend the whole night in the snow!"

Grania's fingers were numb. Her feet were so weary, she shuffled through the snow. But she prodded every step with the stake and, leaning against it, was thankful for its support. She zigzagged between rock and hole, marvelling at the way Bogtrotter could climb that road in the dark, yet carrying a heavy load.

"Poor child! You're worn out!" said Eily's soft voice. "But listen! The waterfall! We're coming home!"

A long thin whine and then a storm of barks welcomed them. The door was flung wide and, the dogs leaping before her, old Mrs O'Hara came through the snow to the causeway, blinking and peering at the hand-cart and the two Rattigan boys.

"That Judy's the divil!" she shouted. "But I give her the rough side of me tongue! I shamed her! Bring up the cart! An Desmond, put them lads in wid yersel tonight, they'll not be goin back!"

To come into that warm lighted room without the ceaseless torment of the snow made Grania dizzy. She brushed the cold moisture from her eyes, looked at the steaming kettle, the heap of potato cake cut in wedges and dripping with butter, steaming before the fire, and Judy playing cards with her brothers and pretending not to see them.

Then she saw her grandmother gazing at her and, smiling back, squeezed in at the fire between the dogs and the wall.

22

Midnight Mass at Kilvaragh

Grania always wanted to go to Midnight Mass. She knew it was very grand in Dromard for she had once been with Uncle Christie and her cousins. But Bridgie didn't like it at all.

"Morning is the right time for Mass!" she declared. "And let me tell you, they won't have it in Dublin!"

So they all went to six o'clock Mass on Christmas Day.

But the O'Haras would far rather stay up late than rise early and Grania was one of them. On Christmas Eve they had salt hake, bread, and tea. Eily had soaked the hake all day and cooked it in goat's milk, and the tea was freshly made.

"Sure if we were Christians we'd ate it plain!" said Mrs O'Hara, "wid dry bread an no milk or sugar in our tay. Wasn't that the way in the old days?"

Phil was smoking one cigarette after another. He and his brothers hadn't touched a card all day and he was restless. Only Judy was content, thinking of her green dress.

"Don't they ever read or do anything?" wondered Grania.

"Will you stop staring at me!" exclaimed Phil. "Do a

painting – do a drawing! Get up and do a black sketch on the wall – d'you hear me?"

Grania felt her face growing red.

"I won't do it!" she thought. "What right has he to order me!"

"Do you hear me?" demanded Phil. "Do I have to make you?"

When Phil was angry his voice dropped. His eyes frightened Grania but she set her lips obstinately.

"I'm not a baby!" she told herself. "What can he do?"

"Why wouldn't you do what Phil asks?" she heard her mother say. "There's time to begin before we set out."

"I'll get the sticks for you!" said Desmond eagerly.

Grania looked round. Eily and Desmond were silently urging her to obey. She stood up and took the burnt sticks Desmond handed her.

"The wall's too dirty!" she protested.

But she was really proud that Phil should bother to tell her to draw, and she began to mark out the lighthouse, the harbour, and the fishing boats, going out, sails set to catch the wind.

"No wonder he's such a bully!" she thought, resentfully. "Everyone gives in to him! Everyone but Judy!"

But she could see his face out of the corner of her eye. He stopped smoking and watched every line she drew. He sat so still he scarcely seemed to breathe. Then Grania forgot Phil in the pleasure of the scene she was creating on the dingy wall.

The crash of a chair flung to the floor startled her. The burnt stick broke in her fingers.

Jer, fidgety and uneasy, had pushed away the sugar box which concealed the hole where floodwater came in.

But the hole had been neatly filled with stones and cemented over.

Phil had sat watching this, wondering what it meant. His interest in Grania had put the matter out of his mind. Suddenly he remembered that he had forbidden Desmond to touch it.

"Didn't I tell you to leave the wall alone?" he demanded, seizing the astonished boy by the shoulder and shaking him. "Did you mend the bank, too? Answer me?"

"Phil!" said Mrs O'Hara warningly.

He let Desmond go and stood frowning, his fists clenched. His mother gazed up at him calmly.

"Do ye forget tis Christmas Eve, son? Twas I told Desmond to build up the river bank an stop the hole in the wall to save us from the flood. We've put up wid it these years back to plaze ye! I'm tired of the rheumatiz, an I'm yer mother. Sit down there, behave yerself an stop frightening the child. Sure, Phil, I'm beginnin to be shamed of ye!"

Desmond, rubbing his shoulder, backed against the wall, where the new stones showed clearly. He tried to conceal his pride, but Grania shared it.

"We should be going," murmured Eily.

Phil turned to his mother.

"If you're upset, I'm sorry. But if that Desmond defies me again I'll have his life!"

Judy jumped up.

"Wait!" she said. "I'll try out the green frock!"

"You'll spoil it!" cried Grania in dismay. "And who'll see it under your long coat?"

Halfway up the stairs, Judy hesitated and came back.

"Maybe you have the rights of it. But I'm sick and tired of waiting to wear that frock. If only we could live as we should with servants and horses and carriages, I could wear my green frock all day and every day!"

Grania expected Phil to jeer. Instead he looked at his sister silently, then walked round the table to her.

"Judy!" he said. "If I have any luck I'll make a lady of you. You shall wear pearls and silks, and marry a gentleman. I promise you!"

His face changed. As he looked up at Judy there was kindness in his smile and Grania was bewildered.

Her grandmother squeezed her arm.

"Sure, ye don't know Phil yet," she whispered. "Ye don't understand him. If he had his rights Phil would make us all proud an happy! I'm his mother. I know!"

"Get the cart ready!" Phil told Desmond. "And don't keep us waiting!"

"Why won't Phil be a bit kind?" thought Grania. "Can't he see Desmond thinks the world of him?"

Desmond was back in a few minutes, far too quickly to have harnessed the pony, and he came alone.

"Bogtrotter's lame!" he announced. "No animal could stand the pulling and hauling that one has to manage!"

"When I want your advice I'll let you know!" snapped Phil.

He turned to his mother.

"I'm sorry about this. I should have kept another horse when I had the chance. You'll not like missing Midnight Mass."

"Bedad, I'd not like it! An I won't!" declared the old woman. "I'm starting now an if I put me best foot foremost, I'll not be too late!"

"You can't walk that road at night!" protested Judy. "Keep the fire blazing and the kettle boiling. We'll need both when we've finished that journey going and coming!"

"I'm the best walker in this family an well ye know it!" chuckled her mother. "Let you, Judy, sit be the fire an suck yer thumbs. I've never missed me Midnight Mass an, plaze God, I never will!"

Phil looked down at her.

"I'm proud of you, mother! Here – take my arm! I'll get you down to Kilvaragh!"

"Ye will not then!" she told him cheerfully. "Me arm ud be tore out of me strivin to keep a grip on ye. Des an me'll hold together. The rest of yez go yer own way. The lad'll see me through."

"Indeed I will!" cried Desmond, darting over to her.

She clutched his arm.

"Pon me word, Des, how I'd have managed here widout ye I don't know! Kevin knew what he was doin when he brought ye here. Come along, now. We'll lead off. Bring the lantern!"

Desmond tried not to, but he couldn't help giving a triumphant sideways smile at Phil. Luckily Phil was staring through the door and didn't notice him.

"Phil! You'll have to get a couple of horses!" grumbled Judy. "You could have kept them. Why didn't you?"

Phil grinned at her.

"Because I paid the bills. There was Eily looking at me as if I was a robber. Grania wanted boots. You wanted a frock. Those brothers of mine hadn't enough clothes between them to cover their skins. But before the New Year, Judy, there'll be horses in the stable and I'll teach the young one to ride!"

"Oh!" cried Grania delightedly.

"We must be going!" said Eily.

Grania obeyed.

"I wish I could ride properly!" she told her mother. "I'm afraid of horses but I'd love to make Uncle Phil proud of me."

"It isn't easy to please Phil," her mother told her.

The snow had turned to slush, and the O'Haras hated walking. But Eily had often walked down to Kilvaragh and back carrying a heavy basket. Phil strode easily beside Judy, who grumbled without ceasing. Jer and Terry shuffled along, blaming Desmond for their troubles.

"Why didn't ye tell us Bogtrotter was lame?" asked Terry.

"Why didn't ye do something?" wailed Jer.

"Keep yer mouth shut!" Mrs O'Hara advised Desmond. "Is the poor baste in pain?"

Desmond shook his head.

"I bathed the leg and rubbed it. There was a stone in the shoe and the muscles were swollen, that's all. I thought he might be well enough for tonight. A day's rest and Bogtrotter will be as well as ever."

Desmond carried a lantern, but the dim light was of little use to the others. Grania and Eily followed closely. Phil walked as if he could see in the darkness. Occasionally the flying clouds revealed the moon and the holes could be seen as dark patches, the stones and rocks like polished silver.

Judy was as clean a walker as Phil. But she grew angrier each moment, while Jer and Terry splashed from one puddle to another.

"And yet they'd spend a night on the bog and never

mind it!" muttered Desmond. "If they won't share the road with the Farrellys, why won't they let me do a few days' work filling the holes with stones?"

"Rest aisy, child!" said Mrs O'Hara. "Wait till the spring. The whole world is better in the spring. There'll be changes even in Castle O'Hara."

Every one in Kilvaragh seemed to be in Main Street, hurrying towards the chapel. There were lights in the houses, doors slammed up and down, people called Christmas wishes, feet in heavy boots clattered over the uneven cobbles. Then they were going through the chapel door, dropping their pennies in the plate, dipping fingers in the holy water font and making the sign of the Cross.

The Crib inside the door wasn't as grand as the one at Dromard. The star was made with silver paper and the figures had been used so often they were rubbed and shabby.

"I wonder would they let me make figures for next Christmas?" thought Grania. "I could make such a grand Crib they'd be coming over from Dromard to look at it."

Judy gave her a push.

"Quit dreaming and go into the chapel!"

There was such a thrill in this crowded Midnight Mass, Grania wished it could happen every week. The salty, tarry smell which almost overpowered the incense delighted her and, when the children in the choir sang *Adeste Fideles*, she was so happy tears came into her eyes.

Yet she hated having to stand all the time or kneel on the muddy stone floor. Judy sat in a corner seat, scornful and proud as ever.

When they came out, even Phil was included in the

Happy Christmas wishes. He returned them politely, taking off his cap each time.

"Sure Phil has the brains an the manners to make his way in the world if only the divil would lave him be." said his mother.

"And now we've to face that climb and there's rain on the wind!" grumbled Judy.

"Twill do ye no harrum!" chuckled the old woman. "Indade it might do yer soul a bit of good!"

Grania was too excited to mind the rain. She wanted to run and dance. Eily was with Judy. She passed them, caught up with Jer and Terry, quarrelling with their usual unmeaning bitterness. Phil strode on alone and she ran after him.

"Can I walk with you?" she asked breathlessly.

He looked down at her.

"Why wouldn't you keep with your mother, or Desmond?"

"You're walking faster," she told him.

Phil at once increased his speed so that she had to run to keep up with him.

"Well, Kevin's daughter!" he said. "You've decided to be an O'Hara and give up the Hanlons?"

"I am an O'Hara!" Grania declared. "But I'll never give up the Hanlons. Why should I? Mrs Hanlon's my aunt every bit as much as you are my uncle, and as for Uncle Christie, I don't know how I had the heart to leave him, I was that fond of him!"

"Tell me about the Fogarty woman!"

"Will ye look at that now?" said Mrs O'Hara to Desmond. "Phil has that young one hanging on to his arm an she chatting away as if he doted on her. I'm thinking she'll take Kevin's place wid him. Thanks be to God!"

"Twas me brought her here!" muttered Desmond. "Yet now she leaves me to talk to Phil. And he's always bullying!"

"Whisht now, Des! Tis me own son ye're blaggardin. Sure Phil's not too bad. He's clever! He's fond of me! He's fond of Judy. An now he's beginnin to have a grah for little Grania! I was afeard he'd be hard on her. Still an all, isn't it a great pity he never took a likin to ye? I had hopes he would."

They were all wet and tired when they reached the castle. They should have been miserable. But soon they were drinking hot tea and eating thick slices of bread and blackberry jam around the fire. Mrs O'Hara began telling of the Christmases of her youth. Phil bragged of the horses he would train and Judy sat back a little, smiling to herself.

Grania sat on a creepy against the wall, Timmy Fuzz purring on her shoulder, and looked from face to face. Phil had told her she should do a drawing of Mrs Fogarty on the wall to remind her of what she had escaped. But it was these faces she longed to draw – as they were now – laughing, yawning, their eyes happy.

23

The Pensioner

On Christmas morning Grania woke so early she was sure no one, not even the dogs, would be stirring. Not a glimmer of light softened the darkness. She put out her hand for the matches and, when the tiny light steadied, she saw Timmy Fuzz's green eyes opening as he sprawled beside her. Lighting the candle, she laughed.

"And I thought I was first!"

Instead of the white ha'penny candle stuck to the table in its own grease, a thick red candle was fixed in a new green enamel candlestick. The black kitten wriggled closer and she saw he had a wide red ribbon tied in a bow round his neck. She was still sleepy, but every second she was seeing more. A pile of parcels was set beyond the candlestick, and as she drew them towards her the door opened and her mother came in.

"I meant to be up first and give you breakfast," said Grania remorsefully. "I suppose it was Midnight Mass made me so sleepy. I'll come now and help!"

"Stay in bed!" ordered Eily. "We'll have breakfast together. I like it best that way. If I don't spoil you, who will?"

"Isn't it very nice of her to like it this way?" Grania asked Timmy Fuzz, who rolled over, kicked, then doubled up his paws and blinked so that Grania had to tickle him.

She was clearing the parcels from the table on to her bed when Eily came back with a heavy tray.

"There's a ham sandwich each!" she said.

"Did you open the present I left for you on the table?" asked Grania.

Eily stood still holding the tray.

"Grania!" she said. "You've made me so happy. But how did you know what poor Kevin looked like? You don't remember him. How could you?"

"Granny borrowed the photo in your room. I drew the picture from that."

"The only photo I had was a little faded thing."

"I imagined him. You've told me so much and granny's always talking about him!"

Eily smiled as she settled herself comfortably on the bed.

"I'll put your coat over my shoulders, Grania. I've been thinking – how we could make this a real castle, clean and bright and grand-looking."

Slowly the old worried look came back to her face.

"But I'm afraid of those four. They're strange and wild! Thank God they've taken you as a real O'Hara! I do believe they're proud of you. But me and Desmond – we're outsiders still!"

Grania tilted her chin.

"I think Judy and Phil are beginning to like me. I wish they would. Then I might get round them!"

Eily laughed.

"Isn't it queer now? One day I feel we're going to be

rich and happy. Then I'll wake up another day and be afraid to open my eyes!"

Grania scraped the sugar from the bottom of her cup and began to unwrap her presents.

"Not last Christmas, but the Christmas before, I was young enough to hang up my stocking," she said thoughtfully.

"I wish you had done it this year," sighed Eily.

"It was fun to wake in the dark and feel all the bumps and knobs, but I'm too old for that!"

Grania's voice sounded regretful.

Suddenly she cried out: "Oh, how lovely!"

She had unwrapped a wide, brilliant blue scarf and a tammy with a pompom to match.

"Who made them?"

"Your granny did the scarf. Twas I made the other. We had a terrible time not letting you know. Desmond helped us. He'd call you to give him a hand with the turf or bring in a bucket of water. Sometimes you were real vexed with him."

"Which is Desmond's present?"

Sally had sent her a box of sweets. As she lifted the lid the gold and silver and speckled papers gleamed like jewels. There were handkerchiefs from Norrie with a golden 'G' embroidered in the corner. Uncle Christie had put a ten-shilling note in with the biggest card he could get for twopence. At the foot of the bed was a heavy, square brown-paper parcel.

Grania laughed as she opened it. Sheets of cartridge paper!

"I'm always grumbling I haven't enough paper. Isn't it like Desmond to give me what I ask for – just that!"

"He's a good lad!" said Eily. "The best in the world. I wish I knew what to do about him! Now don't be asking me questions with your eyes. We've a hard day before us – to do all that should be done and to keep the peace. Come along, Timmy Fuzz, you can go out and look at the world."

"O'Hara uncles and aunts don't give presents," grumbled Grania, as she pulled on her stockings.

She washed in icy water, longing for hot water at the turn of a tap, which Desmond had promised, put on her best frock with the overall on top, and hurried down to the fire.

Desmond was piling sods against the wall. Grania stood on the bottom step and watched him. He built up the sods as if they were bricks and swept the dust and small pieces into the fire. She saw a woven rug before the hearth and a plaid shawl on the back of old Mrs O'Hara's chair.

"Who made the rug?" she asked, hoping to startle the boy into dropping a sod.

He looked over his shoulder.

"I made the rug!" he answered proudly. "It's time the granny had a bit of comfort."

Grania swung on her heels to view her own work on the whitewashed walls.

"When we make it into a real castle, you'll have to paint proper pictures!" said Desmond, still on his knees before the fire.

"Proper pictures!" exclaimed Grania indignantly. "You don't know about pictures!"

Desmond stood up carefully, so that his boots wouldn't scuff the rug.

"I do know about pictures! Haven't I been watching you for weeks and months? And you can't do proper pictures on walls with bits of burnt wood!"

"Lave the child alone!" said old Mrs O'Hara, coming out in her red petticoat and stockinged feet. "Sure she's made the place gran – gran to the world! I can sit all day an look at them pictures! Bedad! What's this? A rug under me two feet an a shawl to me back. Pon me word! Who did em?"

"I made the rug for you!" Desmond told her. "I wanted to have the footstool too. But I hadn't the time. Twill be ready for Easter, maybe!"

The old woman sat in her chair and drew the shawl about her.

"Was it Eily done the shawl?"

"It was Eily!"

"I don't deserve it. This is a dote of a Christmas Day! I feel that good I'd love to go to morning Mass. But tis too late!"

"I'd like Midnight Mass always!" declared Grania.

She came over to the fire and frowned.

"I haven't a present for you, Granny, and you made me that lovely scarf!"

"Wisha, ye poor scrap! Haven't ye made the room fine and beautiful? Me! Red Sarah that was – a knitted shawl big enough to cover her, a worked rug to her feet, an a picture on every wall! Sure I'm a lucky old divil, God help me! Is there a sup of tay in the pot, Grania?"

"We'll all have a cup of tea together," said Eily. "Then we must work. There's a goose in that oven. There's a ham yonder, and listen to the pudding! I wish those four would come to their breakfast!"

"Sure there's only the praties an the cabbage waitin, an a few odd jobs of clanin an puttin right," objected the old woman. "An aren't we better this way?"

Grania and Desmond had decorated the kitchen with holly and long strands of small-leaved ivy. In front of the door they planted a small fir tree and tied bits of fat and bread to the branches, so that while they had dinner the birds had theirs.

"If you haven't the queerest notions, Grania!" exclaimed Judy, looking up from her plate as Grania drew back the upper half of the door and stood watching a robin, its breast glowing, singing a clear winter song.

The moment Grania cleared away the plates and mugs, Jer brought out the cards.

"Ye're no better than a haythen!" exclaimed Mrs O'Hara. "Aren't ye ashamed to have nothing better to do wid yerselves on Christmas Day?"

Phil took the pack of cards from his brother and put them up on the mantelpiece.

"What is there better?" he asked. "If we had horses, we could ride. If we had friends, we could entertain. We do what we can!"

"Why wouldn't ye keep yer promise to the child?" she asked.

He looked puzzled.

"Promise! What promise?"

"That ye'd tache her to ride the way she should. She's an O'Hara an the only one that can't ride properly. Des! Is Bogtrotter aquil for the job?"

"He's grand!" declared the boy. "I'll make him ready. Phil won't have much trouble teaching Grania. She's been up and down to Kilvaragh on him and never turned a hair!"

"Off wid ye, lad!"

Grania was frightened. But she was determined not to show it. Her mother was excited and the old woman, wrapping herself in the new shawl, sat out on the stone seat to watch.

Desmond groomed the pony so that when they came to the door Bogtrotter's thick coat was trim and glossy as if he were racing.

Even Jer and Terry lounged out and Judy stood in the doorway.

"Get up on the riding stone!" said Phil.

There was a big square stone at the edge of the causeway. Grania stood on it and Phil led the pony close alongside.

He folded an old rug carefully and laid it across Bogtrotter's back.

"Put yer hand on the neck, there! Now give a bit of a jump. Hold the reins low and grip his body with your knees."

"Shouldn't there be a saddle and things for me feet?" asked Grania appealingly.

This wasn't the same as jogging along the mountain road with Des at the pony's head.

She felt terribly insecure and longed to clutch her uncle's arm.

He looked at her gravely.

"Did you ever see me with a saddle and stirrups?"

"I've never seen you ride!" declared Grania.

He nodded.

"No. We've had no horses since you came. Never mind. You can begin with Bogtrotter. Once you learn to sit and to hold the reins, you're started!"

He laughed and gave the pony a slap.

Bogtrotter kicked up his hind legs. Grania gasped and tugged the reins.

"Go easy!" warned Phil.

"There never was a O'Hara yet fell off a horse!" called Mrs O'Hara. "Mind yerself, Bogtrotter!"

Grania heard her voice. The pony was trotting and she bounced up and down. Phil ran beside her.

"Don't look at me," he said. "Grip harder with your knees and look over Bogtrotter's head. You'll not feel anything then."

A narrow track led straight to the bog. It was the way Desmond went to cut turf. On one side the ground dropped to the Rocky Valley.

"Where's Des off to?" asked Phil suddenly, stopping the pony.

They could see the boy running down into the valley, shortening the way by leaping from rock to rock. He swung a basket and the gay tune he whistled rose on the cold air. Bogtrotter whinnied but Desmond did not look back.

"He's going for eggs," replied Grania.

"Eggs!" muttered Phil. "Ah, Thady Connor! Maybe we'll pay the Pensioner a visit. We'll see how you shape."

Bogtrotter was rested. He had enjoyed his feed and Grania's light weight was nothing to him. He stretched his neck and set off at a gallop without any troublesome cart to hinder him.

"Oh!" cried Grania.

The bushes and rocks seemed rushing to meet her. But she sat more easily, sure now that she would not fall. Phil was left behind, the track widened and ended in the crumbling brown mould of a turf bank.

The pony stopped and Grania turned, smiling at Phil as he came running after them.

"You'll make a good rider, and why wouldn't you? Isn't riding in the O'Hara's blood?" he said, his eyes sparkling. "But you'll never come up to Judy! To see her flying over hedges and ditches on a fast mare, her red hair streaming! Ah, she's a great girl!"

Grania was thankful to sit quietly, gazing over the bog.

"Every bone I have feels broken," she thought.

Phil turned, following another track, which sloped towards the middle of the Rocky Valley.

"Could I walk for a change?" asked Grania.

She spoke softly and, if Phil heard, he did not answer.

"This isn't the way home," protested Grania, drooping over the pony's head.

"Sit up!" said Phil sharply. "If you slump that way you'll ride like a sack of praties. It isn't home we're going. We're visiting the Pensioner."

Grania remembered now. Desmond had told her how Phil and his brothers tormented the old man.

"I shouldn't have told you where Des was going," she said. "I'd forgotten you don't like Thady Connor!"

He laughed.

"Why should I like him? When we tried to get our rights, Thady Connor backed the Farrellys. He got a queer drop when we won. And now Eily sends to him for eggs! I didn't think it of her."

"If we kept fowl she needn't do that," said Grania, watching his face.

But he was still good-tempered.

"You rode well, so I'll humour you. You can ride by your lone to Thady's. Keep to the path and sit up straight. His place is where it ends. You can give him my respects!"

The path was steep. Bogtrotter went carefully with a lurch at every step, as if they were going to Kilvaragh. When Grania was able to look back, Phil had gone. The pony stopped so abruptly she fell forward and, dropping the reins, flung her arms about the startled animal's neck.

"Bedad, that's the way to larn him!" she heard. "Ye should know better, Bogtrotter, than to frighten the child that way!"

"I'm not frightened," protested Grania.

The pony had stopped at a blue gate in a high holly hedge. Desmond was standing inside and he swung it open. As the pony trotted through, a small thin man standing on a butter-box, with a pair of shears in his hands, bowed to Grania.

"Ye're very welcome. I seen ye many a time at the chapel, but I never dared speak wid all them O'Haras about."

He stepped from his box as Grania slid thankfully to the ground.

"How do you do, Mr Connor?" she said.

He was so pleased and confused at being called *Mr Connor* he blinked and smiled without saying a word.

"Was Phil pleased with your riding?" asked Desmond. "He should be. It's your first real ride."

She nodded proudly.

"But I'm terribly stiff," she confessed. "It's grand to be standing on the earth again."

"I know!" Desmond told her. And they both laughed.

Thady Connor looked at her in bewilderment.

"Wasn't yer mother very rash to trust ye on a pony an wid Phil to learn ye ridin?" he asked. "I've been troubled over ye livin wid them divils of O'Haras! Des says they're not too bad. But I know them. Oh, indade I know them! But come along in now. We'll find the eggs later on."

"Can you spare a dozen?" asked Desmond.

"I can. I can let ye have a whole dozen. Mind ye're lucky, for these times Peg Lanaghan takes all I have. She's a gran woman. Only yesterday she gave me a whole three-pound jar of jam – gooseberry jam! Tis a pity ye can't be friends wid Peg!"

He took them to his cabin built against a rock. The door was bright blue like the gate, and the path leading to it was made of crushed shells. Grania saw that already primroses were opening in the shelter of the hedge and fragile white and green flowers swayed though there wasn't the smallest breeze.

"Ye're admirin me snowdrops?" asked Thady. "I had them from Peg Lanaghan."

"Are they snowdrops?" asked Grania.

Thady pushed open the door.

"Take a seat on the settle," he said. "Mebbe ye'd like a turn at the wheel, Grania?"

Thady did not burn turf but dried furze. He had roots and thick branches piled on the open hearth. Striking a match he lit a crumpled piece of paper and thrust it into the heap, while Grania turned the bellows wheel. At once there was a golden blaze with showers of sparks and a pleasant smell.

"Ye'll take a sup of tay wid me? Ye'll not mind the tin milk?" asked the old man.

Grania gazed about the cabin. It was neat and gay, like a doll's house, with a small dresser, and blue and white delph ranged on it. There were statues on the mantelpiece and an altar lamp with a red shade threw a glow on the sacred picture hanging on the wall. It was opposite the door and Grania remembered the first night when she had ridden to the castle with Desmond and had seen Thady's lamp gleaming through the darkness.

There was a shelf of books beside the window. They didn't look the kind that had pictures in them, for Thady was a bit of a scholar.

The little black kettle began to sing above the spluttering of the furze flames. Desmond went out for more fuel and came in with an armful of roots.

"Sure I have plenty!" protested Thady.

"Ye'll need more," the boy told him. "We're in for a wild night and it won't do you any good to be running in and out."

He piled the roots almost as neatly as if they were sods, fitting them into one another until a big square pile rose against the wall.

"Pon me word, I'll have a gran night wid me papers an the fire," cried the old man, rubbing his hands gleefully. "Look now! Tis Peg Lanaghan got them for me – the whole bundle for threepence!"

He held out a parcel of American magazines with coloured covers and full-page pictures.

"I hear ye're terrible clever at the paintin, Grania," said Thady. "Mebbe one day ye'll be makin pictures like these. That'll be the time, Des, when we see her name in the papers an she'll be a rich lady living up in Dublin."

Desmond looked at Grania as if he did not know her.

"Would you like that?" he asked.

"I would. But I'd want to come back. I don't believe I'd ever be happy away from Castle O'Hara!"

The tea was weak and Grania didn't like the tinned milk, for she had grown used to strong tea with plenty of goat's milk in it. But Thady had a big currant cake and he cut thick slices for them.

"We should be going," said Desmond at last.

"The eggs!" exclaimed Thady. "The eggs!"

They stood up to go with him.

"If I let yez see where the hens lay, ye'll never let on to a soul?" he asked.

"But Eily knows!" said Desmond.

The old man laughed.

"Why wouldn't she? I'd never mind Eily knowing – nor Peg Lanaghan. Tis only the O'Haras I hide from!"

"Is Peg Lanaghan afraid of the O'Haras?" asked Grania curiously.

Thady drew nearer.

"Listen," he whispered. "She threatened to take them into court. They'd be ashamed of that. She fixed them!"

"And you wouldn't do that?"

Thady looked at her in horror.

"Is it to *inform* ye'd have me? Me that's descended from kings – from the great Conor Mac Nessa himself! Sure, child, ye couldn't mane it! Ye see – a poor simple woman like Peg might threaten that – a Connor couldn't!"

"Phil sent his respects," said Grania. "I don't think you've any need to be afraid of him."

Desmond whistled.

"He did that!" cried Thady, looking very pleased. "Phil O'Hara sent his respects. Mebbe he was jokin! Still an all! Pon me word, Grania – if ye could civilise them ones – twould be gran work, gran work! But Phil sent his respects. I'll tell Peg Lanaghan. She'll find it hard to credit. But the eggs now, the eggs!"

24

The Christmas Ceilidh

On St Stephen's Day the O'Haras had tea early. They were all very stiff and grand in their best clothes. When Judy came slowly down the stairs, wearing the green dress, Grania gave a little gasp. It was lovely!

Old Mrs O'Hara stood up and peered at her daughter.

"Ye'll do the O'Haras credit, Judy! I'm proud of ye!"

Judy laughed and sat in her old armchair. The full skirt of the dress flowed round her as she leaned back.

"And you've to ride in that wretched cart!" said Phil. "There'll have to be changes here. I'm going to give you a chance, Judy!"

Eily poured out the tea.

"Des has put rugs in the cart. It won't be too bad," she said.

They were all excited as they set off. Judy sat in front of Phil. Eily and Mrs O'Hara were in the back of the cart. Halfway down, Phil jumped out and walked with his brothers.

As the cart came to the top of Main Street the Wren Boys were standing in the middle of the road singing:

The wran, the wran, the king of all birds,

On St Stephen's Day got cot in the furze,
Though he is little, his family's great.
Now Mrs O'Hara, please give us a treat.
Our box would speak, but it hasn't a tongue,
An a penny or two won't do ye no wrong.
Sing holly, sing ivy, sing ivy an holly,
A penny for sweets sure would cheer melancholy.
Now please do give us of your best
An we hope in heaven your soul may rest.

They swarmed round Bogtrotter. There were girls as well as boys, but it was hard to tell which were which, for the boys wore skirts and the girls wore trousers. They all had coloured paper caps and their faces were blackened. The tallest boy carried a wire cage decorated with tinsel. A queer bird made of crinkled paper and cock's feathers was hanging inside.

"Listen to that rubbish!" exclaimed Terry. "The impidence of them stopping our horse!"

"What harm are they doing?" asked Grania. "I like it. This is fun!"

She ran towards the singers. Grania knew Sean and Patsy Rattigan when they grinned at her, and she was delighted to see Mrs O'Hara leaning down to give them money.

As she stopped, Phil caught up with her.

"A pack of beggars!" he said.

"We're not beggars!" exclaimed Patsy Rattigan, who seldom spoke. "We're Wren Boys. We sing our song and we've a right to what's given us!"

"The boy is right," said Eily. "It's an ancient custom."

The children who were clambering over the cart

dropped away. Grania saw their smiles fade and turn to scowls. Their black faces made the change terrifying.

"Lave the childer alone, Phil!" protested Mrs O'Hara. "Why shouldn't they have a bit of fun? Sure, they're only young once."

The Wren Boys marched off. When they were at a safe distance the young leader, who carried the bird, called back: "Tinker! Tinker!"

The others joined hands and danced in the snow singing "Tinker O'Hara! Tinker O'Hara!"

Only the Rattigan boys stood alone, without joining in.

Phil was about to rush after the children, when Judy jumped down and caught his arm.

"Are you crazy! Do you want us to be the laughing-stock of Kilvaragh?"

"If I laid my hands on them, tisn't a laughing-stock I'd be!" he muttered.

The school flashed lights from every window. A motor lorry, loaded with men standing up and clinging to one another, crashed by. Motors were ranged at one side of the courtyard – carts at the other, where horses and donkeys had the shelter of an open shed.

Grania stayed with Desmond to help him fix the nose-bag and cover Bogtrotter with two big sacks.

"Hasn't Uncle Phil a shocking temper?" she said, wondering where Judy and the brothers were.

Eily and Mrs O'Hara were going up the crowded steps, through the wide-open doors.

"It's the O'Hara temper," exclaimed Desmond.

"I'm thankful I haven't it," declared Grania. "I'd be ashamed!"

Desmond chuckled. Grania flushed and turned on him.

"Are you telling me I'm mad?" she asked.

He shook his head.

"Not like Phil. But you must know you have a temper?"

Desmond was smiling and his eyes coaxed her.

"I could have a temper," he said. "But where's the sense in arguing and quarrelling about nothing?"

He stroked Bogtrotter's quivering ears. The pony shook the nose-bag and began munching.

"Do I look clean and tidy?" asked Desmond as they went up the steps.

Grania glanced at his brown face, serious grey eyes, and the lock of fair hair standing straight up at the back, the clean shirt and gay plaid scarf carelessly knotted.

"I'll paint a big picture of you next," she said. "If we were home I'd start this very instant."

"Don't do to me what you did to Granny – paint me with a squint and a crooked mouth," he laughed.

"I didn't!" cried Grania. "But if I see you that way, that's the way I'll paint you. And it wasn't a squint!"

"Tickets!" demanded the young man at the table inside the door.

"Tis Phil has them, and well you know it, Peter Hannigan!" Desmond told him.

"I've me orders not to let Finn MacCool himself through widout a ticket! But where's the use of makin rules and regulations when dalin wid the O'Haras!" retorted Peter.

"And he isn't an O'Hara," said Grania, pulling off her coat and tammy and squeezing by.

"Isn't it well for him?" asked Peter with a grin.

The big library was decorated with paper chains and the lights had coloured shades. Branches of fir were grouped in the corners with Japanese lanterns tied to the twigs. The floor was still white with French chalk and, through open doorways, Grania could see other rooms as gay and bright.

She could hear motors continually coming up, the sound of horses' hoofs on the flags. The doorway was crowded and Peter Hannigan was red and confused as tickets were pushed at him, dropped on the table or the floor, so that it was impossible to keep track of them all.

Grania was pleased when she saw Thady Connor coming in with Andy Mahon. Thady was clean and smart, but Andy hadn't bothered to put on a tie, though his hair was combed and he wore a white collar.

Eily came hurrying towards them.

"Come with me, Grania," she whispered. "I'm asking Mr O'Neill to let you join the drawing class. Try now and be very nice to him."

"I will!" promised Grania.

She clutched Desmond's hand but he tugged it away and gave her a little encouraging push. She was so excited the lights became blurred and she knocked against people. But nobody minded. They were all feeling gay and friendly after Christmas.

Mr O'Neill was waiting for them in the supper-room. Chin in hand he scowled at the long tables, covered with stiff white cloths and decorated with vases of flowers. Grania wondered at the number of knives and forks, even while she was watching the drawing master, admiring his neat blue suit, his white linen, and bushy hair.

"So this is Grania," he said. "Grania O'Hara!"

"There's so much I want to know," said Grania, her voice trembling. "I can't learn by myself."

"You're not in the class yet," Mr O'Neill told her. "I'm remembering what happened when we had O'Haras here before."

"Sure that was years ago," protested Eily.

"What happened?" asked Grania curiously.

Mr O'Neill flung out his hand.

"Your Aunt Judy came to the dressmaking. She tore up the dress one girl was making. She flung the sewing machine through the biggest window, and beat the whole class out of the room."

Grania tried not to giggle.

"Why?" she asked.

"Why!" repeated Mr O'Neill. "You're asking me why. What does it matter – why?"

"It should matter a great deal," said Grania.

"They called her a tinker!" explained Eily.

"There you are!" cried Grania, and she looked straight into Mr O'Neill's eyes.

He was used to pupils who cast down their eyes or looked sideways when he spoke to them and yet he wasn't displeased with Grania.

"Your Uncle Phil was in the carpentry class and he fought the whole pack of them," went on the drawing master, sticking out his chin. "The Technical School wasn't built for the O'Haras and their kind."

"The O'Haras aren't cowards, anyway!" said Grania.

"Ah, don't be annoying me!" exclaimed Mr O'Neill.

"Will you keep quiet, Grania," pleaded Eily. "If you're so rude, how can you expect Mr O'Neill to have you in his class?"

Grania stood silent.

"She's a clever girl, Mr O'Neill," said Eily. "And I want

her to be happy. If Judy and Phil could have settled to learning something they wouldn't be the way they are. And shouldn't you be able to stop the scholars calling names?"

"If they want to call me tinker I don't mind!" declared Grania.

She could see her red hair, with the bows on each side, and her blue frock, in a mirror.

"I don't look too bad at all," she thought, feeling delighted with herself.

"I've brought some of her pictures to show you," and, unwrapping a parcel, Eily held out one drawing at a time.

Mr O'Neill took the first scornfully. He was convinced that nothing good could come from an O'Hara. But when Eily held up a little black-and-white sketch of Desmond carrying an armful of sods, he whistled softly.

"Well, Grania O'Hara," he said. "If you can put up with what the class call you for a day or so, I think you'll have the laugh of them. The school opens in a week's time – Monday and Thursday, at three o'clock!"

"Only twice a week," sighed Grania.

"Thank you, Mr O'Neill," said Eily. "Say 'thank you,' Grania!"

"Thank you, Mr O'Neill!" repeated Grania obediently, with such a radiant smile the drawing teacher smiled back.

"She's like her father," he thought. "And he was an O'Hara."

25

The Walls of Limerick

Grania looked for Desmond to tell him the great news but could not find him. Suddenly she stood still and backed against the wall.

"I mustn't go pushing and squeezing," she thought. "I'll have to mind my manners now I'm going to an Art class."

She looked about her eagerly. Across the room Desmond was moving slowly, staring at the dancers, who stood waiting for the music, peering at those who sat on the chairs against the walls and looking glummer every moment.

"He's hunting for me," decided Grania, and she began to edge her way towards him.

She was stopped by the crush around the platform, where a plump, grey-haired woman in a tight black satin frock was sounding a note on the piano for the two fiddlers to tune their instruments. Beside her a tall, very thin young man was playing the flute softly for his own pleasure.

Grania was impatient for now she had lost sight of Desmond.

"Let me by, please," she implored a broad, short man who blocked her way.

Then, over his shoulder, she saw her aunt.

Judy had taken off her coat and was walking slowly into the room with her brothers. For once nobody looked at them. Everyone was looking at Judy.

"She's like a princess, and it's my green frock has done it!" thought Grania proudly.

She forgot the hours Eily had spent, stitching the long seams and the yards of hem.

"There's the Farrellys!" exclaimed the short man. "Farrellys and O'Haras in the one room! Now there'll be slaughter!"

Bill Farrelly saw Phil first and his face slowly crimsoned. He stepped forward and Grania felt little shudders of expectation along the room.

"There'll be the divil to pay!" muttered one of the fiddlers.

"Tis the O'Haras is the cause of all the trouble!" declared the young man with the flute. "Look what they did to the Farrellys! Could any one expect Big Bill to forget that!"

He gave the grey-haired woman a poke.

"Here's Father Coulahan coming through the door. Now we'll have sport!"

The pianist craned her neck to see and Grania squeezed away from the platform.

Even the O'Haras thought well of Father Coulahan, but they walked straight by when he came up with his hand outstretched to Big Bill.

"How are you, Mr Farrelly, and how's herself? Is she here?"

Before Big Bill could answer, the priest turned to Phil.

"We don't often see you nowadays at ceilidhs, Phil,

though I hear you're a grand dancer. Judy! I have a partner for you. Come along, now!"

He kept his hand on Big Bill's arm until several people separated them from Phil. Then the priest and Judy walked on alone, and the dancers made way for them, staring curiously.

A big young man, with hair so bleached it looked almost white against his tanned face, stood bolt upright at the end of the room, his eyes gazing over the heads of the crowd as if he didn't see one of them.

"Steve Farrelly!" said Father Coulahan. "I want you and Judy O'Hara to lead *The Walls of Limerick*. Barring Phil O'Hara, you're the two best dancers here."

Steve looked slowly from Father Coulahan to Judy. His eyes were startled but he ducked his head.

"I'll be proud!" he said.

Judy's eyes flashed. She pressed her lips together.

"I've set my heart on you two leading *The Walls of Limerick!*" said the priest.

He looked at Judy.

"The one dance, then!" she said slowly. "Not another one!"

"Mr O'Neill!" called Father Coulahan quickly. *"The Walls of Limerick!"*

Mr O'Neill acted as MC at all the ceilidhs and dances held in the library. He came hurrying out with Eily.

"Sorry, Father, sorry!" he said. "Didn't know it was time yet!"

He glanced up at the big round clock over the door and pulled out his watch.

"And it isn't!" he added. "Another five minutes, though they're all ready and waiting."

"Start now!" urged Father Coulahan. "At once, to oblige me! Judy and Steve Farrelly will lead!"

Mr O'Neill saw Judy and Steve Farrelly standing stiffly side by side. He opened his mouth, then nodded.

"Form up for *The Walls of Limerick!*" he called loudly.

So many obeyed that Grania was able to reach Desmond, flattened against the wall behind Peter Hannigan, who had left his place at the door to see what was happening.

"What's aitin em?" asked Peter. "I never seen such a rush in me life for *The Walls of Limerick*. If twas a sixteen-handed reel, now, or a waltz?"

"Judy's going to lead with Steve Farrelly!" Grania told him.

"That's a good un!" chuckled Peter.

He went back to count the tickets.

"You're joking!" said Desmond, though he knew she wasn't.

"Look for yourself!" Grania told him.

Desmond stepped up on a chair.

"It's the truth!" said Desmond solemnly. "Grania! It's the end of the quarrel. We can be friends with the Farrellys. We can rebuild the bridge and the new road will be for all of us. But I can't believe it!"

Peter laid down the tickets and came over to him. He scratched his head when he saw Steve opposite Judy and smiling at her.

"I never did believe in miracles!" he announced. "Not ornary ones. Will ye look at Phil's face. There's murder in it! He'll slaughter Judy. He'll have her life!"

Desmond scowled.

"I might have known," he muttered. "Tis always Phil! He spoils everything!"

Grania was so happy she couldn't bear to see Desmond disappointed.

"Don't mind him!" she said. "If Judy wants to be friends with the Farrellys, Phil's too fond of her to want to stop it. Besides, if he has a temper, so has she!"

For an instant Desmond looked helpful. Then he frowned again.

"Judy'd never cross Phil!" he declared. "She's just doing this to please Father Coulahan."

"Listen, Desmond," Grania whispered, for she didn't want Peter Hannigan to hear her, "Mr O'Neill is letting me join the Art class!"

"That means you'll go away," the boy grumbled. "And we'll be left alone again!"

"You've made up your mind to be unhappy," Grania told him, laughing at his serious face. "Why should I go away? But let's dance. The music's lovely!"

"I can't dance!" he protested.

"I'll teach you. We'll waltz! It's easy! Norrie was teaching me. Come into the hall down there and we'll practice the steps."

"I don't want to dance!" said Desmond. "I'm going out to Bogtrotter!"

"Go in an enjoy yerself, ye young eejit!" exclaimed Peter. "There's the waltz beginning. Boys, Oh boys! If Judy and Steve aren't keepin on! Phil will be ragin! Go along, now, Desmond, an hop round wid Grania! Twill make ye feel young."

He grinned at Desmond's cross face.

"Do come, Des!" coaxed Grania. But he hung back.

Phil came over to them.

"I'll take you round," he told Grania. "I'll not let this bunch of omadhauns think Judy's upset me. Come along now!"

"I've only started learning," said Grania, shyly. "But I'll do my best."

Phil gazed blankly at her. He wasn't listening. He was thinking.

Grania's head barely reached his shoulder. He swung her round and she tried to dance on tiptoe – one, two, three! One, two, three! Suddenly she forgot to count, but now her feet moved with the music.

"I never knew dancing could be so lovely!" sighed Grania.

She looked at Phil. He was smiling now. But the smile was uglier than a frown.

"He's very angry!" thought Grania anxiously.

The other couples followed one another up and down down the long hall. But Phil was cutting across. Sometimes they knocked against other dancers. Nobody minded. Even if they had, one glance at Phil's face stopped complaint.

Grania saw her mother and Mrs O'Hara watching the dancers. She tossed her head proudly, but they were looking at Phil and didn't notice her.

"Now!" he muttered, whirling Grania right against Judy and Steve Farrelly.

At that moment the music stopped. Steve backed against the wall and left Judy standing there.

"A nice show you've made of yourself!" said Phil.

Judy was excited. But she spoke as softly as her brother.

"I came to dance and I danced. I didn't choose my partner. If you object – there's Father Coulahan waiting to talk to you! When you're finished you can dance with me. Twill save trouble. Be sure *you* don't make a show of us all!"

Judy walked with Grania to where Eily and the old woman were sitting.

"I didn't think ye had it in ye, Judy!" exclaimed Mrs O'Hara. "Sit down now and take the weight off yer feet!"

Judy sat beside her mother. She smoothed the green frock over her knee and laughed.

"Father Coulahan's like a child," she said. "He believes in a kind happy world. Tis in Tír na n-Óg he should be."

"But you did like dancing with Steve Farrelly, Judy!" put in Eily. "You made a lovely pair!"

Judy brushed back her hair.

"Here's another believes in forgiving her enemies," she said.

But she looked at Eily with a friendly smile.

"Why not give it a try?" asked the old woman. "For one night in a year twill do ye no harm! Where's Phil?"

"Where's Steve?" demanded Judy.

She stood up. Her mother pulled her down.

"Stay here!" she said sharply.

Grania saw Peter Hannigan go out through the door, Desmond at his elbow. From the courtyard came shouts and Phil's voice high and clear in anger.

"If tis dancing you want, dance!"

Grania darted out. She heard her mother calling and then she was out in the snow. Over near the gates she saw Phil and Steve – a circle of men round them.

"Hammer the tinker!" called one.

"They should be run – young and old!" growled another.

"No interference now! No interference!" ordered a little man, who was hopping round inside the circle.

"I don't want to fight!" said Steve loudly. "Tis Christmas and if you're willing to shake hands, I'm willing to!"

"Fight, you coward!" was Phil's answer.

Steve aimed a blow at him. The blow was straight and heavy, but Phil wasn't there to meet it. He wasn't in the one place a moment. His fists were tapping away at Steve's face, so that as Grania watched, the blood poured down and his eyes were closing.

"What's this! What have I done?" And Father Coulahan swept through the circle, seizing Steve and Phil by the elbows, forcing them apart. He was a tall man, as tall as Big Bill, but as thin as Phil.

"You have no right to interfere," said Phil quietly. "Better let us finish!"

Steve wiped his face.

"We must finish!" he said.

Father Coulahan would not give in.

"Listen, Phil! If any one's to blame over the dancing, tis myself. But to fight at the Christmas ceilidh is a disgrace. You'll not do it, Phil O'Hara! Not in my parish!"

Grania could hear them all agreeing: "That's right, Father!" "Steve's a decent lad!" "Them O'Haras is always out for trouble!" "They should be run!"

"That's enough!" cried Father Coulahan. "You're all very wise now. But not one of you tried to stop the fight!"

He was troubled and disappointed. Steve went away slowly, for he could hardly see. Desmond had harnessed Bogtrotter and now led him over, the empty cart swaying and bumping. Judy came down the steps and, after her, Eily and Mrs O'Hara.

The music had stopped. The dancers had followed them out. Steve tied a handkerchief round his head and stood arguing with his father. Mrs O'Hara and Eily climbed into the cart and, as Judy stepped up, a boy put his hands to his mouth and shouted: "Look at the red tinker!"

Judy swung round.

"Don't be foolish!" Father Coulahan warned her. "I'm waiting here to see you safely away. Do have the sense to stand by me!"

She sat down without a word.

"The rest of you can walk," said the priest. "I'll be here till you're out of the town. Good night now!"

"I'm terribly sorry this happened, Father!" cried Eily.

The priest sighed.

He wouldn't look at Phil who was humming softly. As Bogtrotter set off through the gates, Terry and Jer ran across the courtyard, a shower of snowballs following them.

Father Coulahan laughed.

"I'd quite forgotten you boys," he said. "Now be off home! May God give you sense!"

When Grania looked back he was standing in the gateway, his arms stretched out and behind him, in a noisy mass, were the people. The lights streamed out on them and the moonlight shone down.

"That's a grand man!" said Mrs O'Hara. "I do wish Phil could have waited to start the fight till we'd eaten our suppers an heard a bit of a song!"

26

Grania in Kilvaragh

"Is it tomorra ye're off to larn the paintin?" old Mrs O'Hara asked, as she sat knitting with Eily beside her darning a pile of socks.

"It is!" answered Grania.

She was sharpening her pencils but was so excited she made the points too long and fine and they kept on snapping. Desmond took them from her and made the points just long and sharp enough. They lay side by side from thick, soft BBs down the the thin, hard ones.

"You'll do your best?" asked her mother anxiously. "You will mind your manners, Grania?"

"She'll be a credit to the O'Haras!" declared the old woman. "But isn't it quare now for a fishy, poor bit of a place like Kilvaragh to have an Art class when a grand lovely town like Dromard hasn't."

"If she can't do better than the brats of shopkeepers and fishermen she should go digging praties for the Farrellys!" muttered Phil, slapping down a card.

"God be good to me! You've taken me last threepenny bit!" groaned Jer.

"I wonder you haven't more pride than to go down there!" said Terry. "You're the first O'Hara to be humble."

Grania was too happy to mind what Terry said.

"If the child bates them all at the drawin – isn't that one way of havin our revenge?" chuckled Mrs O'Hara. "That bumpkin O'Neill doesn't know what's comin to him."

Next day the snow was so deep Grania had to ride Bogtrotter. Desmond went with her to bring back the stores.

"Will I come as far as the door?" he asked. "I could wait a while to see what happens."

She bit her lip, then decided.

"No, Des! I'll drop off at Rattigan's and walk in like the others. I'm not afraid."

"It's only three hours," he said consolingly, as she slipped to the ground.

Clutching her drawing-book and the big paint-box, Grania walked in at the door of the Technical School. Two girls were ahead of her and she followed them to the cloakroom. She hung up her coat and tammy while the crowd of chattering girls became silent, watching her.

The journey down from the castle had left her half-frozen, but now her face was hot, her eyes smarting, and she longed to run out after Desmond. The whispering and laughing began again.

"At me," she thought furiously. Then she felt sad. "Why must the O'Haras be hated by everyone?"

Through the open doorway she saw Mr O'Neill striding across the hall and followed him.

When he saw Grania with the others crowding after her into the room, his eyes twinkled.

"Since you're all here we'll start at once," he said. "I'll call the names, then we'll set to work. Those who have neither pencils nor paper can buy them from me. For next class you'll need paints and brushes. Now – the new students first. There's only one, Grania O'Hara!"

"Present!" said Grania.

"Tinker!" came a whisper and several giggles.

"I'm not like Judy! I don't feel mad at them," thought Grania. "But I wish I knew which one it was called me *Tinker*!" "Besides, what's wrong with being a tinker?"

"To begin with," said Mr O'Neill, "I want you to draw in pencil something you remember. I'll give you twenty minutes."

Grania opened her book and ranged her pencils before her. She had chosen the desk in front nearest the door and her back was towards the others. But she was conscious that a note was being passed and the giggles and scuffles were so continuous, she wondered that the teacher paid no attention.

The note was dropped over her shoulder, a scrap of drawing paper folded in three. Slowly she opened it and read two words, one printed, *TINKER O'Hara*.

Grania placed the paper carefully in her book and began to draw. After the first stroke she forgot the girls and boys who were now scraping, rubbing, and shuffling.

At the end of twenty minutes one after another glanced at the clock and ceased working. Only Grania drew on.

"I'll collect the drawings now," said Mr O'Neill.

He walked along the desks taking the papers held out to him. Beside Grania he stopped and looked down at her work. From all over the room, bright, inquisitive eyes were watching.

"I'm sorry, Grania!" he said. "The time is up!"

She leaned back reluctantly.

"I haven't finished!" she complained.

"Enough!" declared Mr O'Neill. "Maggie Scully, will you pin up the drawings and we'll judge!"

Grania was disappointed.

"Twenty minutes!" she thought. "If he'd given me an hour I'd have shown them!"

A board was fixed along the wall above the master's desk and Maggie Scully, a tall dark girl with a Spanish look, fixed up the drawings with brass-headed pins.

Grania frowned as she sat with her elbows on the desk, her head in her hands, considering them.

"That's a good collie, but the ears are wrong," she thought. "The girl who drew that baby should be at home washing the delph. Mm-mm. Not too bad, that ship. It's moving! What's happened to my drawing?"

There were thirty in the class, more girls than boys. As each drawing was pinned up, Grania saw that Maggie Scully was arranging them in a hollow square.

There was only one left!

Mr O'Neill looked at the youngest O'Hara's anxious face. She was like her father and he had been fond of poor Kevin. Maybe the girl wouldn't turn out too bad.

Maggie Scully picked up the last drawing and fixed it in the centre. She looked slowly round the class, her dark eyes flashing, then stepped away.

Grania was startled. She had drawn a caravan being pulled up a mountain road by a rough, sturdy pony – Bogtrotter. Her grandmother was driving. Phil lounged beside her and Eily was gazing out between them. Judy trudged on one side of the pony, Terry and Jer on the other. Desmond marched ahead, the dogs at his heels, and far down the mountain road, almost out of the picture, was a girl with a tousled mop of hair – Grania herself!

Nothing was finished. The figures were only suggested. The mountain was shown by three heavy lines. But Grania knew her work made the other twenty-nine drawings look foolish.

"Shall we judge?" asked Mr O'Neill.

"There's nothing to judge!" exclaimed Maggie Scully. "There's one picture there and the rest should be on the fire!"

"That'll make them mad!" thought Grania, looking at Maggie Scully in wonder.

A boy at the back thumped on his desk. At once all the desks were thumped and Mr O'Neill listened patiently with a smile. At last he raised his hand and, after two reluctant thumps, the class was still.

"Should we hang it on the wall?" he asked. "We haven't had one good enough for that for a year!"

"On the wall! On the wall!" chanted the students.

Grania turned in her seat. She saw flushed smiling faces, admiring eyes. She ruffled the pages of her drawing-book and took out the note.

"Give me that!" demanded Maggie Scully. "It was a silly joke!"

Grania covered it with her hand.

"I'd sooner keep it," she said.

"Now to work!" ordered Mr O'Neill. "That corner where the bust is on the press and the shadow falls across the floor: see what you can make of it."

He walked from student to student, correcting, explaining. Grania sat with her open book before her, scribbling, making a few strokes. She could not see them. She kept hearing again, "On the wall! On the wall!"

Mr O'Neill stood beside her. He glanced at the almost blank page. Yet he was not vexed.

"I'm very pleased with you, Grania O'Hara!" he said.

Grania could scarcely breathe. The bare ugly room swung round her. The only fixed thing in it was her picture in the place of honour. If only she could have finished it! But she'd do more and more!

Without knowing how it happened she was walking down the dark road with Maggie Scully. "Goodbye, Maggie! Goodbye, Grania!" sounded behind them.

"You're lucky," said Maggie. "If I could only draw, or sing, or play something really well, my father would be just crazy with pride. Anyway, we're friends. How are you going home?"

"Des is waiting for me at Rattigan's. We'll ride the pony up."

Maggie looked at the darkness which shut in the town.

"I'd be scared!" she cried. "I couldn't live up there away from lights and houses."

Grania glanced around her at the few dim lights.

"There's the bog and the mountains and, in the middle of it all, Castle O'Hara!"

"Castle O'Hara!" repeated Maggie Scully. "It sounds grand! I must run. Dad's ship is in tonight. Goodbye, Grania!"

She ran away down a narrow alley leading to her home by the harbour and Grania went on. There was Desmond coming towards her and, at the corner, Bogtrotter tossed his mane and stamped impatiently, indignant at having to carry two creels instead of drawing a cart.

"How was it?" asked the boy eagerly.

"Oh, Des, it was wonderful!" began Grania.

She was still telling him when they reached the castle and the dogs rushed barking to the door. One glance at her radiant face told Eily that one O'Hara was finding the world a happy place.

"They were good to you?" she asked.

Without taking off her coat, Grania sat on an upturned creel. She was shivering with cold and excitement.

"Listen!" she said. "My drawing was the best. It's to be hung on the wall. And Maggie Scully – her father's Captain Scully and she lives in that house leaning over the harbour, and she's going to take me over his ship – she's my friend!"

"Whisha, child! Drink a sup of hot tay. Ye're perished!" protested her grandmother.

"Let her talk!" laughed Eily. "She'll get warm and eat and drink when she's told us everything!"

"I drew a caravan," said Grania. "You were sitting up in front, Granny, with Uncle Phil and my mother. Judy was there and Terry and Jer. Bogtrotter was the horse. Des was the leader and I was coming on behind!"

"Ye drew all that!" cried Mrs O'Hara in admiration, banging her stick on the hearth.

Judy flung down the cards.

"You made us a pack of tinkers!" she exclaimed.

Grania smiled happily at her.

"They called me Tinker O'Hara and I showed them I didn't care! What does it matter what they call me if I can draw better than any of them? And they clapped me and – oh, it was gorgeous!"

Eily laughed again to prevent herself from crying.

"Mr O'Neill was surely pleased?"

"He was," agreed Grania. "He said he was proud of me."

"Tinker O'Hara!" muttered Judy.

"And we were run out of the Christmas ceilidh!" exclaimed Phil. "I suppose you forgot that while you were amusing that pack of young hucksters and upstarts! If you'd a decent bit of pride, you'd have walked out of the school. But no, you sat there and let them call you Tinker O'Hara! I've a mind to skelp you!"

"I'm glad I stayed!" declared Grania, hugging her knees. "I've made a friend and I've drawn a good picture."

Phil glared at her and she looked back at him with an expression so like Kevin's he turned away.

"Drink the tea, child!" urged Mrs O'Hara. "And eat the hot apple cake. Ye must be wore out!"

Grania leaned against the old woman. She was tired now, so tired she did not notice the three men going out with the dogs, or Judy yawning as she went upstairs, a lighted candle sending her shadow dancing along the wall.

"Now we're together," said Eily, "tell us everything, everything!"

Grania glanced over her shoulder. The cards scattered on the table had a desolate air. But with Timmy Fuzz rubbing his head against her cheek and those three friendly faces near, Grania was happy.

27

Phil is Kind

One night, when Grania stood on the causeway before she went to bed, the grass sparkled with frost and the air tingled. When she came out the next morning, the darkness was tinged with gold and a blackbird whistled beyond the sheds.

"Tis an early spring, thank God!" said Mrs O'Hara. "We've the light and warmth of the year before us."

Grania took her aunt's breakfast over to the table.

"Tell me fortune, allanna!" Judy said. "Wait, I'll have a sup of tea first."

Grania started. Judy had never called her 'allanna' before. Hearing the kindness in her voice Eily stood with the teapot in her hand, forgetting to pour in the boiling water, while she hoped that Kevin's dream of happiness for Castle O'Hara might yet come true.

Grania went to the back of the turf pile. Desmond had left an empty creel upturned and she filled it. But it was too heavy for her to carry, so she piled her arms with sods and went slowly back to the castle.

At every step she paused. The air was filled with chirps, whistlings, and a gay careless song that enchanted her.

Eily was cutting bread at a table by the window and she was half-singing, half-humming.

"Now why didn't you call me?" she asked. "We could have brought the creel between us. We'll do it now. Come along!"

"Grania! Didn't I ask you to cut the cards for me?" complained Judy.

"While I'm eating my breakfast," promised Grania. "And I'll do it in the teacup too."

"I don't like this fortune-telling!" said Eily, as they stood beside the turf pile.

"It's only nonsense," Grania told her. "Half the time I'm just making it up."

"But that's telling lies!" exclaimed Eily in horror. "Grania, you musn't do it!"

"Isn't it worth while to keep Aunt Judy in a good temper?" demanded the girl.

Eily sighed.

"Maybe it is," she agreed. "But I hate to hear you telling all that nonsense. It was wrong of Bridgie to let you learn the cards."

"There's Phil!" cried Grania. "I'll run and have his breakfast ready."

"There's Jer and Terry behind him," said Eily mischievously. "But I notice you're not wanting to pour their tea?"

Grania laughed.

"I"m not. But sometimes I think Phil is wonderful. Then more times I don't like him at all."

"We'll fill the creel first," said Eily. "Mrs O'Hara can pour Phil's tea."

"My mother is always like that," thought Grania. "Whatever happens, she'll never drop what she is doing."

Phil was in a good temper. The dogs knew and sat on his feet, their heads uncomfortably resting against his knees.

Grania put a saucer of stirabout on the windowsill for the black kitten, then leaned over the half-door, calling, "Timmy Fuzz! Timmy Fuzz!"

"Never mind the cat. What about my fortune?" asked Judy. "You're a great one for promising. Come over here and do the job."

Grania laid out the cards and gave Judy the kind of fortune she thought best for her. Judy suddenly swept the cards from the table.

"You little cheat!" she stormed. "You're not even looking at the cards. Read that teacup, and if you don't do it properly I'll box your ears for you!"

"Whisht, Judy, whisht!" protested Mrs O'Hara.

Phil laughed.

"That's no way to treat the fortune-teller!" he said.

"How can I do fortunes when I'm wondering what's happened to Timmy Fuzz?" cried Grania. "He hasn't been home all night and I can't find him anywhere."

"I saw him up on the stable last night. He was safe enough then," said Desmond comfortingly.

"That's hours and hours ago!" said Grania, bursting into tears. "He's never stayed away so long before!"

"Some cats stay out every night," Eily told her.

"Not Timmy Fuzz!" declared Grania, trying to wipe away her tears.

At dinner-time the little black cat was still missing, and Grania had to go down to the Art class wishing for the first time she could stay away.

"You must never miss a class or be late," her mother said firmly.

"You'll keep on calling him?" Grania asked Desmond.

"I'll keep on!" he promised.

During the class Grania forgot, but as she came out of the school, the sight of a big tabby cat washing itself on a step reminded her.

"I'm in a desperate hurry!" she told Maggie Scully, and ran off to meet Desmond, who had ridden Bogtrotter down to Kilvaragh.

"Is Timmy Fuzz home?" she called before he was close enough to hear her.

But Desmond guessed what she was asking and shook his head.

During tea strange sounds kept her jumping up, only to realise before she reached the door that wind in the chimney, among the rocks, or the waterfall caused them. She couldn't draw or read or help Eily with the mending. She could only sit with her elbows on her knees, fretting.

Judy went to her room. Phil was out and Jer and Terry slipped away. The lantern flickered and Desmond turned down the wick. The old woman took her candle, but Eily went on sewing by the light of the fire.

"Go to bed, child!" she said. "You're half asleep."

"I'm frightened about Timmy Fuzz," protested Grania.

Eily put a lighted candle in her hand.

"The one who's down first will find Timmy Fuzz waiting at the door. Go along now!"

She rolled up her sewing and laid it on the dresser. Grania went slowly up the stairs, watching her shadow.

The full moon shone into her window, so she blew out the candle's tiny flame. The pictures she had painted on the walls looked strange and fantastic. But a little drawing of Timmy Fuzz curled asleep sent her to the window.

"Where's the use of a window that won't open?" she thought crossly. "I'll never hear him call!"

Slowly a bank of clouds drifted over the sky and the room darkened. Grania had no matches, so she undressed and went to bed in the dark. The sound of rain beating on the window roused her. She leaned on her elbow, restless and uneasy. A shrill mee-ow of pain sent her running across the room. Her hand trembled so that she could hardly open the door. As she stumbled down the stairs she heard it again.

"Timmy Fuzz!" she called. "I'm coming!"

Her eyes blinked as she came into the lighted kitchen. Someone had refilled the lantern and it stood on the edge of the table, casting a circle of yellow light on Phil, sitting in the old woman's seat. His brothers were bending over him and Desmond crouched on the floor with the dogs.

Grania stood motionless. Timmy Fuzz lay stretched on her uncle's knees, Jer holding his hind legs, while Terry's fingers made a cage over his chest. Phil was binding a stick to one of the kitten's front paws, twisting long strips of a torn-up handkerchief round and round.

"Quiet!" he said. "Weren't you a foolish animal to go running wild over the bog and you with a good home? Easy now! Easy. You're in the trap no longer!"

Grania had never heard that gentle voice, or seen that grave intent look before. Phil's long clever fingers were stroking the kitten from head to tail. A piteous mee-ow answered him, then whimpers and purrs, then only steady purring.

"Is the milk warm, Des? Put a drip of tea into it and a spoonful of sugar. Twill comfort the poor little beast!"

"Uncle Phil!" said Grania. And she couldn't say another word.

He looked up frowning.

"Come over here and take him. No need to cry. He'll be hopping round tomorrow, and in next to no time we'll be able to take off the splint."

Phil stood up, motioned her to sit down and put the kitten in her arms. He lifted Mrs O'Hara's shawl from the back of the chair and wrapped her in it. The dogs squeezed up and enjoyed the fire.

"We could all do with a sup of tea, Des," said Phil. "And I'm famished!"

He put his hands in his pockets and leaned against the wall.

"Any cigarettes, Jer?" he asked.

Jer was half-asleep, his elbows on the table, but a lighted cigarette was stuck in the corner of his mouth. He did not answer. Terry poked in his brother's pockets, pulled out a packet of cigarettes and flung it to Phil.

Des, making a pot of tea, lifted a bit of blazing turf with the tongs and Phil bent to light his cigarette. Puffing leisurely, he glanced over at Grania.

"Why are you looking at me that way?" he asked. "Do I look queerer than usual?"

Grania gazed at him with puzzled eyes.

"You were so good to Timmy Fuzz – and yet!"

Phil laughed.

"And yet I don't go round loving the Farrellys and Thady O'Connor and all the ignoramuses of Kilvaragh! I'll tell you why. The kitten can spit and scratch, look at my hands" – he held them out, and she saw long scratches and spots of blood – "but he can't call me *Tinker*. He can't gossip and slander the O'Haras, that's all!"

Grania almost said "But we are tinkers!" only she was too grateful. Instead she murmured, "I'll never forget what you've done this night, never!"

Her voice was choked and Phil smiled at her, a friendly, crooked smile that made her happy.

"Is that tea ready, lad?" he asked. "The young one is in a state. Are they bacon sandwiches?"

"They're ham sandwiches," Desmond told him proudly. "And I've cut off all the fat, the way you like it."

"You have your uses, Des," said Phil.

He told them how Bran, barking and whining, had led him to Timmy Fuzz, caught in a trap. The kitten had been frantic and it wasn't easy to free him. But here he was!

Grania saw her uncle's clothes were torn and muddy, his boots thick with wet, bog mould.

"I'll brush them for him in the morning," she was thinking, when Oscar stood up and whined.

He walked swiftly to the door, his head alert, his short tail out straight. Bran rushed over barking while Finn stood on his hind legs scratching at the doorpost and Maeve lay on the ground, her nose to the crack, sniffing. The uproar brought Judy and Eily running down the stairs, their coats flung over their shoulders, buttoned at the neck, and the sleeves flapping.

Mrs O'Hara shuffled out from her room in her felt slippers, and Grania thought how the O'Haras were always ready to gather about the fire even in the middle of the night.

"What's going on here?" asked the old woman, flopping into her seat as Grania stood up and moved away, holding Timmy Fuzz carefully. "Is there a sup of tay in the pot? Pour it out, Des, there's the lad!"

Phil flung open the door and the dogs leaped out. He stood staring, then sniffed.

"There's smoke on the wind," he said, and walked out into the rain.

"If you're not going to your bed, put something on, child!" Eily told Grania. "It's desperate cold! But what's happened, Timmy Fuzz? Oh, the poor wee thing!"

"He was caught in a trap and Phil saved him," explained Grania. "Twas Phil fixed the paw."

"Put a cushion on the floor in your room," said Eily. "He'll not be able to jump from the bed. Though maybe he'd be better in with Des."

"I want him upstairs with me," pleaded Grania.

"He'll try to come downstairs and hurt himself," Desmond warned her. "I'll take great care of him."

Reluctantly Grania put the sleepy little cat into the boy's arms and groped up the stairs. She pulled on her clothes and was halfway to the door when, glancing through the window, she saw beyond the river, in the direction of the Farrellys' farm, lines of sparks flashing and glowing through the darkness.

"There's a fire over at the Farrellys'!" she called, jumping down the stairs and bruising herself against the wall at the bend.

They were all crowded at the door. Mrs O'Hara pushed to the front.

"Tis trouble at the Farrellys'!" she announced. "Tis hard to tell wid the rain comin down, but I'm afeard a rick is on fire!"

28

The Burning of the Ricks

"Be off wid yez!" cried the old woman. "Stir yerselves! If the Farrellys don't know what's happenin, rouse them. Lend the crathures a hand!"

"Is it us go help the Farrellys?" asked Terry in amazement.

His mother gave him an impatient shove.

"Where's Phil? I'm wastin me time talkin to the pair of yez. Phil!"

He appeared suddenly in the doorway.

"What is it, mother? You called me?"

"I did, son! Is there fire at the Farrellys'?"

"There is. A rick or the house. I can't tell for the wind and the rain. I think it's a rick."

She reached up and put her hands on his shoulders.

"Go across the river and help them, Phil. If I weren't an old woman, I'd be there. Remember, I'm a farmer's daughter and ye're me son!"

Phil frowned as he looked down at her wrinkled face.

"You're asking me to help our enemies?" he said.

"To plaze me, Phil, an because tis right!"

"I'll go!" he said, and without another word, rushed off through the rain.

Terry and Jer gazed at one another in horror.

"Sure, he can't cross the river! Didn't we break down the bridge?" exclaimed Jer.

"Haven't the childer crossed?" demanded the old woman.

"Not on a dark night, with the rain spilling and the river rising!" protested Terry. "Phil will be drownded, that's all – and to help the Farrellys!"

"Bring the lantern, Des, and we'll go!" ordered Judy, pulling on her coat.

She snatched the lantern from Desmond and ran across the causeway towards the bridge, the boy keeping close behind her. After them went Grania and, a long way behind, Jer and Terry.

Mrs O'Hara shook her head, propped open the upper part of the door so that the firelight streamed into the darkness, and sat down in her chair. Eily leaned out, staring through the rain.

"Cut a good, thick sandwich for the two of us," said the old woman. "I'll make a fresh pot of tay. Twill rise the heart in us!"

Eily shivered as she came over to the fire.

"I shouldn't have let Grania go," she sighed. "Tis no night for a little girl to be running wild."

"Sure, that young one's the spit of me at her age!" chuckled Mrs O'Hara proudly. "She'll be as happy as Larry fallin in the river an scramblin out. Twill do her no harrum at all. An isn't Judy there? If I was a bit younger I'd be wid em meself. I do hope Phil won't get his head split. He has the divil of a timper and so has Big Bill. Wouldn't it be a gran thing if they were to come together an end that tiresome old quarrel!"

"How kind Phil was to the kitten!" murmured Eily.

"Sure he has a great likin for Grania, an the lad's not too bad. Tis this place an the idleness has him destroyed. He should go out into the world. I'd hate to be parted from him, but I know well he shouldn't stay here."

Eily couldn't stay by the fire listening to the rain streaming by on the wind but went back to the door and saw the sparks fanned to flames, quenched by the rain, then leaping and tossing, growing fiercer and steadier as she watched.

Grania caught up with Desmond and Judy as they reached the bridge.

"The plank is fixed," said Desmond. "Phil's crossed over. Be very careful!"

The wind blew away the sound of his voice, but she guessed what he was saying and crossed just after him.

Phil had fixed the planks right across, so they were not delayed. But the river was rising and swept over their feet as they walked on the swaying strips of wood.

The rain ceased as they scrambled through the wire fence and the moon came out. Judy was away beyond them, running as if she were in a race.

"There's two ricks on fire!" exclaimed Desmond. "Isn't it lucky it isn't the house! But where are they all?"

"There they are!" said Grania. "Look! Between the ricks! And there's Phil and Judy!"

The young Farrellys were bringing water from a tank used for watering the cattle and flinging it on the flames. Mrs Farrelly stood silent, gazing mournfully at the fire. Suddenly Big Bill turned, seized two buckets and sent them rolling down the hill.

"Are you mad, Bill?" cried Mrs Farrelly.

"Nothing can save the ricks!" he exclaimed despairingly.

Then, by the leaping blaze, he saw Phil standing irresolutely near the farthest rick. Behind him was Desmond, who had picked up a spade, hoping to beat out the flames.

For a moment Bill Farrelly stared in amazement. Then, catching up a steel-toothed rake lying on the ground, he rushed at Phil.

"You'll pay for this, you robber!" he shouted.

"Go back, you omadhaun and save your ricks!" cried Phil. "I came to help you!"

"You'll not make a mock of me!" and the farmer raised the rake above his head.

Phil ducked and ran, darting between the trees, turning suddenly, while Bill Farrelly blundered on.

Desmond caught Grania's hand.

"We'd best go home!" he said.

Moon and flames made it easy for them to see where the wire fence had fallen and they jumped over. As they crossed by the planks, the water threatened to sweep them away, and when they reached the other side Jer and Terry were standing there watching them.

"You've taken your time!" said Desmond scornfully. "Mr Farrelly doesn't want our help. He's after Phil. There they come!"

When Phil reached the bridge he pulled the first plank after him and flung it to the bank beside his brothers. Big Bill came up, red-faced and panting. He glared at Phil across the rushing stream.

"Ye'll suffer for this!" he shouted. "I'll have ye driven out, ye and the boy. I saw ye! I'll have ye gaoled!"

Desmond was startled.

"You can't think I fired the ricks, Mr Farrelly!" he exclaimed. "Why would I?"

Phil put his hands to his mouth.

"Go back home, you're raving!" he shouted. "We came to help you! But now, if the house was burning over your head, I wouldn't lift a hand to save you!"

He strode on towards the castle. Bill Farrelly flung the rake after him, but it fell short and splashed into the river. Grania and Desmond watched until Mrs Farrelly came down and led her husband away. Still the ricks burned.

The O'Haras sat round the fire drinking tea. Their wet boots were in a row by the wall, with tiny streams of water running from them.

"Tis a judgement!" declared old Mrs O'Hara. "Ye tormented and plagued one after another an got away wid it. Now ye went out to do a good turn to a neighbour an ye're blamed. I know Bill Farrelly! He's put up wid all he's goin to. Ye have him roused. He'll drive us out an not a soul will stand by us."

"Tis our own place. No one can put us out!" declared Eily.

The old woman sniffed.

"There's more ways than one of doing that, an mebbe ye'll larn what tis before ye're many days older. But where's Judy? Why didn't she keep wid ye, Phil? I'm beginnin to be troubled about her!"

"You needn't worry about her!" said Phil bitterly. "She's gone over to the enemy. I saw her talking to Steve Farrelly while the old man was chasing me. That's her now!"

The dogs were barking at the door as Judy pushed it open.

"Ye're drownded!" cried her mother. "What happened ye?"

"I slipped down the bank," Judy told her. "I'll change my clothes."

As she passed Phil he caught her hand.

"Traitor!" he sneered, and flung it from him.

"You can't blame Steve for his father!" she said, over her shoulder.

Phil was sitting with his head in his hands when she came back in dry clothes. Desmond put a cup of tea and a sandwich on the table before her.

"The three ricks are gone!" she said.

"Three!" cried her mother. "I thought twas two?"

"Big Bill wouldn't let them save the third," Judy told her. "They could have saved it easy and they've no insurance. He was raging!"

"The man's mad!" declared Phil.

Grania couldn't keep her eyes open. But she wanted to stay there listening.

"Will we have one game before we go to our beds?" asked Judy.

Phil picked up the pack of cards and flung them into the fire.

"Oh, Phil!" cried his sister. "That's the unluckiest thing you could do! Pull them out, Des!"

Desmond raked out the cards with a twig, but they were too burned and charred to be of use.

"We'd better be sleepin the rest of the night away," muttered Mrs O'Hara, blinking round at them all. "Musha, I feel terrible onaisy. Now what ails them dogs! Maeve! Are ye demented?"

The dogs were growling and leaping at the door. Phil strode across and flung it open. There stood Bill Farrelly!

"Come out and let me hammer ye with me fists!" he roared, making a grab at Phil. "I'll teach ye to burn me ricks!"

Phil stepped back and the farmer lurched after him. The dogs snarled at the stranger.

"Down!" he said to them, quietly but so fiercely they slunk against Phil, showing their teeth.

"What do you want here, Mr Farrelly?" asked Judy.

She stood up fearlessly, staring straight back at him.

"I've come to give the O'Haras a taste of what's owing them before they're run from the parish!" answered the farmer.

"Listen to me," pleaded Eily. "Phil didn't fire your ricks. He went to help you. They all went to help you. On my word, they've done you no harm!"

"I'm sorry, ma'am," he said, without looking at her. "But I seen them with my own two eyes. Phil an that young lad, an the others egging them on!"

Jer giggled; Terry yawned.

They were half-asleep and scarcely knew what they were doing. But the farmer thought they meant to insult him. Catching up a wooden stool, he aimed a blow at them. Jer slipped one way, Terry the other and, when he swung round, they were at the far side of the table.

"Will you get out!" exclaimed Phil. "We didn't fire the ricks. I don't want to hurt you, but you're not wanted in Castle O'Hara. There's the door!"

Big Bill rushed at him. Phil stepped lightly away and the farmer brought up with a crash against the dresser. He swept every bit of delph to the floor. Phil caught him by the shoulder. But Mrs O'Hara pulled him off.

"Lave the man alone!" she said. "Do ye want murder

done? He's been druv out of his mind wid the worry and the turmoil. Put up wid him!"

"We didn't touch the ricks!" protested Phil.

Mrs O'Hara sat back in her chair. Eily stood beside her. Judy sat upright at the table, her arms folded, while Big Bill battered their home.

The knowledge that he was innocent bewildered Phil and, while the farmer was smashing a big dish on the floor, he opened the door softly and went out followed by his brothers and the dogs.

Big Bill Farrelly began kicking at the sods Desmond had piled neatly against the wall and stamping them to powder.

"Lave my turf alone!" cried the boy, darting out of the corner where he was huddled with Grania.

"Don't ye dare raise yer voice to me, ye young ruffian!" shouted the man.

He waved the stool threateningly. But he was tired out and it slipped from his hand, striking Desmond on the side of the head. The boy staggered back, blood trickling down his face.

Steve Farrelly came in at the door and clutched his father's arm.

"Have you gone stark, staring mad?" he demanded. "Come home, father, before you do any more mischief!" He turned to Judy. "I wouldn't have had this happen for worlds!"

Big Bill gazed about him and rubbed his eyes as if he were just waking.

"Sorry, ma'am," he said to Mrs O'Hara, and went quietly off with Steve.

29

Boycott

Grania woke thinking of a pen-and-ink sketch she was to take in to Mr O'Neill.

She pulled on her clothes and looked out of the window. Rain had washed it clean and through it she saw the grass, bushes, and rocks, glittering in the sunlight.

Then she remembered the ricks blazing, Phil standing staring, and Mr Farrelly rushing at him. It was a picture in her mind. But not a picture she wanted to paint.

Grania no longer troubled about windows that wouldn't open, dark rooms, and rough furniture. Freedom to paint all day if she chose, the half-admiring interest in her work, meant more than comfort. The kitchen, the only bright room in the place, had to be her studio. But her paper and pencils, her paints, were never touched. Castle O'Hara was home.

She went thoughtfully downstairs. Eily was sweeping broken delph out through the doorway. Desmond was fixing the dresser.

"There isn't a cup left," said Eily. "Wasn't he the terrible man! What will we do?"

"I'll bring in some tins," suggested Desmond. "We'll

have to make do with them for breakfast. Afterwards I'll go down to Kilvaragh and get some delph."

Grania finished sweeping the floor, while her mother considered breakfast. She gathered up the broken pieces of crocks into a creel. There was a rubbish dump at the back of the sheds and, as she emptied her load there, Desmond came running after her.

"I'll put the tins in the creel," he told her.

"Tins from a rubbish heap!" said Grania, twisting her mouth in disgust. "I'd sooner wait!"

"Don't be foolish!" cried Desmond. "I'll wash them as clean as can be. Heaps of tinkers use nothing else."

Grania looked at his solemn face with laughing eyes.

"Don't let Phil or Judy hear you talk that way!"

When they brought in the clean tins Judy and her brothers were at the table. Desmond stood by the door looking nervously at them. Grania took the tins and ranged them neatly, one before each, and the rest at the end ready for Eily to fill with tea.

"You'll have to do without plates or saucers," she said.

"Tins on the table! Is this a joke?" asked Phil.

He spoke quietly. But Grania backed away against Desmond and stared at him with big, serious eyes.

"We've no cups. What else can we do?" asked Eily. "You wouldn't want to wait till we get some from Kilvaragh."

Phil stared moodily at the table. Kicking his chair, so that it fell backwards, he strode through the open doorway, giving Grania and Desmond a push that sent them sprawling.

"Ye cudn't blame him for bein vexed," muttered Mrs

O'Hara. "I'm not too plazed to be suppin me tay from an old tin."

Grania was very indignant as she scrambled up. But Desmond rubbed his arm where he had fallen on it, felt his bandaged head, made a grimace of pain, picked up a creel, and went calmly off to bring in more turf.

"Where would Phil be off to?" said Jer, disconsolately.

"Mebbe he's having breakfast with the Farrellys!" suggested Terry with a grin. "They won't have to drink from tins."

"Neither would the O'Hara's if they had the sense of mountain goats!" retorted Judy, putting her elbows on the table.

Her mother gazed at her so earnestly that Judy coloured.

"Sure, I'm tired of all this hugger-mugger," she said, turning away. "Tisn't civilized, the way we live!"

Grania looked at the desolate dresser that had been so gay with flowered plates and dishes glittering in the firelight. Even Mrs O'Hara's lustre jug had been broken!

"Mr Farrelly's every bit as bad as Phil," thought the girl. "He's no better than a robber!"

She hated drinking her tea from a tin. But Judy didn't grumble once. Jer cut his lip and this so impressed Terry that he wrapped a handkerchief round his tin, knotted the corners into a handle, and drank his tea as contentedly as if he had never bothered about a cup in his life.

"Eily, you should have sent the lad down to Kilvaragh for cups," complained Jer.

"I'm on my way!" announced Desmond, looking in over the half-door. "Have you the list for Rattigan's, Eily?"

"Take your breakfast first," she told him.

"If a tin isn't good enough for Phil O'Hara to drink from, tisn't good enough for me!" he declared, taking the list she held out.

Grania stared after him. He swaggered as he led Bogtrotter across the causeway, then jumped on to the cart and drove off, standing up.

"That lad's comin on," said the old woman admiringly.

"I didn't think he had it in him," agreed Terry.

"Imitating Phil!" said Judy scornfully. "Grania! Run after Des and tell him to bring a new pack of cards!"

"I put them on the list," Eily told her.

She flushed when she saw Grania's surprised look.

"Judy needs a bit of comfort," she whispered apologetically.

Grania was folding clean clothes for her mother to iron when she heard the sound of hoofs and wheels, and ran to the door.

"Isn't Des back quickly!" she exclaimed. "And will you look at the way Bogtrotter is swinging along! You'd think the cart was empty."

"I'm thinking it is!" said Eily.

"I'll soon find out!" And Grania ran out to the causeway.

Desmond was crouched on the seat, his head hanging down. Grania wondered what had happened. But Eily was gazing into the cart.

"You've brought nothing but a few old herrings!" she cried. "No cups, no tea or sugar or meal! We've hardly any flour and you can see the bottom of the salt jar. You knew how short we were, Desmond!"

Desmond lifted his head. The old sulky expression had come back.

"Rattigans wouldn't give me a thing! They nearly drove

me out! I've tried every shop in Kilvaragh. Not one will deal with us! A man at the harbour sold me the herrings. He was a stranger."

"But why?" asked Eily. "We don't owe so much, and we always pay in the end. I can't understand it. You weren't rude, Des? It isn't like you to be rude!"

Desmond laughed, the kind of laugh Phil might have given.

"Twas they were the rude ones, not me. At Hogan's they threatened to set the dog on me, and old Clancy said we should be gaoled! The young Clancys threw stones."

"Are they all mad?" asked Eily.

"Mr Farrelly was in the town before me," Desmond explained. "He's told a pack of lies and they've put the boycott on us!"

Eily put her hand to her mouth.

"I can't bear it!" she said. "The disgrace! I'll go back to Dromard!"

Desmond jumped from the cart.

"You take care of Bogtrotter," he said to Grania. "I'd better clean the fish!"

Grania looked at her mother.

"Does it matter so much?" she asked.

"Matter!" echoed Eily. "It's treating us like spies or informers. No one will sell to us, no one will talk to us. And it's all wrong! How could Mr Farrelly do it?"

Bogtrotter started off towards his stable and Grania hurried after him.

She was proud of being able to back the pony into the shed, so that the cart was ready to be drawn out. Then she unharnessed him, shook out his feed, and went back to the house.

Eily was grilling the herrings on a shovel. The smell mingled with the odours of turf and rabbit stew. They were all hungry, but only Eily cared for the herrings. Desmond's story of his reception in Kilvaragh was making the O'Haras thoughtful and none of them grumbled.

"Tis a pack of old nonsense!" declared Terry. "We never had hand or part in burning Farrelly's ricks – the old fool!"

"That's no way to spake of a dacent man an a good farmer!" protested Mrs O'Hara.

"Tis that same decent man that's put the boycott on us!" muttered Judy.

"An tis only he can take it off," sighed the old woman.

"Mr Farrelly should be ashamed!" cried Eily. "He's smashed every bit of delph we had. He's left us like tinkers, and then he tells a pack of lies to put the boycott on us. I never thought it of him!"

They ate the herrings in their fingers, for they had no plates. Grania disliked herrings for the tiny bones stuck in her teeth, and Timmy Fuzz had most of her fish.

"Maybe I could try the Rattigans when I go to the class," she suggested.

"When she's going, put the creels on Bogtrotter," Judy told Desmond. "There might be a chance!"

"Divil a chance, unless the people is changed," chuckled Mrs O'Hara. "An Grania may not be let into the class. Mr O'Neill won't go against the dacent people of Kilvaragh. He's none so set on the O'Haras himself!"

"Anybody'd think you were glad of the boycott!" protested Judy, while Grania stared at the old woman in horror.

"I'm glad of anything that'll bring the O'Haras to their senses," said the old woman severely. "Something like this was bound to happen."

Grania put her pen-and-ink sketch carefully in her drawing-book. She couldn't believe the boycott would touch her drawing class.

When Desmond brought Bogtrotter to the door, and she thought how awkward it would be to ride behind the creels, Grania almost wished she hadn't offered to go to Rattigan's.

"I'll give them the list when I tie up Bogtrotter," she said, doubtfully.

"Maybe I'd as well come too," suggested Desmond.

He was looking uneasily at her.

"I'm not afraid!" declared Grania.

"If they throw stones!" murmured Eily. "Grania!" she spoke firmly. "Suppose you're turned away from the school? You're not to go!"

But Grania was on the pony's back and pretended not to hear. She dropped her book and pencil-case into one of the creels and, clutching the reins with one hand, held on with the other.

The road was slippery and Grania was thankful the pony was so surefooted.

Then she forgot everything but the view of Kilvaragh between the rocks. Always it made her dissatisfied with her own work, discontented with her progress, doubtful if she would ever be a good artist.

"And I have to make my living at it," she thought. "It's fun for Maggie Scully and the others. It's real for me!"

The Rattigans' yard was empty, but the back door

swung open. She tied Bogtrotter in the shed and crossed over.

"Can I leave the list with you, Mrs Rattigan?" she called.

Mrs Rattigan was moving a clothes-horse from before the fire. There were so many Rattigans that every day was washing day, and in wet weather the house reeked with the smell of drying clothes.

The big woman came over to the door. She stood there with her arms folded, gazing so fixedly at Grania that the girl was tempted to run, but she stood still.

"Didn't Des tell ye about the boycott?" she asked.

Grania's mouth felt dry, her lips so stiff she could hardly speak.

"He did, Mrs Rattigan. But my mother couldn't believe it!"

"Tis the truth, Grania! There's not one in Kilvaragh will buy or sell with the O'Haras from now on."

"But we must buy food, Mrs Rattigan, and all our delph is broken! Mr Farrelly came in and smashed it up!"

"Ye're lucky, me dear, he left one stone on another up yonder. While Phil O'Hara is home, not one here will dale wid his family. The boy's in it too! I know well he had to do whatever Phil told him. But he'll suffer!"

"Mrs Rattigan," said Grania earnestly. "The ricks were on fire before one of us left the house. I was there! I saw it all!"

Mrs Rattigan looked doubtful.

"Ye were put up to say this."

"My mother will tell you the same. I am telling the truth. Indeed I am!"

"Isn't it very quare then how Mr Farrelly declares he saw Phil and the boy setting fire to the ricks?" asked the woman.

"There's not one in this town will think twice if they're to choose between the word of Big Bill or an O'Hara!"

"And yet Mr Farrelly's quite wrong," said Grania, turning away.

"Wait, child," said Mrs Rattigan. "Come in and have a bite an sup! Ye're not responsible! Neither is Eily. Ye're both welcome here. But I can't sell ye an ounce of flour or male!"

Grania walked out of the yard without speaking, leaving Mrs Rattigan gazing at her with a very troubled face.

"Sure, the child can't help what her uncles do, an I don't like being bad friends wid Eily," she murmured. "What if Big Bill did make a mistake? Don't we all know he's a very headstrong man?"

Mrs Rattigan shook her head and went through to the shop.

Grania was halfway down the street before she thought of Bogtrotter.

"Should I leave him there?" she asked herself. "Ah, the Rattigans are much too kind to boycott a pony!"

She walked on, not daring to enter another shop.

The Art class had started and Mr O'Neill was talking when Grania slipped into her seat. She opened her drawing-book and laid her sketch on the desk.

Was it really good? she thought, longing to be praised by the master and envied by the other students.

She had forgotten the boycott. Nothing mattered now but her drawing.

She looked up. Mr O'Neill had stopped talking and was gazing at her. Everyone was staring. Only Maggie Scully looked away and her face was anxious.

"I didn't expect you today, Grania," said Mr O'Neill.

Then he turned to the board and, with a piece of chalk, showed the meaning and use of perspective. Listening to him, Grania looked down at her sketch.

"It's all wrong," she thought. "How could I imagine it was good!"

She propped her chin in her hands and watched the teacher's strong fingers drawing lines as straight as if he used a ruler, all meeting at one point. Suddenly the chalk snapped and the slight sound made Grania realise the background of whispering, shuffling, inattention which destroyed the atmosphere of the class.

"What ails them?" she wondered, turning her head.

On almost every face she saw the hostility which had greeted her the first day.

"They've heard about last night!" decided Grania. "And they've heard it wrong! I'll have to explain!"

Maggie Scully pinned up the sketches. Grania's, though she was now so dissatisfied with it, was still the best. But no one clapped.

Maggie Scully tossed back her long dark hair.

"It's the best drawing Grania has ever done!" she declared.

"It is," agreed Mr O'Neill. "But drawing isn't the only thing in the world!"

Grania looked at him proudly.

"It's the most important thing in the world for an artist! You told me that!" she retorted.

He threw up a bit of chalk and caught it again. Mr O'Neill always did that when he was going to argue. The class settled down, prepared to hear Tinker O'Hara told the truth.

"You're wrong there, Grania!" he said. "Drawing may be the biggest thing, or one of the biggest things for an artist, but it shouldn't be the whole of life, and it couldn't be. There are other things."

Grania's eyes were still scornful.

"Everyone, even an artist, has to respect public opinion," he added.

A buzz of agreement rose in the room. Maggie Scully stepped from her seat and squeezed in beside her friend. Grania pretended not to notice, but she was thankful for that warm reassuring hand clasping hers.

She stood up quickly before she could feel afraid.

"I know you're all thinking the O'Haras fired Mr Farrelly's ricks," said Grania, speaking very distinctly and in a rush. "But you're wrong! We were in the kitchen and the dogs made a fuss. When we found out what was happening, that there was a fire at the Farrelly's, the uncles, Aunt Judy, and me and Des, we went over the river to help them."

She stared defiantly at the unbelieving faces.

"That isn't the story I heard," said Mr O'Neill thoughtfully.

"It's the true story!" Grania told him.

"Then why is young Desmond's head tied up and why has the boycott been declared on the O'Haras?" he asked.

"A boycott!" repeated Grania indignantly. "People boycott informers, not neighbours who have done no wrong."

Mr O'Neill walked up and down the platform.

"The O'Haras have done their last bit of mischief, Grania! They'd best stay away from Kilvaragh."

Grania slammed her desk.

"It's wrong!" she cried. "They did no harm last night!"

Mr O'Neill rubbed the board clean.

"Then they'll be punished for the harm they did other nights," he said. "It's justice, even if it's a bit slow."

Grania didn't wait for the end of the class. Without even saying goodbye to Maggie Scully, she caught up her book and the paint-box she had been so proud of, lifted her coat and tammy from the hook, and ran out of the school. People gossiping at corners stared after her, but she did not stop until she came to Rattigan's.

Bogtrotter's friendly nicker was comforting but, when she looked in the empty creels, it was hard to keep back her tears.

She led the pony out and there was Maggie Scully running towards her.

"Come home to tea with me, please, Grania!" she called, panting and trying to laugh. "Daddy's home!"

Grania stopped. She had never been so fond of Maggie as now.

"Then you're not going to boycott us?" she asked eagerly. "You don't believe we fired the Farrellys' ricks?"

Maggie came right up to her.

"Grania, of course I don't!" she said. "And if you did – well – I'd still want you to come home to tea."

"I can't come," replied Grania. "But, Maggie, you can have that sketch I brought today for your own. Here you are!"

Maggie's dark eyes sparkled.

"Oh, Grania," she murmured. "I'll frame it and one day –"

She laughed and shook her head, not knowing how to finish.

Grania was singing when she came to the causeway,

and Desmond, hearing her, looked with startled eyes at Eily, who had been helping him milk the goats.

"Maybe the boycott's off!" he exclaimed. "Or the Rattigans thought she wasn't in it and they've given her the flour and meal."

Eily smiled.

"I'm afraid it's just that Grania's forgotten the boycott and the O'Haras too," she said.

Desmond ran to meet Grania. He scowled when he saw the empty creels.

"You've done no better than me!" he grumbled. "Did you try for the cups?"

"I didn't!" Grania told him. "Mrs Rattigan was sorry, but she wouldn't give me anything and I couldn't bear to try anywhere else."

Eily came over and, like Desmond, looked first at the empty creels.

"Then it really is a boycott!" she said. "I wonder what we can do. But Mr O'Neill did let you stay at the class."

Grania nodded.

"He did. He doesn't know who to believe. But, of all the class, Maggie Scully is the only one who really believed me."

Phil was lounging at the table, a new, untouched pack of cards before him. He looked round inquiringly as Eily and the boy and girl came in.

"Did ye have any luck, allanna?" asked Mrs O'Hara.

"She didn't!" Eily told her. "They treated Grania the same as they treated Des."

"They didn't throw stones at Grania," muttered Desmond.

"Aren't we to have a sup of tea?" demanded Judy. "Surely we're not that poverty-stricken!"

Eily emptied out the caddy and made a good strong pot of tea. She mixed a cake with the shakings of the flour sack, a handful of meal from the tub, a packet of cornflour, and a spoonful of bread soda. There were chopped figs in it and, while it baked in the pot oven, they sat talking.

Terry was very scornful about the boycott.

"I wouldn't be bothered going near Kilvaragh!" he declared. "Can't we sell rabbits in Dromard?"

"Nobody in Dromard eats rabbits," Grania told him. "They'd as soon eat rats!"

"Have sinse, child!" protested her grandmother. "Doesn't the whole world eat rabbits? Isn't that the raison there's so many of em?"

Eily looked up. Her eyes were anxious.

"Grania's right," she said. "I never ate rabbits till I came to live here. Very poor people in Dromard do eat them. But they'd want them given. They wouldn't buy them!"

"Couldn't ye do somethin, Phil?" asked the old woman. "Ye were sayin about a coupla horses ye were after."

"Twas through Tim Rattigan," explained Phil. "I'm finished there and I'm beginning to wish I had fired the ricks!"

There was such anger in his voice, Grania let the tin she was drinking from fall with a clatter.

"Thank God, you didn't!" retorted Judy. "I'd never have forgiven you."

Phil stared at her, his face twisted in a sneer. But he didn't say a word.

"I'll draw him that way," thought Grania. "He won't like it, but twill be a lesson to him."

Her book was on the table. She began to draw. Eily stood watching her.

"Don't let the cake burn," Mrs O'Hara reminded her.

Eily started, lifted out the cake, turned it on a plate, and began to lay the table for tea. She was cutting the cake into slices before Grania realised they were all waiting.

Phil jerked his head and spoke to his brothers. They carried the table over to the fire, drew forward the settle, and sat round talking of what they could do and reaching out to the yellow slab of butter on the wooden platter.

Judy pushed over her tin.

"There's not another drop," said Eily. "But I'll fill up again, the kettle's boiling. Would that do?"

"I'll not drink washings!" declared Judy. "There must be tea in the caddy!"

Eily shook her head.

"Not a leaf! I turned the caddy upside down!"

"Fill up, Eily! Fill up, give it a boil in the griseach, an add a pinch of bread soda," suggested Mrs O'Hara. "Many's the time I made a potful last the week, that way! Sure we'll have to larn all the old tricks now they've put a boycott on us!"

"It's a mercy we have the goats," said Desmond.

Phil slapped him on the back – a hard slap that made the boy's sore head tingle.

"You've saved us, lad! We'll sell the goats!"

"You can't do that!" protested Eily. "We need milk."

"We can buy milk," Phil told her. "We need cash to deal in Dromard. I'll not be beholden to the Hanlons!"

Mrs O'Hara laughed.

"Ah, Phil, aren't ye very sure of yerself? Where will ye sell the goats?"

He looked at Grania, his head on one side.

"I suppose they don't milk goats in Dromard?"

"They don't," she agreed, laughing.

Then, shyly, she pushed over her drawing-book.

"I'll do one smiling, when you smile," she told him.

Their heads crowded together over the sketch of Phil.

Jer whistled.

"She's caught ye, Phil! She's caught ye! That young one has the divil in her fingers."

"It's cruel," sighed Eily.

"Tis true!" said Mrs O'Hara, her head close to the paper, her eyes blinking. "Take it to heart, Phil!"

He stared at Grania, his face stern. She stared back, frightened but proud.

"Maybe I will take it to heart," he answered with a grin.

30

Desmond Goes Away

Grania came down the following morning so early that only her mother and Desmond were about. Eily was scrubbing potatoes, Desmond, sitting cross-legged before the hearth, blew up the fire with the old battered bellows.

"I forgot to take up a new candle," said Grania. "But I can easily go to bed in the dark now."

Desmond took one look at her.

"But you couldn't see to comb your hair this morning, that's sure!"

Grania laughed.

"I did comb it, but I'll do it again when I have a light."

"There aren't any candles," said Eily.

"There's a drop of oil, enough for tonight," Desmond told her cheerfully. "Something's sure to happen today!"

"I'd forgotten the boycott!" and Grania looked mournfully at her mother. "I suppose there's nothing to eat or drink?"

Eily smiled.

"Sure, you won't starve, Grania! We have plenty potatoes and goat's milk. Tomorrow, maybe, there'll be rabbits."

"I might make some cheese!" suggested Desmond. "Could you spare a jug of milk, Eily?"

"Why not? Twill make a change. There is some milk nearly sour. But it's hard to manage without flour or tea!"

Phil came down. He nodded to their "good mornings" and went over to the tobacco jar. It was empty!

He sat on the settle, his head in his hands. Old Mrs O'Hara saw him there, when she walked out from her room, yawning and heavy with sleep.

"I never wanted a sup of tay more!" she began, then remembered and sat down in her chair with a shiver. "Grania! Pick a bowl of blackberry leaves, there's a gerrul! If we can't have one kind of tay, we'll have another!"

"There isn't a bowl left," thought Grania. "But a tin will do."

She went slowly towards the door.

"What nonsense is this!" exclaimed Phil. "Blackberry leaves for tea! I'll get you tea in Kilvaragh. They'll not treat the O'Haras this way!"

He jumped up.

"Don't, Phil!" said the old woman. "Don't go down to Kilvaragh. Tis ye're the one that darsn't go!"

"Not go down to Kilvaragh! Who'll stop me?"

He pushed by Grania.

"Blackberry leaves!" he muttered. "My mother shall have tea!"

Jer and Terry entered the kitchen as Phil strode out.

"What ails him?" asked Jer.

"Go after him, Terry!" pleaded Mrs O'Hara. "Don't let him go into the town."

Terry stared at her in amazement.

"Is it me to stop Phil? Sure, you know I couldn't do that!"

Judy ran down the stairs.

"Is Phil going down to Kilvaragh?" she demanded.

"He is, allanna!" replied her mother. "All because I wanted a sup of tay! Sure, I don't mind blackberry leaves. Wouldn't they make as good tay as a dale of the old rubbish they do be sellin nowadays!"

Judy turned to her brothers.

"Are you going to let him face the eejits of Kilvaragh alone? Go after him! They won't set on three as they might on one!"

"Tis his own wish to go! Why should I try to stop him?" grumbled Terry. "He wouldn't thank us for following him!"

But he pulled on his coat.

"Wouldn't after breakfast be time enough?" asked Jer. "I'm famished with the cold and the hunger!"

"There's praties and goat's milk, an nothin else!" Mrs O'Hara told him. "An ye'll not be gettin any of them till ye sit down with Phil!"

"Ah, well!" said Jer. "We might take a look round."

He strolled after his brother.

"Which way have they taken?" asked the old woman. "I don't think too much of Jer's courage, though Terry would always stand by Phil."

"We're in a bad fix, I suppose?" asked Judy.

"We are! We are! Never in a worse! There's only one way to improve our desprit case!"

Judy looked at her mother without speaking. Mrs O'Hara wrapped her shawl closely round her and gazed back firmly.

"If Mr Farrelly could be made to understand he was wrong, he's a dacent enough man to take off the boycott. I wouldn't be surprised but he'd be glad to do it."

"Didn't Phil tell him he hadn't touched his ricks?"

"He did, Judy. He did! But the Farrellys haven't much likin for Phil. If ye went across the river, yer own self, an spoke to Mrs Farrelly, I wouldn't say but what ye might end the trouble!"

"Mrs Farrelly!" exclaimed Judy. "I've never spoken to the woman since I was a child!"

"Mrs Farrelly, or Steve?" murmured the old woman. "Ye've spoken to him!"

Judy stood thinking. She shook her head impatiently.

"How can I? Twould drive Phil crazy! He'd never forgive me. Never!"

Eily walked out quietly. For the first time since the fire, she looked hopeful.

"Ye'll think about it, Judy?" asked the old woman. "Tis as much for Phil's sake as for anyone's. We can't go on the way we're going!"

"I'll think!" promised Judy. "There isn't much else I can do."

Grania and Desmond, filling a creel of turf, saw Phil take the road to Kilvaragh. A little while, and Terry, followed by Jer, came out, but they went towards the Rocky Valley.

Desmond, his arms filled with sods of turf, stood staring after them.

"Phil is going down to Kilvaragh alone," he said. "You couldn't tell what might happen! I'm going after him!"

He dropped the turf and, racing back, crossed the causeway and was out of sight before Grania realised what was happening.

As he neared the waterfall a voice hailed him:

"Des Burke! Des Burke!"

He stopped. That wasn't Phil's voice, or Jer's, or Terry's. It didn't come from the castle, or up from the road, but from over the river.

He turned. Halfway across, standing on the centre part of the ruined bridge, was Steve Farrelly.

He was coatless, the sleeves of his blue shirt were rolled up, the wind blew his yellow hair on end, and he was showing every tooth in a friendly grin.

"I'm wanting to have a word with you!" he called.

Desmond scowled. He hadn't heard Mrs O'Hara talking to Judy about Steve and, if he were to keep Phil in sight, he'd have to be quick! But he was too curious to go without knowing what Steve wanted. He walked to the water's edge.

"How's the head?" asked the young man.

"Better! No thanks to you!" answered Desmond.

Steve laughed.

"Me father's terrible when he's roused!" he said. "But don't be vexed with me. I'm wanting to be friends."

Desmond wrinkled his nose.

"You know as well as I do there can be no friendship between the O'Haras and the Farrellys. Our side may have been in the wrong to start! Yours is the worst now!"

He looked at Steve Farrelly with regret. Hadn't he always wanted to be friends? But now it was too late!

"Don't be too sure we can never be friends," retorted Steve. He lowered his voice so that Desmond could scarcely hear him for the noise of the waterfall. "How's Judy?"

Desmond was puzzled.

"Did you say "How's Judy?"

Steve nodded.

"I did indeed. How is she?"

"She's all right. Why do you want to know?"

Steve's bright eyes glanced all round, as though he were afraid of being overheard.

"Did she never say a word about me? You know, wonder what I'm after doing?"

Desmond shook his head.

"Of course she doesn't! She hardly knows you. You're just one of the enemy!"

Steve looked straight at the boy.

"Can I trust you?"

"I suppose so," said Desmond, doubtfully. "I'm not a tell-tale, if that's what you mean."

"You wouldn't let on to the brothers?"

"N-no! I wouldn't!"

"Well, listen now! I'm planning to marry Judy. I've never seen anyone like her – with her lovely red hair and the proud walk of her!"

"You must be mad!" declared Desmond. "How could you marry Judy?"

Steve smiled.

"When I marry Judy I'll be a good friend to you, lad! Would you tell her I was asking for her? Wait till the brothers are out of hearing and just tell her, casual like!"

Desmond was angry.

"You talk of marrying Judy! Don't you know your father's put the boycott on us? And Judy hasn't a sup of tea, or a cup to drink out of! Your father smashed up the place, and now not a soul in Kilvaragh will sell anything to us!"

Steve gazed blankly at him.

"I never knew! Believe me, I never knew! I'll stop all that! Tell Judy! I'm off this minute!"

Desmond marched away indignantly.

"The cheek of him!" he muttered. "Marry Judy, and starve her first! And now, as like as not, I'll lose Phil!"

He wasn't looking where he was going, but racing along, avoiding stones and holes by instinct, when a hand, grasping his shoulder, brought him to a stop.

"You young traitor! You turncoat, you beggar's brat! I'll slaughter you!"

Phil's face, pale and furious, was close to Desmond's.

"You don't understand!" exclaimed the boy, trying to twist himself free. "He only wanted to know how we were getting on. He hasn't done anything. And I'm no beggar's brat!"

"God give me patience!" declared Phil. "Bill Farrelly smashes our place, puts the boycott on us, makes us a laughing-stock and, when Steve asks how are we, you run round wagging your tail! You make me tired!"

"And you make me tired!" retorted Desmond. "Tis you brought all the trouble on us. We'd have a road only for you! We'd have friends!"

He returned Phil's glare with a steady look. But he was dismayed. Because he longed to be friends with Steve, it was no reason for talking this way to Phil.

"What else did Steve Farrelly want to know?" demanded Phil.

"Find out!" answered Desmond.

Phil lifted his fist. Desmond, wrenching himself free, rushed down the road. His injured head ached, his feet dragged, and he staggered. But he kept on until he came to Rattigan's. Sean and Patsy were tossing stones inside the gateway. They looked shyly at Desmond as he passed and he thought of the fun he'd had with them the night they stayed at the castle.

Main Street was empty and he walked slowly, looking at the shops. If only he had some money it would be grand to go to one of the little hucksters where they mightn't have heard of the boycott and buy all kinds of things to eat. He imagined himself swaggering over the causeway with a heavy load and being welcomed by Grania, Eily, and Mrs O'Hara.

But he knew it was only a dream.

"And Phil wouldn't care if he never set eyes on me again!" thought the boy miserably.

As he came to the harbour he saw the *Princess Margaret*, ready to steam away. The gang plank was still out and Captain Scully stood there talking to Maggie.

Desmond had often seen the captain, but had never spoken to him. They were laughing and Maggie was holding her father's hand.

"She'd like to go with him, I know!" thought Desmond. "So would I!"

The Scullys looked at him. Maggie waved her hand and beckoned. Desmond hurried towards them.

"Dad, this is Des Burke," said Maggie. "He lives at Castle O'Hara."

"I've heard of you, young man," the captain told him, gripping Desmond's hand so firmly the boy thought his fingers would crack. "What happened to your head?"

"I got a whack on it!" replied Desmond.

"Anything to do with the boycott?" asked Captain Scully, stepping on the plank.

Desmond suddenly made up his mind.

"Take me with you, sir!" he begged. "I'll work hard. I can do anything. I've quarrelled with Phil and I don't want to go back to the castle. Do let me come!"

The Captain looked at his daughter.

"Does Grania know?" she asked.

Desmond shook his head.

"It never hurt a lad yet to go on a sea trip!" declared the captain. "I'm a bit short-handed and I know you're a good worker. Maggie, let them know up at the castle. We'll be back in a week. The boycott will be settled by then. Goodbye, child!"

Desmond helped to pull in the plank. He waved to Maggie, then turned to coiling ropes, with a sailor who told him what to do and watched him do it.

As the ship passed the lighthouse he looked back.

A tiny figure still waved from the quay – that was Maggie. His eyes wandered over the houses, climbing the rise, a jumble of roofs and chimneys, and glittering windows. On, on, until they rested on a square grey building almost invisible against the mountains.

Desmond felt the deck dancing beneath him. Great green waves rolled to meet the *Princess Margaret* and the salt wind was on his face.

He ran to the side. How could he go from Castle O'Hara without a word? The potatoes weren't planted. The turf wasn't cut!

The captain's hand fell on his shoulder.

"You can tell me what's wrong when I've time to listen. Till then rub those brass fittings till you can see your face in them. When you're at sea never think about the land!"

31

Grania Goes Over to Dromard

Grania was mashing the potatoes and mixing in some chopped chives when the dogs rushed out barking. She put down the big fork and ran after them.

Travelling Finn, stick in hand, the sack on his back, was coming over the causeway. Pegeen, a bit nervous, was keeping close to him, though her tail wagged in greeting to the O'Hara dogs, who formed up two on each side and brought the visitors into the kitchen.

"God save all here!" said the old man, raising his battered hat.

"God save you kindly," answered Eily.

"Ye're very welcome," added Mrs O'Hara. "Come along in an take the weight off yer feet. Bedad, that's a load ye're carrying!"

"It is, ma'am," he agreed, laying the sack at her feet. "But, thanks be, I'll not be needin to take it furder. Tis a bit of a present I'm givin ye! Just a few bits of things!"

He took out a packet of tea, a blue bag of sugar, a piece of bacon, and a lump of cheese.

Grania had drawn over to see what was happening. She leaned on the table and cried out in amazement:

"But that's what you take when you're going the roads! You told me yourself!"

The old man frowned.

"Tis what I've brought an I visitin Castle O'Hara! Haven't I the right to make a gift to me old friend?"

"Ye're a kind man, so y'are!" declared Mrs O'Hara. "The best in the world, an I thinkin we were back in the days of the famine!"

Judy's face was flaming. She knew the old wanderer was giving them his provisions and she was helpless.

She walked to the door.

"Will ye not wait for yer dinner, Judy?" asked her mother.

"I'm going across the river," said Judy, "to do what I should have done before!"

The door slammed behind her and Eily gazed at the old woman.

"Don't tell me Judy is going to make peace!" she exclaimed.

"She is indade! Let's hope she'll succeed," replied Mrs O'Hara. "Ah, Judy's a good gerrul when she lets herself see raison."

"If we had a rabbit or two to go with the bacon we wouldn't be doing too badly," said Eily. "Maybe Jer and Terry will bring some."

"Wid a bag of flour an some male we'd live out the boycott!" chuckled the old woman. "But where would they be comin from?"

"Couldn't I ride over to Dromard?" suggested Grania. "Uncle Phil said I'd soon be equal to it. They'd all love to see me and Aunt Bridgie would get the flour and the meal!"

"You'd be lost!" objected Eily. "But Desmond might go. I wonder where he is?"

"I'm afeard ye'll not be seein Desmond today, nor tomorrow nayther," said Travelling Finn. "I met wid young Maggie Scully an she bade me tell ye the lad is sailin the salt say on her dadda's boat!"

They stared at him in silence. At last Grania spoke.

"He never told me he was going. He never said a word!"

"What could make him leave his home?" asked Eily. "He was happy here. Something unexpected must have happened."

"Maggie said he came rushin demented through the town at the last minute, as the captain was steppin on board. The poor lad went down on his knees an implored himself to take him away, for he'd had a desprit quarrel wid Phil, an darsn't come home."

Grania looked over the half-door. Suppose Desmond never came back!

"Let her ride to Dromard," whispered Mrs O'Hara to Eily. "Twill take her mind off her troubles. Travelling Finn will show her the way."

Grania stood away from the door as Jer and Terry strolled in.

"Did ye find Phil?" asked the old woman anxiously.

"We did!" answered Terry. "And he sent us about our business. I don't know what's happening to the O'Haras at all!"

"Were ye in Kilvaragh?"

"Not at all! We came up with him at the end of the Glen. He was making for Barnakeel. If ye'd seen the look he gave us! Follow me if ye dar! Ah, I'm afraid Phil's not the man he used to be!"

"What would Phil want in Barnakeel?" demanded Eily.

"He was meeting a man who wanted him to take a horse to sell," said Jer sulkily. "And he wouldn't have his own two brothers with him!"

"After all we've done for Phil!" sighed Terry, lifting his eyebrows slowly, one at a time. "Is there any dinner going in this house? I'm famished!"

The brothers were disgusted with the dinner, but Grania didn't know what she was eating.

Eily poured out the tea.

"I'm sorry we've nothing better than a tin to offer," she said to Travelling Finn. "We've had trouble here and all our delph is broken!"

"Sure, Eily, I'd sooner have a tin than a cup any day," returned Finn. "Aren't they more natural?"

They ate and drank without speaking until he stood up.

"Get the pony ready, girleen!" he said. "We must be on our way."

Grania stared at him in amazement, then looked at her mother. Eily smiled.

"You'll not be frightened?" she asked. "You do want to go?"

Terry helped Grania fix two creels on Bogtrotter. His slowness was vexing, for she feared her mother might change her mind. Terry hummed a dreary little tune of a few notes until Grania hated the sound.

Travelling Finn came out with his sack hanging flat and only his billy-can and the frying-pan in the bottom of it. Eily stood in the doorway with a note for Aunt Bridgie.

"You'll take care of her, Finn?" she said. "Tis a long, long way."

She was troubled about the journey to Dromard. She never considered that Grania would have to return alone.

Bogtrotter tossed his head impatiently and whinnied. Finn lifted Pegeen and stowed her with his sack in one of the creels. They were about to start when Timmy Fuzz, sitting on the stone seat, his paw still in a splint, gave a leap and landed awkwardly in front of Grania.

"Come outa that!" chuckled Mrs O'Hara, who had come out to bid them farewell. "Bedad, tis a lucky ride, Grania, when a black cat strives to go along wid ye!"

Grania cuddled the kitten for a moment, then handed him to her grandmother. Now she was riding over the causeway, Travelling Finn beside her. She turned to wave, but had to clutch a creel to save herself from falling.

The path was steep and she looked down over the pony's head. Grania trusted Bogtrotter, yet, each time one of his hoofs sent a stone rolling into the Haunted Pool, she listened for the distant splash and started when it came.

"Ye're a great little rider," said Finn, his hand on the creel. "When ye're comin back give the baste his head an never mind."

"W-will it be dark?" stammered Grania.

She hadn't thought of the return.

"Not till after nine, an then the moon will be risin. Tis at the full. Ye've no need to vex yerself!"

He began to sing:

There were three beggars in the town;
One was tall, an lean, an brown;
One was fat, an bald an jolly,
The third of the three was melancholy.

Grania sang it with him.

"I'll sing it when I come this way tonight," she thought. "Then I won't look down."

"How do ye go wid Peg Lanaghan?" asked Finn, as they passed below a cabin perched on a shelf of rock. A stout woman, so wrapped round she was as broad as she was long, was loading a donkey cart. The donkey brayed defiance at the passing strangers and Peg shaded her eyes to watch them.

Finn put his hand to his mouth and halloed a greeting.

"I've never been up there," said Grania, regretfully. "I was never so near her cabin before! She's bad friends with the O'Haras!"

"So she is," agreed Finn. "Sure, I forgot! But she's a dacent woman an very larned. If ye saw the shelf of books she has over her bed! An she never goes down to Kilvaragh widout she buys another. I'm sorry ye're not friends wid her. Why don't ye ax her to let ye paint a picture of the donkey? She loves the crathure!"

"I will!" promised Grania. "I'm friends with Thady Connor! Did you know?"

Travelling Finn sniffed scornfully.

"Thady Connor! He's a poor, mean-spirited class of a chap! If twasn't for Peg, the O'Haras would have druv him out, bad cess to them! Beg pardon, Grania! Tis Phil an them joyful brothers of his, I'm manin!"

"It's queer, I know it is," said Grania, "but I'd sooner have Phil for an uncle than anyone else in the world, except, of course, Uncle Christie! If only he hadn't driven Des away! What makes him so strange and unfriendly?"

Travelling Finn shook his head in bewilderment.

"Yer father was the same, always the good word for Phil! Mind ye, while poor Kevin was alive, the brothers weren't too bad. Though they were always down on Eily, her and that young lad. I don't think she laughed since Kevin went, till ye came along. D'ye know, Grania, ye've put a windy in Castle O'Hara that lets in the light."

Grania glanced sideways. Was he joking? No! Finn's face was grave and he stared straight ahead.

He began singing again:

I had three wishes given me,
Given me, given me.
I had three wishes given me,
One, two, three.

The first I wished was a pure white mare,
The second a purse of glittering gold,
The third a triumph quick and sure –
I had them all, ere the day was old.

Ere the day was old I rode the mare
An won the race an the purse of gold.
Ere I was old, the mare had died,
I'd nothin to ride and I'd spent the gold –
Ere I was old!

"Look back now, Grania, at every turn, so that ye know the road goin and comin. Tis tonight, when ye're on yer lone, ye'll need to know the looks of the High Bog.

"Remember – this side the Gap ye're on the old road till ye come to the silver birches. Keep the Rocky Mountain on yer left till ye see the three rocks come out foreninst ye. Turn till they're alongside. Keep away from the heather an listen for the sound of the stone an Bogtrotter's hoofs."

"Des jumped over the pools when he came this way. There was one pool so deep you'd never find the bottom!"

"The lad was showin off! Ye'd think he was an O'Hara, instead of a Burke. But I'm tellin ye!"

They went over the steep rise and the chimneys of Dromard lay before them.

"Could I leap down the way Des did, the day he came for me?" thought Grania.

As she wondered, Bogtrotter gave a scrambling leap and landed in the roadway in front of Hanlon's.

Grania held back a scream and sat clutching the reins, while Travelling Finn climbed slowly down the bank.

"Ye've done one half the journey," he told her. "Watch out on the way back and ye'll be safe enough. Hand me out poor Pegeen an me sack!"

Pegeen barked and raced along the road, thankful to be on her legs again. But Grania looked pleadingly at Finn.

"Wouldn't you call here for me and we could go to the castle together?" she asked.

The old man patted her hand.

"Don't be scared, child! Bogtrotter will take ye safe and sound. An sure, I'm on me way to Cork. Ye'll not rest eyes on me again for a while."

He set off at a run, Pegeen leaping beside him.

Grania slipped to the ground and, holding the reins, opened the door of the shop and peeped in.

The tinkling of the bell made everyone in the shop

look round. Aunt Bridgie was on the stepladder lifting down a box of children's jumpers. She glanced over her shoulder and, when she saw Grania's brown face and tumbled hair, nearly dropped the box.

"If this don't beat all!" she gasped. "Tis Grania herself!"

"I've Bogtrotter here," explained Grania. "I'll take him round!"

As she closed the door a buzz of excited chatter followed her. The gate of the yard was unbolted. Grania lifted the latch and led in the pony.

Seated on a bench in the sunshine, Uncle Christie was sorting out nails, while his paint brushes soaked themselves clean in a tin of hot soapsuds and turps. He looked up smiling.

"Be all that's wonderful! Tis me own little Grania! Come in, pet! Come in! Bedad, ye have the horse wid ye! Did ye ride him? Is Eily wid ye, or the young lad? Come in! Come in!"

He talked away, asking questions and never waiting to have them answered, his eyes puzzled but happy. In time he would know what had brought her. Until then, it was great good luck to have her there.

"Ye're thin and wild-looking," he said. "D'ye know, Grania, I do believe you'll grow into a beauty; not a regular, ordinary kind of a beauty, mind ye! Still beauty's beauty, when all's said and done!"

Grania tied up Bogtrotter, fixed the nosebag, and sat down beside her uncle.

"We're in trouble, Uncle Christie. The boycott has been put on us because the people think Phil and Des fired the Farrellys' ricks and they didn't. But no one believes us, and Des has gone away to sea along with Maggie Scully's father!"

Christie Hanlon pursed his lips, his face grew red, his blue eyes were indignant.

"I never heard the like! To boycott Eily an ye because of the Mad O'Haras!"

"Travelling Finn gave us his tea and sugar, and bacon and cheese. But we haven't any meal or flour! And what he brought us won't last long!"

"Don't worry, child! While ye can ride the pony, we'll fill the creels. But I don't like it. I don't like it at all! The boycott wasn't meant for people like yer mother. Tell me all about it – everythin! Sure, I'm wishin we'd never let ye go. Wait! Here's Bridgie!"

Bridgie Hanlon flung open the back door.

"What's wrong?" she asked. "Is it Eily?"

"No! No!" exclaimed Grania. "She's well! But, Aunt Bridgie, we are in trouble!"

"It's my belief trouble and the O'Haras are just two ways of saying the same thing!" declared Mrs Hanlon. "Come along inside and tell me the whole story. We don't want an open-air meeting!"

Christie swept the nails into their box, put the box and the tin of brushes in the shed, gave Bogtrotter a friendly slap, then hurried in after his wife and Grania.

Norrie and Sally were having their tea. When Grania came in Norrie laid down her knife and fork, while Sally, still clutching hers, put her elbows on the table.

"Poor Grania!" said Norrie. "What's happened you?"

"She's been dragged through a hedge backwards," declared Sally. "Or, maybe, she's only turning into a real O'Hara!"

But when Grania hugged her, she hugged back.

"This is a comforting house," said Grania. "Even Sally!"

"What's wrong now?" asked Sally. "Have the darling uncles turned you out or beaten you black and blue, or what's happened?"

"We're boycotted and Des has run away to sea!" Grania told her.

She couldn't help a feeling of triumph at the thrill she was giving.

"Boycotted?" cried Norrie.

"Des run away to sea!" screamed Sally. "Hurry! I must hear all about it. Miss Mooney can do her own hairdressing for once!"

Grania tried to tell about the ricks as quickly as possible. But every one of them, even Norrie, asked questions, gave opinions, and interrupted so continuously it was a wonder she could talk at all. When she had finished they gazed at her curiously.

"What do you feel like, now you've left off being a Hanlon and turned into an O'Hara?" Sally wanted to know.

"Eily should go to the priest!" declared Aunt Bridgie. "He'd believe her and he'd stop this boycott!"

"He doesn't like Uncle Phil," said Grania. "But I do believe he likes Judy."

She told them how Father Coulahan had made Judy dance with Steve Farrelly.

"Judy has a grah for Steve, I know that," added Grania. "We all like him – only Phil, and – of course – Terry and Jer!"

"Listen to me, now!" said Mrs Hanlon. "There'll be no peace in Castle O'Hara till Phil takes himself off and his two brothers with him. He's a tinker and no tinker ever rightly settles down!"

"My father did!" Grania pointed out.

Her aunt smiled.

"Eily never thought of him as a tinker. Maybe he took after old Mrs O'Hara. Isn't it queer now the way Eily gets on with her?"

"I'm hoping all this trouble won't stop Grania's becoming an artist," said Christie, wrinkling his forehead.

"I have to go back," Grania reminded them.

"We'll fill the creels first," murmured her aunt. "And you keep on eating!"

She smoothed her apron.

"Grania! Is it safe for you to ride alone over the High Bog? I can't understand Eily letting you do it. I'm terrified of the place and the night's coming on!"

"What can we give them?" asked Christie, knocking out his pipe.

"All we've got!" said Bridgie, opening the doors of the big press where she kept her stores. "There's flour – take it, Christie! Meal; you can't live without meal! How about rice? Will their lordships eat rice? Christie! Run down and get a round of beef and a couple of pounds of sausages."

"I'll go!" offered Grania, jumping up.

Her uncle pushed her down.

"Remember the hard ride there is before ye, child!"

She ate all they gave her. Then she sat on the bench looking up at her drawing of Timmy Fuzz, growing faint and smudged. Wasn't it strange how lonely she felt?

"I'm neither here nor there!" she thought. "Mebbe it's because I'm a tinker too!"

The window was open at the top and the evening air had a touch of cold. Grania shifted closer to the fire and tried to count up how long it was since the first time she had seen Desmond.

"He'll be bringing in turf, or straining the milk, or breaking sticks," she told herself, smiling.

Then she remembered that Desmond had left Castle O'Hara with all its quarrels and vexations

"You're shivering, pet!" exclaimed Mrs Hanlon. "I'll close the window."

"Tisn't cold I am. I was just thinking Des won't be there when I go home," Grania explained.

"I hate to hear you call that desolate place home!" protested her aunt.

"Don't fret about Des," Christie told her. "He's having the time every lad dreams of an he'll be back before you're used to him being away."

He had wandered in, loaded with a huge piece of beef and sausages which escaped in a long string from the brown-paper bag.

"If you're not holding the bag of sausages upside down," cried Mrs Hanlon. "Thanks be, you didn't forget the child's sweets!"

Dumping the beef and sausages on the table he sat beside Grania.

"When I was Desmond's age, I'd have given the two eyes out of me head to go off to say," he said dreamily. "Many's the time I wish I had!"

"Hark at the bold pirate!" joked Bridgie.

She moved backwards and forwards from the press to the table, while Christie tied parcels and told Grania what was happening in Dromard.

"Mrs Fogarty is goin to have a shop-front fitted to the house an the whole place painted up grand. An yer Uncle

Christie is the chap that's goin to do it! Twill be a shockin time for me, shockin! She's the world's worst to work for! Sure, ye're well away from her. She'd have ye heart-scalded! The way she gives out to them young ones is desprit!"

"The creels won't take another inch of anything," announced Mrs Hanlon.

She leaned against the table, her arms folded. Grania looked round the clean, comfortable room and thought of all Desmond had hoped to do for Castle O'Hara.

"I don't want to go back!" was in her mind. "I don't want to go back!"

Yet she stood up.

"There's an easy way on to the High Bog," Uncle Christie was telling her. "I wandered up the mountainy road last Sunday. Tis better than leaping up the bank the way young Des would do!"

He was trying to keep her as long as he could. Grania understood.

"I'd better go the short way," she said.

"You'd better not!" snapped her aunt. "You've forgotten those loaded creels!"

Yes! She had forgotten those loaded creels. But she had remembered the wild bog, the pools, the loneliness.

They came out through the yard with her. Mrs Hanlon had closed the shop and, looking back, Grania saw the road, empty and quiet.

"In another few hours they'll be comin down this way to the Fair – the sheep an the cows, an the pigs riding like gintry," said Christie.

"I used to see them out of the little round window," Grania told him. "I meant to paint a picture of them."

"Ye'll paint it yet!" he declared.

"What will I do if Mr O'Neill won't let me go to the class because of the boycott? Even if he does, there isn't one there will speak to me, only Maggie Scully!" said Grania.

"The dacent little gerrul, God bless her!" muttered Christie. "Yonder's the path!"

He helped her up on Bogtrotter.

"Come again as soon as you can," her aunt urged her. "I'll be worrying!"

32

Night on the High Bog

Grania felt very proud as she rode Bogtrotter up the mountain road away from Hanlon's, with Aunt Bridgie and Uncle Christie admiring her. When she turned the pony on to the bog she could see them still watching her from the doorway.

"Safe home!" they called.

"Slán liv!" returned Grania, to show she hadn't forgotten her schooling.

Now she had to give her mind to staying on Bogtrotter, for there wasn't much room behind the loaded creels and, though it was easier to sit sideways, it was also easier to slide off.

When at last Grania was able to look back she could see only furze bushes and clumps of heather. Even the chimneys of Hanlon's had disappeared. She was alone on the High Bog!

Holding the reins loosely in her left hand, Grania settled herself between the creels and gazed over the bog. The sun was setting before her, pools and streams blazed as if they were liquid gold. Bunches of clouds, white, pink, and gold, drifted slowly across the deep blue sky.

"I love colours!" thought the girl. "I could ride on like

this for ever, yet I'd sooner draw little black-and-white pictures. I won't let Mr O'Neill know, or I'll never learn to do oils. I may feel different when I have an easel and a great piece of canvas."

She forgot the boycott, forgot to guide Bogtrotter.

Slowly the golden light faded. The clouds turned grey, the pools were brown. Grania shivered, clutched the side of a creel and, cautiously, sat upright and looked around her.

While she had been dreaming, a mist had been settling on the bog. Now it was rising so that she could not tell low bushes from rocks. It filled hollows and, as it flowed over the uneven bog, Grania felt she was riding into a sea. White waves rippled against boulders and crept up the trunks of trees. When she looked down, Bogtrotter's legs were hidden so that he seemed to be swimming.

The pony's hoofs clattered on stone.

"That shows we're going right," thought Grania. "When we come to the end of the old road I'll have to watch out for Travelling Finn's landmarks."

But already the landmarks were blotted out. The mountains were hidden. The clumps of trees, the tall rocks the wanderer had shown her could not be seen.

"He told me there'd be moonlight," she grumbled. "He never warned me about mist!"

Far away she could hear waves rushing up a stony strand and thought of Desmond out on the sea.

"If he were here it would be an adventure," she told herself. "As I'm alone, it's a bigger adventure," she added, pretending she had no fear of the mist or the coming night.

There were gaps where the mist thinned to a faint veil.

But rocks and bushes appeared like strange, terrifying animals and, when a bramble caught her stocking, she screamed.

"I should be ashamed!" she said out loud.

She tried to sing for the companionship of her own voice, but the timid, trembling sound terrified her and she was glad to be silent.

The bog wasn't silent. All around she could hear splashings and gurglings.

"That's shallow water flowing over stones," she decided.

A fluttering of wings, scratchings and scurryings, eddies in the mist, darker shadows rising and swooping, she explained them all. But that didn't make her any the less frightened.

Didn't she know there were birds and rabbits, creatures of all kinds who made their home on the High Bog?

Grania strained her eyes; she tried to shut her ears. But she shrank from the clutching arms and towering figures which swayed, leaned towards her, and passed on. She could no longer hear the waves and was forced to trust the pony, for she could not tell where Dromard and Kilvaragh lay.

"Make for home, Bogtrotter," she said. "Find the castle!"

The pony neighed and went steadily on. His hoofs tossed up water and he had to wade slowly. Grania remembered the bog holes and shivered.

Now she could see only Bogtrotter's ears and the waving of the thickening mist as he tossed his head. Her hair was wet and she felt damp fingers stroking her face.

Luckily her coat was thick, but she grew colder and colder.

"We must be nearly home," she thought.

She tried to see Peg Lanaghan's light, or Thady Connor's. The left creel scraped against a tall rock and she hoped they were entering the Gap.

Bogtrotter stopped and backed. He was trembling, so was Grania.

"Mebbe we were nearly in a bog-hole!" she thought. "I don't believe we're anywhere near the Gap!"

"Try for home, Bogtrotter!" she coaxed. "You wouldn't want us to be out on the bog all night?"

Bogtrotter spread out his legs, blew noisily, and stood still.

"We're safe so far," said Grania. "Should I get down and lead the way?"

As she considered this, she heard faintly the noise of hoofs striking against rock. She caught her breath. Who could be riding on the High Bog?

She tried to put Mrs O'Hara's stories of mysterious unseen creatures out of her mind. Then the friendly neighing of a horse and Bogtrotter's eager, answering whinny reassured her.

Putting her hands to her mouth she called: "Castle O'Hara! Castle O'Hara?"

To her delight a voice replied: "Who calls the castle?"

"It's me, Grania O'Hara!" she cried. "Who are you? I'm lost!"

She heard a laugh.

"Who would it be but your own Uncle Phil! What are you doing, wandering on the bog?"

Now he was riding beside her, his hand on the pony's neck. Grania reached out and clutched his arm. She had never been so glad!

"Oh, I was frightened!" she told him. "So was Bogtrotter. I can't see anything! Are we near home?"

"We're not! We're at the foot of Carrig Mór. But, answer me, what are you up to – stravaging round on the High Bog in this fright of a mist? You might have lost your life!"

"I've been to Aunt Bridgie's! Something had to be done. She filled these creels."

"So you've been cadging off your decent, respectable aunt!" jeered Phil. "But what made them let you go alone? Had my mother nothing to say? Is Eily quite mad? What was Des doing?"

"Des wasn't there! He's gone to sea with Captain Scully, and all because of you!" said Grania reproachfully.

"He'll come back!" Phil assured her. "The *Princess Margaret* doesn't go to foreign parts. And I'm leaving the castle. I'll take the boys with me. That will settle the boycott. All your troubles are ended!"

"Leave the castle!" cried Grania. "You can't! Don't go, Uncle Phil!"

"Tis Judy that's driving me away!" exclaimed Phil. "Her and her grah for Steve Farrelly! D'you think I'd stay there and be the joke of Kilvaragh? Anyway, twill be best for her. She'll be getting what I wanted for her. Without me you can all be as happy as kings!"

"It will be terrible lonesome without you and Des!" protested Grania, tears rolling down her wet cheeks.

"It breaks my heart to leave the castle!" said Phil. "But I should have done it years ago! Steady now! Don't be falling off! You'll frighten the little mare. She's a nervous creature and I've enough to bother me."

"Don't go!" pleaded Grania. "Be friends with my mother and the Farrellys. We could be so happy!"

She tried to see his face but he was only a darker blur in the surrounding greyness.

"I'm glad you want me to stay. I'll remember that," he said slowly. "I've been unfair to Eily. I'd have been unfair to you, only for that look of Kevin in your eyes. And that poor young devil, Des, I needn't have been so hard."

"He thinks the world of you, Phil! I know he does!"

Grania had forgotten the mist, the cold, her weariness. Her face was stiff, her fingers numb.

"Will you be happy, Uncle Phil?" she asked.

"I will, because I'll be doing what a man should do – work and make his way in the world. I've a mare here you could love, Grania! I'm off to Ballinasloe to sell her for a man and I'll make a good bargain. I'm giving up cards! I'll knock sense into Terry and Jer. I'll be the biggest horse-dealer in Ireland before I've finished! Don't fret for me, Grania! It's the most sensible thing I've ever done. Make up for me to the granny. She'll think she had Kevin back. Moryah! Twill be the end of the Mad O'Haras!"

"Oh!" sighed Grania.

"Oh!" Phil mimicked her. "There's the causeway! There's the castle! Tell the brothers I'm waiting on them. They must bring the dogs. Hold tight now!"

He gave Bogtrotter a slap which sent the pony bounding forward. The dogs barked. The door was flung open and Grania saw her mother standing there.

The dogs leaped about Bogtrotter like friendly wolves, their fangs gleaming, their paws beating the air.

Eily put her arms around Grania as she slid to the ground.

"You poor child! I've been terrified. When the mist came on I hoped Bridgie had kept you. You're perished!"

"There was no mist at Dromard," said Grania, her voice so tired it was only a whisper.

She leaned against Bogtrotter. He stood motionless, his head hanging down. He, too, was cold and stiff, and weary.

Terry and Jer came out.

"We'll see to Bogtrotter," said Terry. "Go along in! There's company!"

Grania's eyes, so accustomed to the mist, were dazzled as she looked into the kitchen. She rubbed the damp from her eyelashes, yet still could not believe what she saw.

There was a white cloth on the table, cups, saucers, and little plates! But the greatest wonder of all was Judy in the green frock, her hair twisted round her head like a coronet and caught up with a high comb, leaning forward, laughing and talking with Steve Farrelly and – could it be – Mr O'Neill?

Eily laughed.

"It's real, Grania! Steve brought it all as a gift from his mother. Go in to the fire! The boycott's off! Thank God you're safe? Mr O'Neill has something wonderful for you!"

Terry and Jer lifted the heavy creels inside the door. They went off to the stable with Bogtrotter. Still Grania did not enter, but stood looking at the strange scene.

"What is wrong?" asked Eily. "Ah, you're worn out! Lean on me!"

A shrill imperious whistle sounded behind them in the mist. Judy started up from the table. Terry and Jer came running.

"Who's that?" cried Eily.

"That's Phil! I'd know his whistle anywhere!" said Mrs O'Hara, from her corner by the fire.

"It is Phil!" said Grania, coming into the room. "I was lost. He brought me home. But he's going away. He said to send Jer and Terry out to him, and the dogs."

Without looking at the others, Grania went over to her grandmother. The old woman gazed up at her and half rose.

"I'll go out to Phil!" she said. "Where is he?"

"We're off! Goodbye!" called Terry.

The sound of their hurrying footsteps, the excited yelps of the dogs died away.

Mrs O'Hara sat down again.

"They'll be coming back," she muttered. "But sure, tis time they went!"

"Phil has a lovely mare," Grania told her. "He's taking her to sell at Ballinasloe. He's going to give up the cards and become the biggest horse-dealer in all Ireland!"

"Whisha, God help him! The poor lad!" chuckled his mother. "Tis time he was out in the world. But ye haven't said goodnight to Mr O'Neill and Steve Farrelly. They'll think ye have no manners at all!"

Grania turned to the table. She was ashamed to meet the Art teacher so dirty, untidy, and weary. He smiled at her.

"Sit down, Grania! You've had a terrible time! But I've news for you! So have Judy and Steve, I think."

"Ours can wait!" said Steve. "But, Grania! The boycott is off! Twas all a foolish mistake!"

Grania looked at Judy. Her elbows were back on the table. Yet in every other way she was different. Judy happy! Laughing, contented! But Mr O'Neill's news?

"You've won a scholarship!" he said. "An Art scholarship. You're to go up to Dublin and study Art for two years, maybe three. Your mother will let you go!"

Grania thought the mist had followed her into the room. Faces, voices were blurred. Her mother drew her down to the settle, pulled off her coat, smoothed her hair. Judy pushed a cup of tea towards her. Steve cut toast into fingers. Mr O'Neill went on talking:

"You have great talent. One day Kilvaragh will be proud of you! These pictures on the walls – they're too good to be lost!"

"How soon must Grania be going to the college in Dublin?" asked Eily.

"All the great artists of Ireland studied there!" said Mr O'Neill. "She'll be walking over O'Connell Bridge, up Grafton Street."

Mrs O'Hara held out her cup for more tea and Grania carried it over to her. She sat on the creepy, and while her grandmother talked of Phil and Kevin, Grania saw the pictures she would paint: they were in the fire – faces, fairs, horses, ships. The voices followed and mingled. It was real, yet a dream!

"She can stay with Lisha Doyle," Grania heard. "Lisha is always wanting me or Bridgie to visit her. We were friends at school. She'll be good to Grania."

"I studied there. But I was the eldest son, I had to come home!"

"Up Stoney Batter, Lisha lives. Within sound of the Cattle Market. I was very fond of Lisha!"

"She'll be home for the holidays before you know she's gone!"

"We'll rebuild the bridge and, where the upper waterfall is, we'll build a house with wide windows!"

That was Steve's voice.

"And electricity!" said Judy. "And taps with water coming out of them. And a stable for Phil's horses!"

"Anything you say!" agreed Steve.

"Tis wonderful! Tis grand! I'm not denying it!" declared her grandmother. "But I'm thinkin tis goodbye to the Mad O'Haras!"